THE MAN WHO LOST INDIA

Simon & Schuster
Celebrating 100 Years of Publishing in 2024

Praise for Meghna Pant

"We enjoyed Pant's raunchy satire of India's cultural mores."

—*The New Yorker*

"Pant is elegiac—a testament to her emotional wisdom as a writer. Her sensitivity to the multidimensionality of the issues and her eye for the detail of social interactions result in intelligent, satisfying reads."

—*The Gulf News*

"Pant is part of the gifted population of Indian writers penning a runaway success story with her rich prose."

—*Khaleej Times*

"10 Young Indian Writers Who Are Changing The Game."

—Scoop Whoop

"Among The Top Indian Women Writers."

—Youth Ki Awaaz

"A skilled writer (who) uses (her) journalistic base to create convincing, sensitive fictional scenarios."

—*The Hindu Business Line*

"Among The Top 8 Female Indian Authors In The Literary World."

—EYuva

"Among India's Most Influential Female Writers."

—Polka Café

"Pant Is Paving The Way For Writers."

—*The New Indian Express*

"Among The Top Trending Indian Authors Who Completed Our Bucket List This Year."

—Word Hazard

"Meghna Pant is an author who wears several hats with elan. She is a journalist, speaker, and a feminist, too."

—*Deccan Herald*

"Meghna Pant is known for taking a strong feminist stance in her writing. She shines through."

—*The Hindustan Times*

"Meghna Pant's short stories stick like burrs. They are small, dramatic pieces that hook into the skin with urgent claims that are not easy to resolve or brush off."

—*The Asian Age*

"With her sparkling writing, Pant's stories capture the horror as well as the beauty of life."

—*Tehelka*

"A pioneer amongst women writers, Meghna Pant empowers women and promotes the beauty of Indian literature."

—*The Indian Panorama*

"Meghna Pant's mastery lies in her ability to hold the reader's interest to the end."

—*Business Standard*

"Pant writes sparkling stories."

—*The Hindu*

"Among 7 Incredible Indian Authors Whose Books You Should Be Reading RN!"

—Delhi Metro

"10 Young Indian Writers Who Are Changing The Game."

—*Frontlist Magazine*

"Top 10 Indian Female Authors."

—*Litgleam Magazine*

"An Honest, Intelligent, Insightful And Downright Feminist."

—*Girl Talk HQ*

"A Survivor And A Hero Of Act Two, Who Started Her Life After A Cinematic Intermission, Meghna Pant Is Among The Strongest Feminist Voices In The Country."

—*Femina*

"Meghna Pant Is A 'Role Model' For Her Chat Shows."

—*Sakaal Times*

"Among the Top 50 Speaker Influencers on Twitter."

—Bloggers Alliance

"25 Witty, Sharp And Fearless Women To Follow On Twitter."

—SheThePeople

THE MAN WHO LOST INDIA

MEGHNA PANT

SIMON & SCHUSTER

London · New York · Sydney · Toronto · New Delhi

First published in India by Simon & Schuster India 2024

1 3 5 7 9 10 8 6 4 2

Simon & Schuster India
818, Indraprakash Building,
21, Barakhamba Road,
New Delhi 110001.

Simon & Schuster: Celebrating 100 Years of Publishing in 2024

www.simonandschuster.co.in

Paperback ISBN: 978-81-946430-9-8
eBook ISBN: 978-81-946430-4-3

Typeset in India by SÜRYA, New Delhi
Printed and bound in India by Replika Press Pvt. Ltd.

Simon & Schuster India is committed to sourcing paper that is made from wood grown in sustainable forests and support the Forest Stewardship Council, the leading international forest certification organisation. Our books displaying the FSC logo are printed on FSC certified paper.

Disclaimer

This book is a work of fiction. All characters appearing in this book are fictitious. The book and its characters are created purely for entertainment and are not intended to hurt the sentiments or feelings of any region, country, individual, community, caste, creed, sect or religion in any way whatsoever. Names, characters, places and incidents are either products of the author's imagination or are used fictitiously. The resemblance to actual persons, living or dead, and/or actual events, and/or organizations, and/or institutions is purely coincidental and unintentional.

The creators, editors, publishers, sellers and/or distributors of the book do not intend to disrespect, impair or disparage the beliefs, sentiments of any person(s), or any country(ies) and their culture, customs(s), practice(s) and traditions(s), or any community(ies) and their culture, customs(s), practice(s) and traditions(s). The use of certain expressions in the book are purely for dramatization. The author of the book and any other persons associated with the book do not support the use of such expressions by any person.

"Man will never be free until the last king is strangled with the entrails of the last priest."

—Denis Diderot

CONTENTS

LIFE AS WE KNOW IT

2032

The headlines read:

China Attacks India!
Chinese Soldiers Decapitate Mazhabi Sikh Jawans
Rohtang Pass Falls in Surprise Attack
PLA Destroys Eastern Naval Command

Seth puts away the *Times of India*; this is not the day for fear. In fact, it's a leisurely Sunday afternoon. Seth is on the terrace with his children, Vakil and Ida. His house help Ram is pressing his feet, indulgent of Seth like only a parent can be. Seth looks at Ida, born of dewdrops and stardust, for morning had slipped into her mother's womb at the moment of her birth. She's flying a kite. Across the road, her friend Nandini Mehra tries to cut Ida's *manja*. The girls laugh. They're at an age where their teeth show when they smile.

Outside the terrace a jacaranda tree holds out its branches in prayer to the day; the burst of its trumpet-shaped flowers a tribute to the clear blue sky. Its lilac petals blow gently in the breeze and come to rest, like holy pilgrims, on the balustrade. A clock chimes to the tune of waltz and singing birds. The smell of hibiscus from the garden enraptures Seth's senses like a lover's caress. He sits back on his chair.

Mine is a life of glow and colour, he decides. As the richest man in Lalbag, one of Punjab's smaller towns, he owns most of the factories that lie to its west as well as a mobile business with many stores. He lives at the Royal Mason, a part of town that few can afford, in a bungalow that no one else can afford. Despite this, he is respected and liked. Seth takes a sip of his adrak chai, allowing its sweetness to embrace him.

Outside, the crows begin to caw. A bicycle pedals away. A pair of kites, yellow with long red tails, watch them like the eyes of the sun. The streets are wide at the Royal Mason, lined with manicured hedges and trees atop which hibiscus flowers sway with vibrancy. His bungalow, The White Taj, has a beveled stonewall overgrowing with red bougainvillea. The stonewall is lined with trees taller than one-storied buildings: pink lapacho trees with tubular-shaped flowers, gulmohar trees with scarlet flowers, jasmine trees with bell-shaped silvery flowers, a spectacular show of colours, like the fan of a peacock's tail.

Soft footsteps click on the bungalow's cobblestone driveway.

"Namaste, Aunty," Seth hears Ida shout to Geeta,

Nandini's mother, who visits Seth's wife Kamala at four every afternoon.

"Namaste, beta," Geeta replies, her voice like the breeze of dawn.

Although war has not come to their town yet, Seth finds Geeta's calm unnerving. It's not been two Sundays since Pramod, her husband, received a letter from the Chinese; a letter that threatened to take him as a prisoner of war. It's rumoured that the last PoW was taken to a Chinese military hospital, where his liver, skin, heart, kidney, cornea and lungs were removed and tossed into an incinerator. Such a fate cannot befall a man Seth has grown up with, a man who once held a funeral for a dead baby sparrow. The Chinese are mistaken about his ties with various freedom fighters.

Seth puts down his teacup. The tea has become cold.

Atop the Himalayas the snowcaps melt, winds hit the Malabar Coast, rivers flow into oceans, possessed only by the need to deliver a change of seasons. If only people had this sense of quiet dignity, thinks Seth.

He sees Urmila collecting clothes from the clothesline.

"What are you doing?" he asks her. "The clothes are not dry."

Urmila looks uncertainly from Seth to her husband Ram. She is a woman of few words and ample action, beautiful in a way that no one would notice or desire.

"On TV they said that the ... the Chinese have banned hanging clothes in open spaces," she says.

Her words slice through the terrace like a knife. Everyone becomes silent.

Quickly Seth says, "You should not believe everything you hear."

"Why not? The Chinese have attacked most of India, haven't they?" says Vakil.

His son, now taller than him, is having none of it.

Seth massages his forehead before replying, "Don't believe rumours, beta. China is not going to attack Lalbag."

"How do you know?" Vakil asks.

Ida turns to her father, her eyes wide with fear. Seth glares at his son.

"We are good people from good families," he says. "War does not happen to us."

His son scoffs. Seth looks at Urmila. She starts putting the clothes back on the clothesline. He nudges Manu, Ram's son, who is holding Ida's spool. Manu tugs the spool, diverting Ida's attention.

Seth looks around his house, The White Taj, with its faux Victorian splendour, its air of congealed money and luxuriant grace. Nothing can happen to them here. He pushes his head back on the chair and takes a long sip of his cold tea. The fragrance of magnolia from his garden is gone.

Across the landscape, a slit of light disappears, as if a giant hand is drawing a veil over the face of this earth. The afternoon shine becomes dimmer.

"Aeroplane bye bye!" he hears Ida shout. Seth looks up into the darkening sky, thankful for the distraction, and sees something black flying above the kites.

"It's not an airplane, stupid," Vakil tells Ida. "It looks like some kind of—"

They hear a loud explosion from the neighbouring town of Kharbag. The children drop their kites and run to Seth.

"What's happening?" they ask, terrified.

Peace does not fall from the sky, but war certainly does. Seth knows this. He also knows that tongues are keepers, not of the truth, but versions of the truth. He pauses with the effort of a poet carefully selecting his words, and says, "Don't worry. Nothing is happening."

"Papa, look!" Vakil says. He holds up his mobile phone that is live streaming *Times How*. A hysterical anchor screams: *The last bastion has fallen. China has attacked Punjab!*

Seth sees his children tremble like electric wires in a storm. Before he can calm them, they hear the roar of a jeep. They run to the parapet and look out at the road. An army jeep screeches to a halt in front of Mehra's bungalow. Five Chinese soldiers in olive drabs jump out of the jeep and storm into the house. Seth hears the sound of glass shattering, utensils clanging and cupboards falling. They're ransacking Mehra's home.

"What's happening, Papa?" Ida asks her father.

Seth says nothing. He pulls his children to the ground. His heart is thumping against his body like it's possessed by a powerful demon. He looks up to the sky and sees a large yellow moon hanging there like a decayed tooth. Where has the clear blue day gone?

He turns to Urmila. Her eyes are brimming with tears.

"The clothes!" he whispers urgently to her. "Get rid of the clothes!"

Urmila runs to the clothesline and pulls down the clothes.

Through the balustrade, Seth looks at his neighbour's terrace. Nandini is gone. He sees the soldiers pull Pramod, Nandini and their two housekeepers out of the house. They make them line up in a row and kneel down on their knees. Nandini and her father huddle together. Pramod's eyes are filled with the sorrow of a man who has lost everything.

Ida starts crying. Shhh, Seth tells her. We can't let them hear us.

A soldier, a boy, a few years younger than Nandini, stands above her. There is no playfulness in him. He rams the butt of his rifle into Nandini's face. Nandini clutches her face and crunches to the ground in pain. Her father gets up and leaps at the boy. The other soldiers grab him and bring him to his knees.

Seth sees a Benelli shotgun. He sees a soldier feed a bullet into the chamber. He hears a loud click, a sound as cold as death, the metallic snap of the shotgun's safety being released. He sees the muzzle of the shotgun pointed at Pramod's head. He sees the soldier pull the trigger. He sees the bullet fire. Pramod's head droops, as if he's asleep. His body crumples to the ground. Dust from the ground rises on impact and covers Nandini's horrified face. The soldier resets the shotgun's safety and slips the shotgun back into its holster.

Seth shuts his eyes in shock. He hears Nandini scream, almost at the same time as Ida. He puts his hand over Ida's mouth. "Quiet! Everyone stay down," he whispers urgently. Ram, Urmila and Manu sit down beside him, no one moves a muscle.

There's a rustle of leaves from their compound's mango tree. Seth cannot believe that the front gate of his bungalow is open. What if the soldiers enter? What will he do then?

They hear gunshots. Seth peers over a baluster and sees that the two housekeepers have been shot dead. Only Nandini remains. She holds her burst cheek, sobbing. She's only sixteen, three years younger than his daughter. Seth watches the boy soldier kick her again. The front of his army boot hits Nandini on her nose. Seth sees blood roll down her face. The soldier's foot rises again, high in the air, and Nandini folds her hands in front of her face. "Daya," she seems to be saying. Her front teeth are broken. The soldier laughs. He picks her up and carries her to the jeep, as though she's as light as a feather.

Seth freezes.

Geeta Mehra comes running out of their house. At the front gate she stops. She looks at the dead bodies. Her eyes become as empty as a gutted animal. She sees her daughter and hurls herself at the jeep. Seth turns his children away.

He hears a shot. He watches Geeta as she falls to the ground.

The jeep pulls away.

It's been less than twenty minutes since it arrived.

No one moves. Sweat streams down Seth's arms and he watches it dry. A jacaranda flower falls quivering to his lap. After a minute or ten, he lets Ida go. She screams.

"Where have they taken her?" Ida clutches him and asks. "Where has she gone?"

Nightmares have pooled around her eyes.

"I don't know," Seth replies.

He holds his daughter and walks her slowly down the stairway. The others follow, crying and trembling. Will his family meet the fate of the Mehra family?

Seth breaks into tears.

Life as we know it, he thinks, will never be the same again.

STARDUST AND FIREBRAND

God is not listening, because not a single prayer is bringing what's expected of it. But if there's a time for prayer, Seth knows, this is it. Over the last three months, without any warning, without heed, China has captured most of India. Millions of people have been killed. Lalbag is one of the last standing frontiers and, at any given moment, a bomb is expected to fall on it.

It's almost midnight and the ceasefire is minutes away. So, the townspeople are praying. They're praying to their beloved Lord Shiva, for it is Maha Shivratri, the holiest day of the new moon month of Maagha. Seth watches their eyes shut tight in devotion. War does not change you, it reveals you, Seth thinks. He admires their piety, the surrender that it brings. But has a single man prayed himself out of the life meant for him?

Seth hears the ring of a large brass bell and watches Swamiji rotate a lamp, throwing fire two feet into the air.

The sandalwood scent of the incense, the rhythmic chant of Om Namah Shivay, and the gentle breeze flowing in from the North ensconce the temple into a calm that can lull the fear in every heart. Standing atop Mount Akaho, the temple casts a golden glow on the town of Lalbag. No wonder man created God.

Seth is here, to show his support to the townspeople, but he cannot bring himself to pray. He possesses neither the fear nor the devoutness of a devotee. He looks at Ram, Urmila and Manu, standing next to him, deep in prayer. Seth's own family has chosen to stay at home, still shaken, still distraught.

Faith is like the sea, it throws back double of what's thrown into it. So is fear.

Suddenly something black darkens the night sky. A shadow falls on the half moon of Seth's face. On the Shiva Linga, glistening with milk and vermilion paste, Seth sees the reflection of a dazzling blaze of light. Light: the colour of blood and ice.

Seth looks up to see that the dark night has revealed something insidious. His mind becomes red hot. He peers into the vast emptiness where the earth joins the sky and sees a light churning the air behind it. What is it? A star with a tail? A comet? No, the light is slashing the air with angry welts. Its fury is as bright as the skin of Lord Shiva. It is ...

"A bomb!" Seth screams, his tongue like scorched water. "Run! Everyone get out of here."

The devotees open their eyes in alarm. They look at each other in confusion. Does anyone believe the rich? No. They turn to Swamiji, where their faith truly rests.

"Save yourselves," Swamiji says slowly, as if God is whispering in his ears. "Run."

The earth begins to quake. The temple bells tremble and crash to the floor. The devotees look up to see that the hot summer moon has swallowed its own light. The vaults of hell have been let open. They drop their bilva leaves and rudraksha malas, their bananas and marigolds. They get up in commotion, ready to flee. But their feet! They find that their feet have frozen. The heavens are lost. What is happening?

They look at each other in panic. Many begin to sob. A man faints.

Seth too finds himself glued to the temple floor.

Ram leans over and puts his arms around him.

"I will not let anything happen to you, Mai Baap," he says.

Urmila and Manu look at Ram with the full force of hurt, till he pulls his arms away.

"Save us, Shiva!" says Urmila, clasping her hands in prayer, tears streaming down her face. "I vow to spend the rest of my life filled with your thoughts and to never speak a human word again."

Seth thinks of Ida, within whom his happiness always finds heart. He hopes the bomb does not make its way to her gentle life.

From behind the Shiva Linga, where the cannonball tree grows—bearing sweet-scented blooms in winter and shading the devotees in summer—there comes a strange noise. Seth sees the buds of the cannonball flowers, twelve in all, quiver, as if gathering their strength. And then—Seth gasps, as do all the devotees—the flowers begin to open their petals, like the hood of Shiva's serpent. They throw columns of shining golden light into the sky. What supernatural thing is this?

Then the Shiva Linga, black and crowned with the Naga, starts to grow. It grows and grows. Longer and longer, wider and wider, crashing through the roof of the temple. This time the shock is too great. Seth can't even gasp. He just stares, mouth open, as the Linga begins to take the shape of Shiva. It is a shape that he knows but does not expect. And then, right before his disbelieving eyes, Shiva turns into a fiery column of light. The Lord has come alive!

Like leaves falling at the foot of a tree, everyone drops to their knees.

"The Neelkanth has arisen," they gasp. The fear in their hearts is gone.

The bomb shows no such reverence. It hurtles towards them, impatient, as if it's a blessing the devotees have long prayed for. And it falls, wreck and fury, in all its destruction, and it falls upon the light of The Lord.

"No!" cry the devotees.

There is a single dazzling explosion. Mount Akaho rattles as if its core has exploded into the sky. A tempestuous wind sweeps through the land, whirling dust in an eddy, shaking trees by their roots, forcing homes to crumble, sending the good earth into that heaven where Gods convene.

Seth shields his face from the flying embers and shrapnel he expects. His ears ring. He feels a powerful force lift him up and drop him to the floor. He hears his body crunch.

Hai Ram!

Then there's silence.

Seth opens his eyes. Everything is the same. The temple. The people. And he's alive! Through the settling gold dust he touches his arms, his legs, his body. He's neither dismembered, nor bloodied, nor killed; only his right leg seems to be broken. Yet, he has no feeling of pain. How is this possible? He looks around. Every single person in the temple is rooted to the spot like seaweed in a tsunami. Every person is touching their body for broken bits and parts. Every person is unharmed.

"How are we not dead? How is this possible?" someone asks Swamiji.

Swamiji looks up at the sky, which is once again concealing its secrets with darkness, and says, "Ours is not to question."

An unseen powerful force has saved them all.

Seth notices that there are three horizontal lines of ash on everyone's forehead.

"Where has this come from?" he asks Ram, who is patting his body for injuries. Ram rubs his forehead in surprise and looks around. "It's the *tripundra tilak*!"

"What does it mean?" Manu asks them.

"It is Shiva's *vibhuti*. We have been marked by his trident," Swamiji interjects. This thought seems to give the priest courage. He rises to the full majesty of his body and says, "It will always protect us."

"Where did the bomb go?" Seth asks.

Swamiji looks around and smiles. "The Lord has swallowed it!"

He points towards the direction of where Lord Shiva's statue used to be. It's no longer there. The bomb has destroyed His statue, the Linga and the cannonball tree.

Ram moans, "This cannot be. Our God has been taken from us!"

"No!" says the priest. "He has come back to us in all his glory." Swamiji points towards a crater in the ground. The devotees walk towards the crater, which is wider than a tree trunk, and gasp.

Seth tries to stand up and falls. Ram and Manu lift him up. They walk forward and peer into the crater. They too gasp! For inside the crater is a water fill, inside which three lingas have appeared. Vishnu, Brahmā and Mahesh. The Holy Trinity for Hindus! Jyotirlinga, Lord Shiva's most sacred shrine, found in only twelve hallowed places across India, is now present in their very own Lalbag. No wonder they've been saved.

Praise The Lord! What a surprise! What a blessing! He has not only saved them, but also shown them that destruction can bring renewal.

Now Seth knows that faith is not unfounded, it is not intangible, it is present before him more glorious than ever. He bows his head and prays.

THE GREAT GALL OF CHINA

As China awoke one morning from uneasy dreams, it found itself transformed into a gigantic arid nation. This was not entirely unexpected, of course. The Chinese, so many of them, had long been tapping into scarce resources and drinking up all of China's water. The government tried to get new sources of water. It launched a one-litre-a-day drinking water campaign. It built dam after dam after dam on rivers Yellow and Yangtze and Sungari and Pearl. It tried to save the melting Himalayan glaciers, two-thirds of which were expected to disappear by 2056. It tried to get the Mekong River breadbasket to bake—speaking metaphorically—fresh buns. Nothing worked. Beijing experienced heat waves. Shanghai saw storms and floods. The citizens were left parched. There was simply no water.

China was left with two options: to become a barren wasteland or to source water from the outside.

That's when the bright Chinese strategists remembered

The Doctrine of Absolute Territorial Sovereignty. This doctrine said that upstream states, like China, were allowed unlimited use of trans-boundary waters regardless of what occurred downstream. Now Tibet, whose ass China owned, happened to be—luckily for them—the world's largest water tank. Many rivers originated from Tibet and flowed downstream to other nations. All China had to do was gain absolute control over these trans-boundary waters. After all, why should China let Tsangpo pour its precious water into the Brahmaputra, when it could keep all the water to itself?

Thus, on all rivers flowing out of the Tibetan plateau, China build dams and canals and pipelines! It wrung out all the lower riparian nations and soon had control of most waterways in Asia. China then diverted most of Tibet's water to its parched North (enforcing the one-litre-a-day drinking water policy on the innocent Tibetans) and rejoiced when liquid fire flowed into the bone-dry throats of their yellowing necks.

The other Asian nations protested.

Make a bilateral treaty on water utilisation, China!

Err ... no, sorry, we talk no English.

Share hydrological data, China!

Err ... no, sorry, we see no English.

Engage in dialogue, China!

Err ... no, sorry, we hear no English.

Then the still-thirsty Chinese throats gurgled: why are we nibbling on the shore when we can swallow the whole ocean? So, in typical covert style, China build a dam on

Nepal's Karnali River and then watched—it worked, this plan worked!—the great Ganga River gasped for breath.

The other Asian countries, pushed to the brink, threatened to attack China.

Well, shrugged China. Perhaps for water to flow, blood must flow. Instead of building dams, we will build graves. And so, China began a war for regional dominance. It wasn't a new idea, or fairly difficult. All of China's greatest leaders—Mao Zedong, Sun Yat-sen, Deng Xiaoping—wanted only one thing for China: for it to become the world's most powerful country. China knew that it could become a superpower only when it had an indestructible military power capable of huge devastation across the globe. And it had that: the world's largest army, with a military budget of three hundred billion dollars, one hundred thousand million troops, and a long-roosting ambition to rule Asia. Despite having suffered a century of invasions and humiliations, the Chinese had not developed a notion of not doing unto others what they didn't want others to do unto them. Like a dog squirting on fire hydrants, China began to mark everything in Asia as its territory.

Taiwan: unification. Vietnam: intimidation. Philippines: incapacitation. Spratly Islands in the South China Sea: reconquestation. Outer Mongolia: reclamation. Japan: old revenge, easy conquest, as it lay crippled by Mother Nature. Diaoyu and Ryukyu Islands: now Chinese. Soon, the winds from the Pacific Ocean to the South China Sea to the East China Sea whispered: China is King.

The autocratic regime showed no remorse in displacing and killing thousands of people.

With Tibet, China owned almost fifty per cent of the world's water supply, and now—with recent invasions—it owned more than sixty-to-seventy per cent. It controlled more than half the world. But, the dragon was still thirsty. It greedily eyed another H2O nation: India, with its mammoth blue lines of boundless gurgling water. How lovely would it be, thought China, to sip from the Ganga, Krishna, Godavari, Yamuna, Kaveri and Meghna, to slurp from the Bay of Bengal and Arabian Sea, to take a gulp from that great Indian Ocean.

India was both a mere downstream pawn and also the mightiest enemy on China's border. It was the only nation that could oppose China in the region. It had to go.

Still. Victorious warriors win first and then go to war, Sun Tzu whispered to the ancient memory of the Chinese strategists. They devised a plan. China exported arms upon arms to rogue Pakistan. And Pakistan, tossed the bone of a promised Kashmir, rolled over and licked China's feet, allowing it full rein on its expansionist plans. Armed and in arms, Little Brother went to war with Big Brother: give me back my Kashmir doll. With Big Brother distracted in trying to, once again, discipline the younger one—"No, chotu! No! How many times have I told you not to take something that does not belong to you? Now give Kashmir back."—the Chinese Premier Mao-ed the nation's menacing battle cry, "Fuck his mum! Hit them hard!" And so China went to war with India.

It was 2032.

China lifted India's skirt up and unzipped both the McMohan Line and the Johnson Line. It fucked India slowly, starting with The Finger: Sikkim. Then it felt its way around the Line-of-Actual-Control, four-thousand-odd kilometers of the Himalayan Frontier, and—using as a lubricant the new Silk Route that it had jointly build with sweet innocent India—it penetrated the chicken neck of the Siliguri Corridor. And where the meandering curves of the Brahmaputra bend over into India, sealing the union with moist glistening lips, China entered from the rear. It took out the inverted palm, the state with the cock's head, and then chopped off India's left arm. As India scurried to stem the bleeding, another Chinese regiment went where grass wouldn't grow, pouring over the Karakoram Mountains where Indian jawans, frozen stiff like tin soldiers, lay with weapons in their hands. Then it went chin down into Aksai Chin, *chup chap* down the Chip Chap Valley, roaring to the Rohtang Pass, spearing even the heart-shaped state. It took the axe, felled the Western Corridor and decapitated a crippled India.

For seventy years—since that 1962 Sino-Indian war, that humiliating Chola incident in Sikkim—China had been gathering its breath. So when it huffed and it puffed, it blew the disputed-border-that-it-never-believed-in down, neutralising most of India. After all, war is won only when the warrior has no collective conscience.

When the border assault was complete, China went down south on India, teasing state borders with incursions, declaring that peace would come only when the state with the slanted face was theirs. Having established, over the previous decade, several strategic access points encircling the Indian Ocean Region (just a little something for our energy need, they'd said then), the militarised Chinese string of pearls choked the Indian neck. It swallowed Andaman and Nicobar Islands as easily as a blue whale swallows an infant fish. There was some resistance by the Eastern Naval Command—go, Vizag!—but India's blue-water Navy, with its blue-eyed status and blue-aged diesel-electric submarines, was no match for the Chinese nuclear submarines—go, JIN-class SSBNs!—the advanced nuclear destroyers and the frigates.

The XXXIII Corps, they were the first to be felled, followed by the Eastern Command, and the rest: Western Command, Central Command, Northern Command, South-Western Command. Those brave Mazhabi Sikh soldiers fell weak to the ground. The multi-ethnic, multi-regional Mahar Regiment succumbed to *Bolo Hindustan Ki Jai!* Even the Training Command headquartered in Shimla disassembled. The sambar-eating Southern Command stood its ground but what match was it for the lion-penis-eating Chinese? The last hope was pinned on that virginal futuristic infantry with its fully-integrated-fighting-machine soldiers, but that sub-unit too disintegrated in no time.

Headless and armless, India moaned. Her simultaneous wars with China and Pakistan, a fifth of China's defence budget, her crumbling infrastructure, her worthless rupee and colonial borders, that inept mountain warfare with its pulmonary edema, sub-zero temperature and Indian troops lugging forty kilo bags containing their lifeline of food, medical aid and weaponry, that Maxwell's 1962 war report showing the military's fault lines, another kowtowing Prime Minister (and, goddamnit, another Mephistopheles Defence Minister in a Savile Row suit); how could she fight back?

For the first few Indian states that China loved, the pretty ones they'd always wanted—Sikkim, Arunachal, Assam, Himachal Pradesh, Kashmir, even Gujarat and Maharashtra—the world's largest military build-up went loco—no navy, no air force, no nukes. Instead, a platoon of The People's Liberation Army of China, using stealth foot soldiers with an eight to one numerical superiority, hand-to-hand combat and mortar fire were put to the task. When those states fell, the PLA brought out the armed drones, the long-range missiles and the bombs, and annihilated the uglier states, the ones whose people and topography they felt were not worth saving.

To stop the war, you lose the war. And so India did.

But a large nation, however clobbered, however crushed, is impossible to occupy, to rule, to control, and impossible to train. Isn't that what those Japs had said about the Chinese in the 1930s? So, what to do with this giant India? How to control its unmanageable one and a half billion plus people? Well, to begin with, integrate the pretty states into China—hello Sikkim, hello Arunachal, hello Assam! And UP, Bihar, West Bengal, Odisha, what to do with them? Give them their chaotic independence! Declare them separate countries! Feign sympathy with splinter groups clamouring for secession from the Union of India. Placate them by offering their vulnerable citizens better education, work and healthcare!

Kill freedom fighters and their bloody movements and clubs! Kill those goddamn journalists and bloggers and liberals. Kill the poor, the ugly, the old. Save farmers who could fulfill China's failed agrarian utopian dream. Ban Instagram. Ban Facebook. Ban X. Ban Google. Disintegrate the mighty India! Make it powerless in front of the Megalopolis of China. Merge the Indian army with the Chinese army! Make it the largest and strongest in the world, with a military strength of over four million! Make military service compulsory by law, so captured Indians become soldiers. Goodbye all!

The cartographers went quietly to work on the shape-shifting border, their ink running dry. They named it something they thought was both innocuous and creative: the Chinawallah border. A faction intelligence group wrote another insipid report—The Henderson-Brooks & Bhagat Committee 2—which too would be spoken about but never seen. Rest in peace all!

Why did no one come to India's rescue? Where was the rest of the world?

The US—distracted by the Iran Nuclear Crisis and China's twenty-first century supremacy and, mostly, by its weak foreign policy that no longer engaged whether it was Iraq or Syria or Gaza or Ukraine—condemned the war but continued to supply arms to the Chinese. Europe had disintegrated into its own economic chaos, and was in no position of authority. The UK labelled the war a localised skirmish.

The truth: they didn't mind India becoming communist. They believed that democracy had given India nothing but chaos and poverty, a population that was out of control and consuming more resources than the world could afford. India needed to be regimented.

Plus, hadn't Napoleon prophesized two hundred years ago that once the sleeping dragon awakened, the world would tremble. Why tremble when one can trade economic opportunities instead?

And what of India's neighbours? Oh, the ones to whom China had, for decades, provided economic, technological and military aid? The ones in which China had setup military bases with the sole aim of creating a deadly necklace around India? The ones in The South China Sea, The East China Sea and The Yellow Sea, on which China controlled all sea shipping lanes, thus blocking aid and war assistance coming to India from the East?

Sri Lanka was indebted to the Chinese after their rebuilding efforts post the island nation's civil war. Myanmar, Bhutan, Nepal and Bangladesh could barely save themselves, leave alone India. Khalistan, India's first separatist state and newly declared enemy, was too doped on Afghani opiates to care. Russia was still fighting a sectarian civil war with the Ukrainians. Neither country would be spared either, soon after, but that's another story, another novel.

At a time when cities and countries were swooning like Victorian ladies, divinity saved the obscure Lalbag. The bomb didn't work. The town could not be annihilated. The world was left astounded. This historic event even made the Chinamen quake. There were unknown forces at work in Mount Akaho, like the Jyotirlinga, that protected the town of Lalbag; forces that their mightiest bomb and bravest men could not defeat. And the Chinamen—despite knowing these things (and these things only): military posturing, anarchism and duck sauce recipe—understood that in war what couldn't be explained had to be respected. They relinquished Lalbag. All that the cartographers had left of India was the town of Lalbag: a tiny dot, a small green-brown blip that was easy to miss on any radar.

But the Chinamen use two brush strokes for the word "crisis"—one brush stroke for danger and the other for opportunity. They know that any crisis can be both a danger and an opportunity. So they setup their outposts, their SIGINT stations, and their troops around Lalbag. They watch the town closely. They wait for the right opportunity to destroy Mount Akaho and finish their conquest of the little town, make the whole of India theirs, and show the world their might.

For it's only a matter of time. It's always only a matter of time.

BOUNDARY OF MEMORY

2036

There is no sound of men, only the sound of feet shuffling against the concrete path, the static whining of walkie-talkies. Seth stands in line holding the National Identification Card in his hands. His forehead is sticky with sweat. His eyes are glued to the ground. His palms are moist, as if carrying a corpse. All around him are troops from the People's Liberation Army of China. He does not look up at them.

An egg doesn't hurl itself against a rock.

A gong sounds. The man ahead of him takes a step forward. It is perfectly executed. Seth follows him. He lifts his right leg straight up to knee-height and brings it to the cross mark in front of him. Then he lifts his left leg, with the same military precision, and places it next to his right leg. He stumbles.

What has he done? The hair on Seth's back rise, like the

hackles of a dog. He expects to hear a volley of shots and see blood trickle down his *kurta*. He waits with his eyes shut. He hears a buzzing sound. Is this what death feels like? He opens his eyes. A large grasshopper lands in front of Seth like a grenade. "Shhh ..." Seth whispers. The noisy beating of its wings will attract further attention in his direction.

There's nothing. The troops haven't seen him.

Om Jai Shri Shiv Omkara. Quickly, before his luck runs out, Seth puts his left leg three inches away from his right leg and holds still. He doesn't breathe. His forehead becomes sticky with sweat. A minute passes. Nothing happens. He is safe. He lets out his breath, happy to be alive.

Seth can now see the border between New China and India, a long wall, seven foot high, lined with outposts and topped with wire fencing—the parenthesis of his life. This border encloses Lalbag, which is all that's left of India. A five kilometres band around Lalbag has been cleared of trees and shanties, and earmarked as the border patrol area. Guard units make rounds of this area on foot, some carrying bazookas, most swinging their hip to the right to avoid hitting the rifles slung over their left shoulder. Every two kilometres, heavy machine guns are mounted on sandbag rises and manned with sharpshooters. With their armoured personnel carriers, their machine gun emplacements—buffed like ancient turtles—and their flamethrower tanks, the Chinamen are heavily armed for border patrol. They're also ready to be mobilised within seconds. They live nearby, in a hutment of low-pitched tents, outside which Seth has seen them gather together to smoke, drink Jin Fo tea and look at pornographic magazines.

I hope we don't get into a war with them again, Seth thinks. The last time Lalbag got lucky. Not a single man was killed and not a single house was demolished when China attacked. Will this happen again? Highly unlikely.

When Seth is in New China—at least the three kilometres he's allowed into—it is a completely unrecognizable place from the neighbouring town of Kharbag that earlier stood there. The roads are paved and leveled, washed every morning, dotted with trees, lined with shiny new buildings. There are no beggars and no dirt. The one McDonald's restaurant has been renamed Mai Dang Lao and sells rice burgers. But in the last four years, Seth has never seen an Indian there. Where have they all gone?

Another thought niggles him—the Chinamen who live there don't act like they're living on occupied land. Seth assumes this is because during the thirty years of Maoist rule their parents had been driven by ideology and broken by famine, so to be apolitical is a privilege. They sit with their families in restaurants eating cold noodles with cucumber and batter-fried octopus, while their young girls go shopping for hair clips with plastic flowers shooting out of them. They desire nothing except immediate satiation. The only other people they allow in are white tourists who throng the marketplace, call it hutong, and buy selfie sticks for Yuan hundred from hawkers. The locals, who barely speak English, ignore them. Why should they care when the whole world is learning Mandarin?

It's a pity that nothing of India is left in New China. Seth remembers Nehru describing India as an ancient palimpsest on which layer upon layer of thought was inscribed, without erasing any previous layer. It's therefore even more astounding to think that China has done what no conqueror in India's long history did: they've erased all of India's layers.

India is being forgotten.

Seth sees a line of tanks pass by. Two troops walk up behind him. He hears one of their growling voices shout, "You Yindu bastard." Seth stiffens. If he dies what will happen to his family? Where will they go? How will they survive the Chinamen? And his Ida, of milk and honey, what will happen to her impending wedding? But the troops are not coming for him. They're carrying a dead body, which they toss on the ground a few feet ahead of him, and leave. A patrolman sends a flare to light up the sky, letting the townspeople of Lalbag know that another dissident has been killed. Seth dare not look up, but he imagines a deep red bleed into the sky. Tonight every house in Lalbag will light a diya on their doorstep—their version of grief eaters—such that, from heaven—where their dead (hopefully) rest—the town will look like a small funeral pyre. There's nothing else they can do for the departed.

The smell of the corpse assails Seth. He can't gag—his face has to remain as impassive as the Chinamen—so Seth swallows his own spit. He wants to bring his handkerchief to his nose and dab his sweat with it, but he keeps his hands firmly pressed against his body. The corpse—judging by his blood not yet dry—has been dead for only twelve hours or so. His hands are tied behind his back. A black hole has punctured his temple that is still lined with a tripundra tilak. His eyes are open, the pupils turned upwards, as is his mouth, the tongue twisted inside. Large flies begin to buzz in and out of his nostrils, probably to lay eggs.

Seth shudders. He remembers the other bodies, their rotting carcasses also gouged by cherubic flies, their eyes wide open, faces like black smoke caught in a gust of wind. These are bodies of men, mostly Chinawallahs: Indians living in the India that China annexed during The Chinawallah War. They try to sneak into Lalbag through the footbridge, the only passage into town, but the footbridge is long and the sentries in the watchtower alert. Do they not read the sign at the footbridge that warns: *You Shot Unless Authority*? Chinese English; laughable but explicit. Do they not know that they will be left for dead, unclaimed, at the end of the footbridge? Do they not know that since the failed 2032 bombing, Lalbag has been declared a buffer zone; refugees are not allowed to come in and no one is allowed to leave?

The Chinamen assume that men should know better.

Seth shuts his eyes and holds his hand up to his chest, a dangerous move. Under his kurta, he's scotch-taped the photo of Lord Shiva to his skin. In New China the Chinamen have banned religion and its motifs, except their own. They've forcefully converted Hindus, Muslims, Christians, Sikhs and Parsis into communists. Temples, mosques and churches have been turned into glass and chrome, white bathroom-tiled office buildings with blue Plexiglas windows, a design the Chinamen love. Religion: the sigh of the oppressed creature, the heart of a heartless world, the soul of soulless conditions, the opium of Indians, is illegal. That's why Seth cannot be caught. But this is something he needs. It calms him down.

A gong sounds again. Seth opens his eyes. The man in front of Seth steps away from the line. Seth takes a goosestep forward, this time with a calf-raise, firmly holding his walking stick, and reaches the patrolman's stand without stumbling. Behind the stand is a blue sign that reads: *Outpost 28934. Secret Area. Not To Enter. You Shot Unless Authority.* Inside each outpost is rumoured to be a Chinese SIGINT station, a signals intelligence-gathering vessel, that allegedly spies on the Lalbag residents and gathers their communication data. The townspeople gossip that there are at least a hundred such PLA outposts, though Seth has counted only thirty-nine in total. Seth imagines the inside of these stations to be stacked with rows of classified documents and somber looking men on black phones, listening in on random conversations.

The patrolman is wearing black gaiters, hot to look at in the sun's heat. His face is hairless and shiny, like a little boy's penny. He has a rifle strapped on his back and a Mauser C96 at his waist. On his stand is the statue of Guan Yu, the God of War, red-faced, clad in black armour, his yellow beard gathered in gloved hands. Seth toys with the idea of lifting his eyes to the patrolman's face, like Guan Yu, and shudders at his own foolishness. The Chinamen are intolerant to the slightest form of anarchy. A few months ago, four Chinawallahs, contracted to pick up the border patrols' garbage, were buried alive, in graves they were forced to dig at gunpoint, for refusing to eat the slugs and frog legs served to them for lunch.

A man should know better than to hit the mosquito that lands on his testicles, Seth thinks. He himself is a testament to this. Despite being the (now) second richest man in Lalbag, he is here, every day, surrendering to the whims of the Chinamen.

He moves forward and places his NIC, facing up, on the stand's cross mark. The patrolman picks up the card and studies it carefully. He takes a sip from a canteen. He notes down Seth's ID number, his Minguo calendar date of birth and his Chinese name, Lao Seth Singh—Lao: a Chinese endearment for "old"—on a computer, and scrutinises Seth's face to see if it matches the photo. His face reveals no recognition of Seth, even though Seth is here almost every day. The patrolman then places the card under a scanning machine and when the light on the machine blinks green, he nods his head to the right and says *Zǒu*; Seth is allowed to pass. Seth scrambles past the stand and onto the footbridge.

Peace, like war, commands the price of men.

Below the footbridge is barren land that peters out into a rocky track. Above him, Seth hears a chopper. I wish I didn't have to go to New China every day, Seth thinks as he walks, his strides as quick as his hobble allows him. But he has no option. Seth's company Chokia sells mobiles and mobile accessories. The company's main supplier is in New China.

Seth is one among only a handful of men from Lalbag, all wealthy with Chinese business interests, to be issued a NIC. Even the Chinese, for whom the once felonious capitalism is now a currency, are not foolish enough to refuse incoming money. A smart hare doesn't eat the grass at the entrance to its own hole.

Over the curve of the bridge Seth sees his beloved town of Lalbag. Lightness fills his chest like a helium balloon and he smiles to himself: I'm home.

THE CHINAWALLAH WAR

In eleven minutes, Seth crosses the footbridge and reaches Lalbag's marketplace. He wishes he could call for his car and go home in the luxury of his Rolls-Royce Phantom. But driving cars has been banned in Lalbag—the Chinamen want to watch everything and everyone—and fuel is rationed so most people use motorcycles, bicycles or scooters, something Seth cannot deign to be seen in. So, Seth walks. His breath still feels caught up inside his heart and he needs to shake off this persistent feeling of being weighed down, heavy, as if something is looming above him. He hates having to go to New China so often.

Seth passes Nandu's tea stall as Nandu gives him a smart salute. In front of the stall is a red signboard on which "India's Last Tea Shop" is written in white. Next to the signboard is a mural with a Chinaman and Chinawallah man shaking hands. Below this is inscribed, "War no more, cooperation will build a new nation". The twenty thousand townspeople know that they are being watched; that the Chinamen have imprinted each of their names, each face, to memory. But Nandu's only customers, three men sitting on pink plastic chairs are unmoved by the gravitas of these signs. They eye the desert-dry laddoos that Nandu has sealed in plastic containers and drink the sweet milky tea concoctions that Nandu brews with ginger, ginseng, lotus leaf root and—rumours suggest—a little bit of snake blood. These rumours do little to dent Nandu's popularity. Milk is now available only in powder form and Nandu is the only one in Lalbag who can still make *chai* taste like *chai*.

"Lao Seth, I heard a Chinawallah's throat was slit for running over the toe of a Chinaman?" Nandu shouts out to Seth.

Despite his cavalier tone, Seth sees worry creased on Nandu's face.

It is said of this town of Lalbag, that it's a town for the dead, existing on borrowed time, a ticking time bomb. It's both a battlefield and a safe house. The townspeople are inside a cage. They have no future. They have nowhere to go, nothing to do. They don't know how long they'll live: a day, a week, a month? All they know is that the Chinamen are watching. And the world is watching too, with reverence—for Lalbag is China's only shame in a war that otherwise belonged to them. This proud sentiment is tinged with fear—for New China will take revenge, most likely with the complete annihilation of Lalbag and its citizens. So the streets are filled with such stories, futile gossip and endless questions: How are the Chinawallahs? How long will Mount Akaho protect us? How will we stay alive?

All they're doing is prolonging survival; but then, isn't everyone?

"Don't believe everything you hear," is all Seth can elicit as he hurries on.

New China controls a lot of what happens in Lalbag, from food supply to information. Internet has been banned in Lalbag; people are not privy to the rest of the world. The townspeople still have mobile services—thankfully for Seth—but calls are kept brief and business-like. People no longer send texts, for even an innocuous message can be viewed as dissident by the SIGINT and invite Chinese bestiality.

Gossip has therefore become the main source of information, gleaned from those with NICs. But Seth doesn't know how to answer the townspeople. They ask him to save them; to get their children out. He sees the helplessness in their eyes. What can he do? When the unknown evokes such fear, how can the known, worse than imagined, allay it?

A horse cart carrying a generator passes Seth and, as he tries to overtake it, he sees Manu squatting under a tree, waiting for him. He is smoking because he's heard its part of the Great Chinese Dream. You the young, Seth thinks. On seeing Seth, Manu stubs his cigarette and runs up to him. He folds his hand near his heart and says, "Ni-maste—" a combination of Namaste and Nǐ hǎo ma. He takes Seth's bag, filled with Chinese goods, and they walk towards one of Seth's three Chokia stores.

Manu is wearing Vakil's new khaki shirt—Vakil will not be pleased—and for a moment it's tough to believe that he's a housekeeper. It is, however, the perfect decoy. The semi-Chinese rule in Lalbag dictates dignity of labour and all forms of menial labour, like house helps and rag pickers have been banned. The haves are annoyed at meting out equal treatment to the have-nots. The poor love that house help is an adjective in China, not a noun, defined by their job and not their identity. But they've also heard rumours that the Chinamen are eradicating the Chinawallahs that they deem a burden to New China's limited natural resources—the poor and crippled and ugly and old. And the Chinamen know how to eradicate things. If they mark Ram, Urmila and Manu as poor, they could be picked up and thrown into wells with hand grenades tossed in after them. To save them this fate, Seth has bribed the district officer (for corruption is still rampant) to obtain a worker's license for Ram and his family, designating them as his personal assistants and offering them above minimum wage, at least on paper. Seth gives them a home and his protection, while they continue to work as his helps. Nothing has changed, yet everything has changed.

"How was New China today, Seth Sahib?" Manu asks, his face in a smile too wide to be unconcerned. Seth knows Manu will not talk about the dead body, though he couldn't have missed the flare. Manu carries a giddy-eyed wonder for the Chinese, like a lover who can't see that his moon has blood clots. "Have you seen the highway they're building to connect Lalbag to New China?" Seth nods. "It must be wonderful! No more potholed tar that passed for roads in India."

They cross a few shops and an old gaming parlour outside which a sign reads: *Women wearing skirts on their knees are not allowed here. By, Order.* The *not* has been crossed out by the Chinamen. Unlike Indians, they genuinely believe in women empowerment.

"The British built our roads and took our jewels. The Chinamen built our roads and took our water," says Seth in Hindi. "Is that fair?"

"What's a little water in return for development, Seth Sahib? This is better than those promises of *apne din* that we poor never saw. We need a million controversies to make one dam. The Chinamen build dam after dam, and the poor pose happily in front of it."

"The poor in India did not have much to eat or wear, Manu, but they had a vote. And it was a powerful thing. Like a tiny mosquito that could make a hijda out of a man, this little vote could make a hijda out of a government."

"Who cares about a vote? In New China I'll be given housing, childcare, medicines, education, all for free!"

"But you'll have no rights. You'll need the danwei's permission for everything, even if you want to have kids!"

"As long as I'm not treated like an average Zhou, all this doesn't matter."

The concern of the youth, Seth thinks. To be seen as unique. To never be forgotten.

He smells chana jor being roasted with desi ghee and chilli powder in an open-air mud oven. Steam rises, like dreams in the air, from a boiled shakarakand cart, where sweet potatoes sit like perfect brown teeth slathered in Amul butter. Nothing's better than Indian street food, Seth thinks. His stomach growls. He wants to stop and eat, but he would rather be in the safety of his own home as quickly as possible.

"These are all things of the past," he corrects Manu. "New China is more unequal than it's ever been. There only a platinum credit card talks; a card you don't have."

Manu nods uncomfortably. Everyone knows the New Chinese government has told people to shut up and get rich. The Chinamen study Marx and Mao, but only dream of money. It's still better to be poor in India than to be poor in New China.

"New China should give us their roads and leave us our democracy," Seth says softly, knowing this will never happen.

A peddler on a bicycle rushes by with a stack of candied apples and raspberries on his back seat. "Congratulations on your daughter's wedding, Lao Seth!" he shouts. Seth nods but doesn't reply. He's superstitious that way.

They reach Seth's store and Manu places the Chinese goods inside the glass top counter. Outside the store's cement wall someone has plastered a poster for Rakshak Condoms. The ad shows two stick figures in white: a man and a woman. "Hum" is written on top of the man and "Tum" on top of the woman. A sperm, also painted in white, points to the man and says: *Sochta kya hai? Ek ho ya anek, condom laga ke dhek.* Such depravity, Seth thinks, shaking his head. He's about to tell Manu to remove the ad when he stops. This work can only be on the dictat of the Chinamen, who are partial to birth control. There's a no-child rule on the Chinawallahs, a sustainable demographic structure the Chinaman is building. Indians are expected to contract the Chinese disease *shoshika*—a society without children—and go from red to grey. What can one do?

Seth tells the manager to shut the store an hour early today in honour of Ida's wedding. Manu's shoulder slump when Seth says this. Youth is really wasted on the young, Seth thinks and asks, "All in order at home?"

Yes, Manu mumbles, and again Seth wonders what happens to the boy every time Ida's wedding is mentioned. He knows there's been more work in the house than usual, but that's the nature of celebration: it's born of hard work.

Seth looks at Manu. He's shuffling behind him. Seth decides to humour him.

Seth asks, "Stop working all the time. Get a girlfriend. Have some fun."

Manu shuffles his feet for a distance and says, "I don't want a girlfriend."

Like the other boys, Manu thinks that war is an obstacle to love and happiness.

"Do you know that your Chinamen have multiple women? But the Chinawoman can only keep one man," Seth says.

"Really? Why is that?"

"They say that one teapot usually has four cups, but have you ever seen one cup with four teapots?"

Manu laughs.

Two feet away, behind Kittu's cold drinks stall and a

pawnshop for pressure cookers, Seth sees a frayed billboard from almost four years ago. It's of that buffoon politician, dressed in khadiwear, eyes squinted, the kind of person who needs flash cards to recognise human emotions. It's rumoured that when India was attacked, this scion of the nation's greatest political dynasty, was the first to flee the capital and move his black money—multi-billion dollars sired from India's kitty—to Switzerland.

Someone has spat on the billboard. Good, thinks Seth.

"You know I have no choice but to marry off Ida?" he continues softly in Hindi. "If the Chinamen take my stores ... I'll be left with nothing. This is the only way to keep my daughter safe."

He thinks of Nandini Mehra and knows he's doing the right thing. He glances to the West. This is where his factories were before the Chinamen seized them and transferred them to business tycoon Deven Shah, his arch nemesis. Deven manufactures sex toys in the factory, a far more lucrative business than Seth's mobile business, for Deven is now Lalbag's richest man. By marrying Ida to Deven's son Harsh, Seth is staging a sort of coup.

"Harsh has a NIC that is transferable to a spouse ... he has money ... means ... he can make Ida a mother before the Chinamen come ... God willing, he can take her to Jerusalem."

Israel has been accepting Indian refugees, the only country to do so. But to get there one has to fly via Dubai. Getting a visa is virtually impossible as the Middle East has major oil contracts with China. Still, money speaks, miracles occur.

"I know, Seth Sahib. I understand," Manu replies. "You've already lost so much weight worrying about Ida."

Seth looks at Manu and smiles. "No one has conducted a wedding on this scale at a time like this. They're sending cops to watch us. What if there's a problem?"

"There won't be," Manu mumbles.

"I hope the dinner tonight with Deven and Harsh goes off well."

"It will," Manu mumbles.

Will it? In Lalbag nothing's for certain. Everything is always changing, Seth thinks.

They turn right on the path leading to the town square, where Seth hears the laughter of children from the Jhande Wala Park. Near the gate, the Indian flag hangs on a flag post, upside down, a sign to the Chinese of surrender. The children, gathered in groups of three, are playing cricock, a popular Indo-Chinese game that involves bowling shuttlecocks to a cricket bat. Some are running around sandbags, pretending to shoot one another. A girl is playing paddleball by herself, the rubber ball banging against the paddle, while her friends gather around her, also in groups of three, giggling for no apparent reason. What I would give to be carefree like that, Seth thinks melancholically.

The children stop playing when they see him. They run towards him, forgetting that they're supposed to come in groups of three. Ni-maste, Ni-maste, they say to him and grin. He can't correct them. Not when they're smiling like that. He holds out his hands that have White Rabbit Creamy Candy, their favourite item from New China.

They ask him:

"Seth Sahib, is it true that the Chinamen hide in the mountain?"

"And at night, when you are fast asleep, the Chinaman sneaks into your room and takes you up to Mount Akaho?"

"And there he chops you into tiny pieces and eats you?"

"There are no Chinamen in Mount Akaho, kids. I am sure of it," Seth replies gently.

He sees a cop in the far distance. Lalbag's police office has come under China's jurisdiction. It's illegal to gather in groups of more than three people, unless one is indoors. Dissidents are jailed without trial and hanged in a matter of hours. If the cop sees them it could all be over.

"Now you have to go away, okay? Fast!" Seth shouts. "Otherwise the Chinaman will see us."

The children see the panic in Seth's eyes and disperse in groups of three. Seth looks at their tiny backs and says to Manu, "The Chinamen have made military service compulsory by law, so Chinawallahs as young as eight are being trained to become soldiers. Can you imagine being made to run miles, work out, and master combat training? It's a catastrophe I tell you."

"I think it's better than our lazy Indian exercises, like yoga, that involve lying around," Manu quips.

Seth keeps quiet. What can he say to a Chinese sympathiser?

"Do you think that the Kurukshetra War was not a real battle, Seth Sahib?" Manu finally says. "That it was a metaphor for our life, the daily battles we have to fight? Or that Ravana was not a demon but the ill inside Shri Ram that had to be destroyed using Sita-ji as a crutch? And that's why Sita-ji was gone once he defeated Ravana?"

Seth looks at the boy, surprised. Since when has he started speaking like this?

"Even this war we're in, that we're not fighting, Seth Sahib—well, it's not a real war, like you know ... like Kurukshetra ... with a battleground and battle line, where you fight the enemy till one side is defeated. The Chinamen dare not attack Lalbag. We have nothing to attack them with. They watch over us. We have no option but to be watched. There is nothing for us to fight, to forsake our life for. It's all in limbo. This is not a war."

"Would you prefer a by-the-book war?"

"No, I'm saying that this is an ideology, not a war. India had to be merged with China to stem the impact of climate change. People had to be killed so others could be saved. The war is not military but tactical."

"What nonsense, Manu! Those Chinese-speaking classes you're going to have brainwashed you. We should have nuked China when we had the chance," Seth mumbles in Hindi. You never know who's listening.

"What? And triggered a nuclear winter? Brought an end to two of the world's oldest cultures?" Manu shakes his head in surprise. "The Chinese would have dropped their No First Use policy for nukes and retaliated. Their nuclear warheads are three times what we had. India would have been wiped out. Actually, not just India. It would have led to a nuclear famine the world over, destroying all agricultural production. Three-four billion people would have died. That would've been apocalyptic."

Seth shakes his head sadly. This is what the war has done to the youth, turned them into cynics. They cannot fight for their country. They cannot take up arms. They cannot bleed on the battleground. All they can do is wait around for a Chinese bomb to land on their head. So they build no future, secure no jobs, marry no women.

"You think too much, Manu. If we'd had enough time to plan and strategise, the Indian military would have defeated the Chinese."

"I doubt it, Seth Sahib. The Chinese had five times India's submarines and tanks, double the warships, three times the number of aircrafts. Even their long-range missiles DF-41 had a range that was twice our Agni-V."

Our life is a story that we tell ourselves, thinks Seth. He is too tired for Manu's ideologies, too tired to assuage his own fears. So he taps his walking stick against the ground and trudges on ahead.

He looks northeast, up at the conical-shaped Mount Akaho, named for the earth (a) in between (ka) the sky (ho) for it was created by the Prajapati, or so Lalbag's legend states. No one, neither the Indians nor the Chinese, have understood what happened at Mount Akaho: the appearance of Lord Shiva and the destruction of the bomb—twenty-five metric tonnes of pure nuclear. It's believed that the bomb was swallowed by the mouth of Mount Akaho and plugged by the Jyotirlinga. Many say that the bomb has become a store of gems in the mountain's heart and its shine, so brilliant, spreads like a quilt of light over the mountainside. The Chinamen, like the Indians, have a habit of accepting their fate. They believe that Lalbag is protected by divinity. As long as Mount Akaho exists, they do not dare to attack Lalbag again.

Seth says a silent prayer as the two men turn right into the gated community area of Royal Mason. Even here, the sense of fear is palpable. Outside every house the Indian flag has been hung upside down. If the flag turns, or is missing, for even a day, a Chai sign—the sign for destruction in Chinese—appears outside the house, and within hours entire families go missing and are never seen again. Many houses now lay abandoned in Royal Mason.

They pass the ten-by-fifteen-foot bunker. It is one of two bunkers in Lalbag, the other being at Comi Area, the posh sequestered part of town where only the local Chinese are allowed to live. The bunkers are a privilege for the rich who the Chinamen want to preserve so they can use them to build New China. They've been told that if they hear a howl from the sky or a siren they are to run into this bunker. Such courtesies have not been provided to the "non-rich", the Indians living and working in demarcated parts of Lalbag that are considered dirty or dangerous. There are rumours that many of them have dug bunkers underneath their houses, as deep as the earth and their resources allow.

The bunkers are not the things that provide balm to Seth

for his eyes seek only his house: The White Taj. When he finally sees it—glistening under the sun, moon of the moons, star of the stars, a place where his breath has come to life every morning for the past sixty years—his heart starts racing and his strides become longer. The day's weariness washes off him like a warrior's blood.

Suddenly there's an explosion from Mount Akaho; the fire from its four pillars rise into the air, like the agitated thoughts of a spurned lover. No one in town knows why or how this happens, but it happens every evening at five, like the countdown to a great historic event. Every year, since the war four years ago, on the twenty-fourth day of the seventh month, a pillar mysteriously appears on either side of Mount Akaho. Each pillar is made of ten thousand eight hundred bricks, all baked and squared, representing each hour of each passing year. A fire burns from each pillar and it doesn't stop come rain or storm. It burns through the day and night.

Some townspeople believe that the Chinamen build these pillars and they contain secret Chinese stockpiles of ammunition and bombs and gasoline. Others say that Chinese soldiers secretly live inside them. There are others who claim that the Chinamen have planted a nuclear-fuelled device inside the pillars to monitor activities in Lalbag, just like the one set up in 1965 on the Himalayan peak, Nanda Devi, by an Indo-US mission to spy on the Chinese. Another section of townspeople believes that it is a manifestation of Shiva's blessings to show that He is protecting Lalbag.

At Mount Akaho's rear are splintered peaks of black

mountains, some streaked with white snow, some with chains of thick fog around their throats, like prisoners behind bars. Everything that frees also imprisons, Seth believes.

Like all great things, Mount Akaho's fame is far greater than the sum parts of its significance. Despite its name and legend Mount Akaho is—in fact—a mere three-hundred-metre-tall hill that is crowned by the temple to which one can clamber by way of one-hundred-and-eighty-one ridged steps. It's harmless.

Outside the four-sided stone gatepost of The White Taj a sign says: "Accident Porn Area", another one of New China's grossly misspelled and useless signboards. At least it's not the Chai sign, Seth thinks gratefully. Manu covers this sign with a thick string of marigold flowers that have been hoisted like tapestry around The White Taj. He turns to smile sheepishly at Seth.

"Should I complain about this to the district office?"

Seth laughs. He puts his arms on Manu's shoulders and replies, "When your house is on fire, you don't throw gasoline on it."

They turn to enter The White Taj.

BRIMFUL OF LADLE

Ram listens to the chatter of workmen putting up shamianas outside The White Taj. In haste, he drives the hammer hard into the nail on the wall. It almost slips onto his thumb.

"Careful, now," he mumbles to himself as his eyes twitch. He hasn't slept in days and the dark circles under his eyes are wider than cesspools. He strings the tapestry on the white stucco wall, no longer able to count which one this is; he's been hanging up tapestries in every room of the mansion since morning.

Job done, Ram steps off the stool and loses his foothold. He is about to fall, smack on the ground, but, fortunately, his stomach—big and lopsided despite his thin legs and arms—hits the wall and he is saved.

As he straightens up, Ram thinks not of potential injuries but of his work. Tonight is their big night—when Ida's to-be in-laws are coming home. Everything has to be perfect. He scans the ground floor of the mansion: the tea lights on the front porch and back verandah, the white lanterns on the ceilings, and the strands of twinkle lights on every wall, which he spent two days hanging up. Ida's wedding planner has a firework display scheduled after dinner tonight, and Ram wants to be certain that the firework is no match for the mansion that at nighttime, he hopes, will glitter brighter than a quasar.

Such pettiness, Ram knows, but this is all he has to give Ida.

"How else can a servant show his love?" he mumbles to himself, grabbing a bunch of marigold threads in his arms. Since childhood Ram has served Seth as his faithful and humble help, without knowing where duty ends and love begins. And now Ida, of milk and honey, whom he held as a baby smaller than his forearms, in whose playfulness he sees the daughter he never had, is getting married. He cannot give her away, he cannot pay for her trousseau or banter with her groom. He looks at the tall gifts stacked up against the wall and knows that he cannot even buy Ida a wedding present—it will be too small or too big, insulting in either case. So Ram doesn't sit, doesn't eat, and doesn't sleep in preparation for the wedding, till at last Seth notices: "Rest now, Ram. You've done enough." His gift has been received, Ram thinks. For how else can a servant show his love?

A tear rolls down his cheek. Ram quickly wipes it away. If the price for love is suffering, he thinks, it's a price a foolish man like me is willing to pay.

Ram hears the front gate opening.

"Seth Sahib is coming," he shouts, running through the large living room and into the kitchen. "He is almost here. Is the house clean?"

Urmila drops her ladle stirring coconut curry, and begins to put away the utensils on the countertop. Ram—in order to please Seth—has been insisting that the mansion, despite being a wedding household, remain as spotless as the bride's face.

Ram continues to shout, "Manu! Go check the rooms on all floors."

There is no response.

Ram looks around for his son. "Where is he? Where's Manu?" he asks his wife.

Urmila shrugs, her dark eyes luminous, her pupils white. She doesn't know. True to her vow, she hasn't spoken since the bomb dropped on Lalbag. No point in asking her.

Ram clucks his tongue. Manu has been disappearing over the past few weeks, like a Murakami cat, barely participating in the wedding preparations and even neglecting his household duties, which he usually performs with the gusto that only the young possess. But there's nothing that can be done. The boy is not here.

Urmila understands that a mother must do what her son fails to do. She picks up a plate of beetroot and leaves the kitchen, which Seth never enters. She goes to the drawing room and looks around at the marble coffee table and its fireplace with a mirrored mantelpiece. Above the mantelpiece hangs a family portrait with the expectant gloss and shiny smiles. Urmila straightens it, knowing it's the first thing Seth will look at when he enters the house. Chandeliers with teardrop crystals light the dining room, dimming any imperfections, but Urmila makes sure the fresh lilacs are in the vase. There's a study room and a library stuffed with thick books that no one reads, neither of which Seth has seen the inside of. The architect has used what Urmila understood as a "byzantine" design for the inside of the house, which means that the house has archways, large square pillars with white marble spheres, and streamlined contours for the lighting fixtures, all of which keep the house effortlessly beautiful and make her job easier.

Urmila looks out at the semi-circular spooled porch in front of which is a garden inset with a gazebo. The gazebo is fanned by tall torches and adjoined by a lily pond where goldfish—that Ida insists sing during the rain—swim. This is also where Seth's wife Kamala used to hold her sought-after monthly kitty parties, back when it was okay to be openly frivolous, with themes like The Queen of Rolex, The Doll of Gucci, and The Duchess of Prada, brands a guest had to wear to be admitted.

Satisfied that the wedding labourers have not spoilt the porch, Urmila climbs up the marble staircase to the first floor, knocks on a bedroom door and walks in. Like all the other rooms, this room too has a tessellated ceiling and a chandelier with a tassel at the bottom end. There's also a balcony with wrought-iron railings on which Ida loves to sit. A pair of golden stilettos is on the floor. Urmila picks them up and arranges them carefully on the shoe rack. Inside the shoe rack she finds Tubby, Ida's stuffed teddy bear. She places it next to the full-length mirror cabinet, where it is usually kept.

Kamala looks up from the couch, where she is sitting amid rows of jewelry cases, a new obsession since the war, talking to herself, "Is it okay for mother of bride to wear more jewelry than bride?" On seeing Urmila she asks absent-mindedly, "Snacks and dinner full ready?"

Urmila nods. She wipes her hands at the end of her sari, stained red with beetroot. A drop falls on the floor, bloodying it. Kamala gulps when she sees the stain and adds, quickly and politely, "I ask only because Sethji worry about tonight dinner. How like headless pigeon he is running up down."

There's a giggle. "It's a headless chicken, mother," a voice says. On a four-poster bed with cascading lilac drapes and plump pink throws, Urmila sees a velvet creamy face onto which almond and honey paste is being massaged. Ida turns to Urmila and asks. "Do you think Harsh will like me, Ayi? Do you think he'll find me beautiful?"

For a second Urmila can't blink. Even though she sees her everyday, Urmila has to agree with the townspeople that Ida, of milk and honey, is the most beautiful woman they've ever seen. How can a woman not know she's this beautiful?

It's the war. It's produced a deep dread in everyone of anything that's good.

Urmila holds her hand in a thumbs-up. Ida smiles. Urmila gives her the plate.

"It's a bride's worst nightmare to get married without

makeup! Do you think they'll notice a little mascara? I have an old bottle from four years ago." While women across Lalbag have hailed the better rights, increased safety and more equality they've got under New China, they detest that—since Chinamen think that only actresses and sex workers wear makeup—cosmetics have been banned. Ida picks up a beetroot and laughs, "I can't believe I have to use beetroot as rouge, lipstick and eye-shadow. It's ridiculous!"

"Stop this nonsense," Kamala quips. "Since morning to night you go like cracked record, am I pretty, will fatso love me? We have more worry. You know people call me Old Mrs? From which angle I be old?"

"Don't you understand that it's important that Harsh likes me? It will save my life, and probably all of ours," Ida says, her soft brown eyes squinted in worry. She lifts her pet pug Lassi, now called Baijiu in public, as he licks her nose with zest. "The dinner tonight has to go off well."

Kamala glares at Ida, remembers that she will be gone in three days, and turns to look at Urmila. Urmila motions her index finger upwards.

"Oh yes, Vakil's room. I'm sure it's clean, not that her in-laws will check," says Kamala. Her son lives on the second floor with his wife Pia. Since the war, the two of them stay locked in their bedroom most of the day, praying to Mount Akaho. They've even shifted the mirror in their room so that it reflects Mount Akaho at all times. Vakil meets the family once a day, during dinner, and does not otherwise like to be disturbed.

But intrusion is not something a mother recognises in her son's life, so Kamala picks up the internal landline and presses two on the dial pad. After a minute she puts the phone down. "No answer he is. Must be doing Om, Om, Om. He think his prayer will stop China from attacking us? Such stupidity I tells you! Manu go and check his room!"

Urmila shakes her head from side to side; Manu is nowhere to be found. She points to herself—she will go up to Vakil's room—and leaves. Ida watches Urmila. She possesses the kind of body that looks like it's taken a deep breath in and forgotten to breathe out. Her face has met the same fate, as if it's been smashed against a window. The war has been a cruel agent. No wonder the townspeople are scared of her.

After Urmila leaves the room, Kamala chides Ida, "How many time I tell you be careful what you talk in front of *her*. You want thing to go wrong before wedding?"

But Ida is not listening. When her mother's notice turns to another diamond necklace, Ida looks at a pair of her panties that are lying discarded on the floor. They are pink with a red rose in the front; Manu's favourite. Ida shuts her eyes and remembers those many moments when she's drawn her curtains to find him standing next to the washing area below her bedroom balcony, holding this panty in his hands. On seeing her, he'd bring the panty to his nose and take a deep sniff: the smell of her, all of her, in his nostrils. His eyes would shut in pleasure. A big smile would light up his face. He's never once washed them.

But since the announcement of her marriage, Manu has

not only stopped standing below her balcony, but he's also been sending this panty back to her, clean and—like a slap to the face—ironed. It comes to her with a shock that this love, Manu's love, of which she's always been so certain, is slowly ceasing and that she misses it.

She rolls over and thinks about her to-be husband, Harsh Shah. Ida doesn't mind that he sniffles his nose a lot, and that, though taller than most men and better built, he slouches at his shoulders. His idea of life is to receive everything that he gets with the simple acceptance of a child, and she hopes this will include her. She's met him only once and can only hope that the premeditated arranged marriage will translate into love. But is love all that a woman needs? Doesn't a woman long to be weighed down by a man's body and be consumed by his agony? Doesn't a woman need a man who stands below her window every night as she slowly undresses for him; a man who is as dark as Harsh is fair, as hot-blooded as Harsh is calm, a man who enjoys smelling her smutty panties? Is love all that a woman needs? No, of course not. Ida, she knows this.

Ida feels feverish, as if she's made of water, and the water is boiling. Her feelings continue to knead and plod her body with such disregard for what they're doing to her that Ida wonders if they're being intentionally cruel. Still, it is only when her mother leaves the room that she gets out of bed.

She picks up her panty from the floor and takes an old red lipstick from her dressing table. At least she can use it for something. She turns to the inside of her panty and writes: *Midnight. Black Taj*. She folds it neatly into a wicker basket of her soiled clothes, picks up the basket, leaves her room and walks down the marble steps.

Behind The White Taj is a large empty laterite field that shimmers like a lake of blood. From this rises hot red dust that engulfs three adjoining decrepit black walls, an unfulfilled mausoleum of Seth's ambition: The Black Taj. Before the Chinawallah War her father had wanted to build The Black Taj as a traditional courtyard home, with a four-sided yard and blood red lacquered doors, flanked by guardian lions with ferocious roars meant to scare away bad spirits from the mortal and immortal world. After the war, he wanted to make it as lavish as The Taj Mahal, which New China now controlled. They reasoned with him. Some thirty thousand labourers built the actual Taj. It took them twenty-five years. Its marble came from Rajasthan, jasper from Punjab, and jade from China. From Tibet came turquoise, lapis lazuli was sourced from Afghanistan, sapphire from Sri Lanka, and carnelian from Arabia. How could they build something like that with the Chinamen watching? Seth persisted. He wanted the fourth wall to be made of red sandstone inlaid with semi-precious stones, like the actual Taj Mahal. It was only when he hired an architect who was later found in a ditch with his fingers chopped off, that Seth dropped the idea. Now The Black Taj is a frail shadow of The White Taj, a dilapidated howling structure with the reputation of an angry ghost.

Dreams sometimes have all the soot of a fireplace with none of its warmth, thinks Ida.

The basket is becoming heavier by the moment and it

is while clutching the gold-plated balustrade in precarious balance that Ida wonders: if no one can find Manu, where is she supposed to find him? She knows. He's been spending more and more time with her father, as if holding on to a remnant of her. He must be with him. On the ground floor, in the dim light, she spots Seth in the drawing room discussing the carpenter's wages with the wedding planner. He's lost a lot of weight, she realises. Best not to disturb him. Kamala is sipping tea at the teakwood dining table, her hand vacantly, and as always, petting a ritzy pendant on her neck. Manu is not there.

Her parents don't see her, so she avoids them and tiptoes to the kitchen. Urmila is there, alone, stabbing a pumpkin with a sharp pointed knife. Never mind. Ida walks to the back verandah and peers at the orchard. This is where the wild things grow, of their own accord, untended and lush. To give this orchard some sense of decorum Seth has kept aside a part of it for a kitchen garden. This is tended to—on most days—by a drunk gardener who manages to coax out spindly ladyfingers and sour tomatoes, with carpetweed being the rare thing that grows there in abundance. Many times behind the big mango tree, Ida has let Manu squeeze her breasts.

Manu is almost certainly not there. Ida goes back inside, debating whether to take her hunt to the coal cellar, when she spots Ram at the gazebo. He is setting plastic chairs for Harsh and Deven, who are expected to arrive shortly for dinner. There are men. And there is Ram. A boy with crow's feet and gray hair, stooped not by wisdom but by servitude, ingratiating to the point of blandness, eager to empty himself into the nearest available mold. Men like Ram always have a smile but never an answer. There is no point in asking him anything.

If Manu is not here, then there's only one other place he'll be. Ida places the basket firmly against her waist and walks outside, quietly past the front door. She looks over the curved driveway. Made from round river cobblestones the driveway is spotted like an alligator and at its mouth are parked Seth's flashy cars: a Jaguar, a 1947 Buick, one Mercedes, a 1952 Packard and his Rolls Royce; none of them have been driven since the war. Along either side of the driveway are foot-high statues of The Ecstasy of St Teresa, meant to demonstrate that Seth's family is progressive and cultured. But brown lines of water run down the faces of the saints, lending the stylised sculptures an oddly stodgy look, almost staid in the evening light. The driveway splits, turning left into the mansion and right into the servants' quarters that is separated from the main house by a stone path and carefully camouflaged behind a row of frangipani trees. This is to where she walks.

Ida reaches the servants' quarters and stands outside it. She doesn't say anything. She doesn't make a sound. She counts to three in her head, and opens the door without knocking. He is there, facing her, waiting for her, as he always is.

It's as if his eyes only seek her.

She walks up to him and puts the basket in front of him. "For you."

He tosses the basket. She sees a hot flash consume his entire body. She smiles.

In the house Manu is an amorphous entity, dangerous of Ida's full attention, but now she can scrutinize his smoldering dark looks like hot coals she wants to walk over. His sleeves are rolled up to his biceps and his trousers show half his lower leg (he's wearing Vakil's clothes that can't keep up with his height). His body is a place where youth has come to reside. It is strong, with the kind of muscles that her rich friends acquire with steroids. His sooty black eyes focalise his exquisiteness, as if they're the earth around which celestial bodies revolve. His hair is like waves washing ashore, and it makes Ida want to run her hands through them. Who would've thought that poverty was a raw savage beast that would walk beside him like a trophy? Her brain becomes fatuous mush, but her body, it wants to be held by him, by those lips and those arms, and be torn apart by them.

Ida ignores her impulse to leave everything behind for their love, for this world is full of responsibilities greater than happiness. For now, she can only leave her lover's house.

Once Ida is gone, Manu sits down on the floor. All he hears is his heart banging loudly against his chest, as if it wants to sear his body. He looks around. This is where he lives with his mother and father, in this structure that was originally intended to be some sort of gardener's shed (which accounts for the flimsiness of its walls). This roomless house is divided by curtains into three parts—his parents' room, his room and a kitchen. The house has two doors: a front door that leads out to the garage and main gate, and a back door that leads onto a small verandah—Manu's favourite part of the house—overlooking the orchard. Attached to the house is an outhouse, a narrow and cold space built as an afterthought to a bathroom. It contains a toilet where iron has stained the bowl a toxic brown, and a black rubber hose for bathing, through which a trickle of water flows in icy coldness. Despite his mother's constant swabbing and dusting, everything in the house remains smutty with grime. This house is the reason he can't be with Ida. It's a symbol of his poverty, the deadly thing that tears lovers apart.

He collects all her clothes and puts them back in the basket, folding each one gently, caressing each one as if it's a baby that has to be coddled back to sleep. He is searching for a message Ida must've sent him. Stop, he says to himself. He cannot fall under love's trap again. But his hand keeps rummaging the basket. You have to stop, he thinks, gathering his strength into determination. Quickly, before his mind changes, he carries the basket outside. Next to the outhouse is a washing area for clothes and utensils, where he dumps the clothes on the hard cement floor and begins to wash them. The soapsuds flow into nothingness, like his feelings.

Suddenly he stops. For beyond the water, beyond the hard floor, beyond the splay of the many coloured clothes, he sees his favourite panty: pink with a red rose in the front. And on it is scrawled that message again: *Midnight. Black Taj*.

This time, he decides, he will not go.

A BREAST OF RED

The window is open but no breeze brings relief. Instead, the heavy smell of summer grass wafts in, a blanket Manu could suffocate under. He brings the panty to his nose and takes a deep inhale. It is there, the smell of dried onion and old cheese; the smell of her. He sniffs again and slumps down. Over the clot of white, that looks like rotted garlic clove, Ida has written her message in bright red; her hieroglyphic writing with long wavery stems and big circular dots.

He will not go and meet her.

The evening sky begins to feast on the day. He watches darkness creep up on him and eat away his shadow, his legs, his arms, his head, till he can no longer be saved. In this blackness he is nothing but a beating heart.

At The White Taj, she's entertaining her future husband, fluttering her eyelashes, making herself palatable to whatever need Harsh may have. She's being anything but herself. All her life she's claimed to love Manu, but last month—without hesitation, without thought, without telling him—she agreed to marry another man. Why? To survive this stupid war? Did she think about how Manu would feel? How he'd live without her? Did she wonder what he would do in this house without her? Did she ever love him? She's broken him, this heart of his, and now she wants to meet him? He will not go.

He sees the light switch, a pull chain hanging from the bulb, and yanks it. The light comes on and there he is, back again, in all his form, shadow and legs and arms and head; the heart already somewhere else.

He will not go to The Black Taj; it isn't right. And it isn't right for Ida to meet another man before her wedding.

He cannot go. He should not go. He will not go.

The sounds of crickets bang against the walls of his temple like squash balls. Something crawls up his leg, a feathery antennae touch, a grasshopper or cockroach, sending a shooting tingle, like that of a spider web, throughout his body. He brushes it aside and gets up from his bed to sit on the verandah where the light from a glass lantern has attracted a hive of glow-worms. With the ceaseless beat of their wings these glow-worms bang into each other, half mad things, frantic like the thoughts in his head.

He looks into the orchard where random life grows: tall thin nandins, orange marigolds, weeds with white pods in their mouths, a funny mix blushing in the afterglow of sundown. When dawn comes, they will light up like twinkling torches under the mesh of the moon and the sun, and become shiny happy things, bathing unabashedly in the delicate shower of dew. There will be a new world. And he? He will remain the same. He shuts his eyes.

Only a few minutes remain till midnight. Dinner with the family must be over. Ida must be back in her room. Manu's parents must be cleaning up. Harsh must be a delighted man.

Manu can go to The Black Taj without being noticed, without being missed, and return before his parents are back.

He should not go. He cannot go. He will not go.

***

It is afternoon and the front lawn of The White Taj is festooned with balloons. Ida is turning thirteen today. There are clowns and magicians, stalls for hair braiding and video games, a rock-climbing wall. Her friends, most of them from the Royal Mason, are playing and laughing. Manu is inside the gazebo, cleaning a bench on which a girl has spilled juice. He moves self-consciously among the children. In school he's a few years senior to them—courtesy Seth Sahib—but at The White Taj he's a servant to them. He's picking up after his juniors, bringing them paper plates filled with Gucci imprinted cupcakes, olive crackers and imported Gouda cheese that he is not allowed to taste, stacking up Ida's gifts on a table. Two boys walk up to him. Where's *your* birthday gift for Ida, they ask. I don't have one, he replies shame-faced. He thinks of himself as Ida's plaything, not her playmate. They scowl at him. He doesn't meet their eyes. They push him to the ground. The large boy gets on top of him, ready to punch. Suddenly Ida is there, yelling at the bullies. They scramble. Manu gets up; he's embarrassed that Ida has seen him like this. He turns to go. Follow me, Ida says to him. She walks through the mansion, past the adults whose liquor-filled glasses clink with ice, through the laterite ground and into The Black Taj. Here, they're alone. He looks wonderstruck at the black walls, shining like the hide of a water buffalo. We are not allowed to come here, he says. Ida walks up to him. Her eyes stare directly into his. "Am I not beautiful?" she asks him. He looks at her as if seeing her for the first time. Yes, she is beautiful. He sees her lick her lips. She puts her lips on his. It's only for a second. His world shifts. He doesn't know what to do. Should he press his lips harder against hers? Should he bring out his tongue? She pulls back. She hesitates for a moment and then lifts her dress, pushes down her panties. He sees that her lips have moved from her mouth down to her legs, and they're standing up! Oh no! Is this punishment for kissing her? He looks up at her face in horror. But no, her lips are still there, pouty and pink on her mouth. Do all girls have two lips? Maybe he's not supposed to look. Maybe it's magic. He turns away. Touch it, she tells him. He turns back. He doesn't dare. Touch it. *No.* Kiss me here like you kissed me there. *No, they will kill me.* A boy in school touched a girl there. She said she liked it. Touch it, she repeats. *Ask one of the other boys.* I don't like them, she says, I like you. I want you to touch it. It will be your gift to me on my birthday. Manu has no choice. He touches it. It's soft. Put your finger in. He puts his finger into the folds. It's grainy. She giggles. She has the prettiest smile in the world. She pulls her panties up. Don't tell anyone, okay? Pinky swear? He nods. She steps outside the walls and is gone. Manu drops to the ground and brings his finger to his nostrils. There is a smell of soft grass and petals, which will become like mercury and curdled milk, as she gets older. Her smell: her gift to him.

***

Manu enters The Black Taj. Blinded by its absolute darkness, he gropes the brick walls till his eyes find light in the flicker of a lamp. His shadow is thrown against the corner of a wall from where another shadow emerges and merges with his.

"I am leaving," he shouts at the shadow. "I came here to tell you ... I want to tell you that it is over between us."

The shadow becomes a bright red cloth, shimmering with a million mirrors. Each mirror reflects his unmet desire. Stay strong, he tells himself. Turn around and leave. Then her face emerges, a face for which the light burns, for which mirrors are built; a face cast in the soft glow of beauty. Ida: Goddess of the Earth, born of dewdrops and stardust, her opaline skin of milk and honey, gleaming golden: for morning had slipped into her mother's womb at the moment of her birth.

He manages to ask, "How was dinner? Is your to-be-husband madly in love with you?"

How does it matter, she says simply.

"Do what you want. I am leaving," Manu shouts.

"Even if I say I love you?" she whispers.

Manu startles for a second. Can it be true? Has she not given up on their love? But she's marrying another man.

"How can you love two men at the same time?" he asks.

"The heart is not a box that gets filled up with love. It expands and it expands, and it keeps loving more."

Her face is contorted with the innocence of a child and the lust of a temptress. It is the only thing about her that reveals the truth.

"What nonsense!" he says.

"If you grow up in darkness, you only love darkness because that's all you can see. So, one day, when you see the light you're drawn to it. It's magnificent! But seeing the light doesn't mean that you'll never turn back to look at the darkness. You love both light and darkness ... and you can't love one without loving the other. You're helpless."

"Are you drunk?" he snaps.

I don't love him, she says simply, and smiles at him like he's an impish child.

He doesn't listen. "How much did you drink?"

"I had to. I had to drink to survive that horrendous dinner," she says.

A tear rolls down her cheek.

Manu walks towards her.

"No," she says. "This is my own doing."

"Talk to me about how you're feeling," he tells her.

"Right now, I don't want to talk."

She moves towards him, like liquid flowing between silk sheets. She runs her hand along her face, over her breasts and her navel. She reaches that mound which Manu so often visits: rubs it and pokes it. Then she moans.

Manu's thoughts slow down and stop, like a train pulling into a station.

Her fingers, wet and shining, rise up again and dip into her blouse. They unbutton the blouse, revealing two full moons of breasts. They tug at her cherry nipples.

The twisted coils in Manu's stomach unfurl and an ember burns; the fire within him reignited.

She steps out of her sari and stands before him, naked like a goddess.

Lust gathers in his throat like a lake.

He remembers the taste of her skin, like molten honey, her vagina like crushed grapes, and her lips like a glass of red wine being poured in the sun.

The dam bursts.

He falls upon her.

***

Today she is doing what she's never done before. Today it's all teeth and nails and deep angry growls, as if they are two clashing swords. Her fingers coil around him like a noose and her tongue forks in his mouth, sending his moans into silence. He pines for her soft eyelashes, those moist lips, their entwined limbs and a gentle caress. He pines for all this but today he lets her be. Pleasure is not the only thing that leaves memory.

***

For even as she prods and explores Manu, Ida sees lights torch the corner of her mind. Her dark spaces are invaded by such ecstasy that she can't reach out to them anymore. The parts of her body that he touches come alive, moist and glistening as if made of dewdrops. Everything within her that is shattered, the niggling bits and wobbles of her life that she can never piece together, become whole when she is beside him. All her stupidity, her mistakes gather in one place, and blanketed by his embrace, they are forgotten.

This stupid *stupid* love. She sees it; it's still there, standing quietly in the corner, whispering to her. She turns the other way and prays for it to go away.

***

Manu gazes up into the night. It's dark. So dark that he thinks that Ida and he are two riverbanks, and the sky is a river that flows between them.

Ida is in his arms, both of them spent like discarded muslin.

This silence is the only time he completely owns her. He's enjoying it.

"They looked at me without seeing me, Manu. How do men do that?" she asks, breaking the silence. Her hand plays with the red-hot sickle moon that she's bitten onto his chest. "Do you know what my father-in-law said at dinner? That he doesn't understand 'all this love nonsense'. He said that even God does not recognise the heart. He said that Brahmins manifest from the head, Kshatriyas from the arm,

Vaishyas from the thighs and Sudras from the foot. There is no manifestation of the heart. Love is meant for buffoons, he said. And Harsh agreed with him." She looks earnestly at him, "How will I marry a man who doesn't believe in love? How will I survive this marriage of convenience?"

In reply, Manu buries his face in her chest and whispers to her, "You were so sweet, so loveable, till you started filling your head with reality, with these stupid ideas of settling down and getting married. If only you'd told me that's what you wanted."

"And what would you have done?"

"I would have asked you to marry me. I'm still saying it: marry me."

She brushes aside a lock of hair falling on his forehead, "You know that's not possible."

"Why not? We can always run away and get married."

"Run away?" she looks at him quizzically. "Run away to where?"

Manu realises the foolishness of his offer. Neither of them have a NIC. Neither of them is a Chinawallah. She is right. Where will they go?

"We'll run over the footbridge. Escape in the middle of the night when the Chinamen cannot see us. We'll go to Jerusalem where our love is free."

"Don't speak so foolishly. You could get into trouble," she says. Her eyes harden. Manu looks into them and sees something he hasn't noticed before.

"I know the war has got to you too," he says, the truth

dawning upon him. He sits up and gathers her roving fingers into his. "But what's really scaring you?"

Ida looks searchingly around her, as if the darkness is a rabbit hole she can escape into. "At any time, we can go," she says slowly, her voice trembling. "We may be taken. We know nothing of what will become of us. If the wedding doesn't go off as planned, as per the rules of the Chinamen, I can't imagine what they'll do to us. I can't watch my father and mother die before my eyes. I am not brave enough for the Chinamen."

"Why are you so scared of them? I will never let them touch you. You will live. I will make sure that you live forever."

"They are animals, Manu. Don't you remember Nandini?"

"Of course, I do."

"She was my friend."

"She was my friend too. We will not let *that* happen to you."

She wipes her tears away and says, "With the Chinamen nothing is ever certain. What you know and what you don't know is the same."

He stares at her and says nothing for a while. Then, "You are all I know, Ida. And I want to know nothing in this world except you. I am begging you, marry me!"

He waits for her reply. But she doesn't reply. She sits up and gathers her discarded clothes. Why is he being punished? Because he's not rich? Can this life take away everything from him even though it's not given him anything to begin with?

"Let's find a way out, Ida. A way for us to be together. I need to become rich enough to marry you. Tell me how?"

"It's too late."

"Give me a few months. I will find a way to become rich and get a NIC."

"It's not possible."

"Help me help us! There has to be a way we can be together."

"There isn't!"

"There has to be! Think!"

"If you marry me, you can become rich. Is that why you want to marry me?"

Manu's face crumples like an avalanche.

"Is that what you think of my love of twenty years?" he snaps. His anger sounds like a spit. Ida startles. She wonders if she's broken his heart. She knows that right now she is not very good with hearts. Not even her own. She looks at him, as the light from the moon falls on his strong jaw and his piercing eyes, his cheekbones that protrude like steroid muscles from his face. His heart is young, it is strong, she decides. His heart will love again. Is that a way out?

She sits down next to him. "You could marry someone else. A Chinawoman. That way you will not be marked. You will get a NIC. You'll be saved."

He looks away.

Ida lifts her hands in exasperation, "To escape. Isn't that what you want?"

Manu gives her a look of the wounded and whispers: "No, that is not what I want."

"I am trying to save you. It may not be what you want from me, but you can only take what I have to give you," Ida insists.

Silence settles between them like an old unresolved argument.

"I don't want someone else, Ida," Manu finally says. "I want you. I want to marry you." He takes her hand and pulls her into his arms. His voice is now a whisper. "I want to wake up next to you every morning, Ida, and spend every waking moment doing what makes you happy. I want you to fall asleep in my arms so that even in your dreams I can be with you. You are my prayer, my dream, my passion, my belief. Every single thing that I've done in my life is so that one day you can be mine. Ida, marry me."

Ida looks at Manu for a long time. Then she releases her hand from his and says, "You have to try to understand me."

"I don't. You are my moon, I am your sun. We are meant to be together."

"The sun and moon are not together, silly," Ida says with a smile. "They orbit around their own separate spheres. In fact, they are the loneliest stars in the universe. What's romantic about that?" She tickles his foot.

He laughs in response and then becomes serious, "I love you and I will save you from those animals."

"Do you think I don't want you as much as you want me? Do you think I don't want love? This is breaking my heart too!" She wraps him around her arms, rests her head on his chest and says in a conciliatory tone, "One day we will marry. One day when you're rich or I end up living in a house like—" she looks around "—like this. That day *I* will come to *you* and beg you to marry me. Okay?"

She kisses his cheek, smiles at him playfully.

Manu doesn't reply. He knows then that Ida has experienced the full extent of his love without ever understanding it.

There is a noise near the wall.

"Someone is here," Ida startles and raises her head.

"I don't care," Manu says.

"Shhh ... they're getting closer. We're going to be seen!" Ida begins to collect her clothes, "I cannot be caught like this. The wedding preparations are done. Everything has been paid for. If Deven finds out, he will send my father and me to the streets. Or to the Chinamen." Her voice becomes a sob.

The sound comes nearer; someone is right behind the wall.

"Hide!"

"Where?"

She looks up again in alarm, "Oh God, they're here."

Lassi, her pug, pokes his head in.

Ida drops her clothes and slacks back to the ground. She wipes a tear from her cheek and giggles. She gathers her pet pug in her hands and says, "It has to be a dog, following me around like a jealous mistress. Only a dog is capable of such devotion."

Manu turns to her seriously, "I am not a dog but I am devoted to you."

Ida laughs and her laughter echoes off the empty walls of The Black Taj. Manu stares at her, looks into her eyes. He never wants that shine to go. He lets her stretch languidly over his arms. He lets her place her little finger under his chin and strokes its underside. He dissolves like ash in her hands and pushes his head back in blissful surrender.

He takes a deep breath and tells her: I will never let you go. I'll eat you up and never crap you out.

THE PLAGUE THAT KILLED THE CENTURY

He stands at the front gate holding up a platter of maghai paan, though the guests are more interested in the cardamom tea that Ram is serving in little porcelain cups. Heat rises within his body, especially from the back of his right hand. He looks down and sees that his hand is on top of the bright orange flame of a diya. He pulls it away. The flame goes out.

These bright, shiny people further darken Manu's mood. He's about to hand the platter to his mother and lock himself in his quarters when he hears Seth whisper frantically in his ear, "What are they doing?"

Manu looks up desultorily and sees Harsh sitting atop a horse—sitting where Manu should be—all smiles. The people around him are also all smiles. "They're fine, Seth Sahib. They're in groups of three."

"No," Seth replies. "The music!"

That's when Manu hears Bollywood's last song from Shah Rukh Khan's last movie in 2032. Since then, the Chinamen have shut down Mumbai's film studios, forced Bollywood actors to become dancers in Chinese films, and declared Aamir Khan—who was trying to make an underground movie about India being the new Tibet—missing. They view Bollywood as something dangerous and combustible, over-stimulating the Indians, making them think and feel. The groom's party is committing a crime.

"Should I send them back?" Manu asks Seth.

"Of course not!" Seth says. He looks at the Chinese cop standing nearby. "But make them stop before she hears them!"

It's too late. The Chinese cop is walking towards them. They both freeze. The cloud-shaped mole on her right cheek seems to get bigger as she approaches.

She hands Seth a grey ticket and walks away.

Seth pats his chest a few times to calm down. "Two more tickets like this and we'll be marked."

Who knows their fate if that happens.

"Don't worry, Mai Baap," Manu hears Ram tell Seth. "Everything will be okay. Look at the groom. He is so fair, like the moon. He looks like a prince, a moon prince."

Seth beams at Ram. Such happiness, I cannot watch it, Manu realises.

Thrusting the platter of paan onto a passing waiter, he escapes to the cooking tent. For a while he walks among the giant bronze pots that simmer and steam. He stops in front of a frying pan, picks up the dough for *naan* and throws it into the pan, watching it sizzle into blackness. Manu then grabs a Blue Label bottle from a crate and starts to drink.

***

"Where's Manu?" Seth asks Ram. "He's supposed to be serving the guests."

"I don't know, Mai Baap," Ram mumbles, bowing his head. "But everything is in order. Look!"

He points to the lady cop who is at the bar sipping beer.

Seth sighs in relief. Today is not the day for mistakes. Deven is watching him like a hawk. At his own son's wedding Deven is standing alone, wearing his customary khaki sola topee, a misfit so becoming of him that it further highlights his specter. No wonder the guests are gazing at him from a distance.

According to Lalbag folklore, Deven Shah was born to a weaver family belonging to the Ghanchi-Teli community in Gujarat. Growing up he befriended his neighbour, the tea-seller's son Damodardas, and was inspired by Damodardas to do good things, great things. Deven served in the 1971 Indo-Pak war where, rumours suggest, he chopped off the head of a royal Pakistani soldier. It is said that a drop of the blue-blood soldier fell on Deven's dusky skin and seeped the ambition of riches into his bloodstream, leading to his legendary rise.

His hold is over the Chinamen as well, for they allow him—the only person they know who is privy to such indulges—to live in New China while also working in Lalbag.

Deven brushes off a flake of dandruff from his satin sleeve, not allowing for even momentary imperfection. A month ago, he'd showed up unannounced at Seth's store and sat down on Seth's ornate magnolia chair. As Seth had clutched the sides of his ebony table, assuming that Deven was here for some sort of Chinaless coup of his company, Deven had said, "My father, the weaver, always said that seemingly random patterns at the loom produce the best tapestry. Chokia reaches the largest number of poor in Lalbag. This is the same demographic that can buy sex toys. All we have to do is tie-up our businesses: your guys sell sex toys from your shops, and my guys sell phones from my shops. We'll have Lalbag's most profitable merger."

"You want us to become business partners?" Seth asked incredulously.

"More than that. Have you heard of a triumvirate, Seth?" Deven asked back. "No? Well, it's a formation of three powerful men that, of course, Julius Caesar started. You, me and my son Harsh, we will be that. Even better. I hear your daughter is a Cleopatra, made of milk and honey. My son, Harsh, is a bee who loves his honey. Your daughter and he are perfectly matched."

Seth gagged. How could he let his precious daughter marry into a family of blood-sucking heartless businessmen? Deven tapped his fingers against the tabletop and Seth saw that each finger had a different ring on it. The rubies and sapphires and five-carat diamonds glinted in Seth's eyes. Still, he held himself in place and said, "I like to keep my enemies close and my family closer, Deven Sahib. Your son and you live mostly in New China. I will not let my daughter live there like a second-class citizen."

Deven didn't flinch. His poker face lent him an air of inscrutability, a carefully cultivated construct that Seth knew belied how cold, calculating and callous he was.

"Have you ever played this game called Monopoly, Seth?" Seth nodded his head. "You know that in order to win the game a player needs to own the maximum number of houses? I play life like Monopoly: to win. Everywhere I go, I buy the biggest and best houses there. I've just done the same in this shitty town. My house here is bigger than yours, you can safely assume. What's even better is that my son will front my business in Lalbag. You can marry him to your daughter, and visit them for Sunday lunch. Let's not forget, your daughter will be richer and safer than you ever imagined."

She would.

"Your son has a NIC, I'm assuming?" Seth asked.

"More than that," Deven said and leaned over. Was he finally going to reveal the source of his clout with the Chinamen? "As his wife your daughter will get whatever he has." Seth waited with bated breath, but there was nothing. "If things get rough here, they could apply for a visa and move to Jerusalem."

They could, Seth knew. "But you make *sex* toys?"

"Morality does not suit business, Seth. Your father was a drug peddler. You know money comes to those who get their hands dirty."

Seth looked away. "You took my factories."

Deven added, more gently, "It wasn't personal. You didn't want to make sex toys because you're Brahmin. I had no such problem because the Chinamen make seventy per cent of the world's sex toys. This business has made me richer than any of my other businesses."

"Why are you doing this?" he asked.

Deven's eyebrow rose and in that Seth tried to surmise an answer. What choice did Deven have? There was no saying what the Chinamen would do when. By having his son marry into Lalbag's second-biggest family, he was buying at least some short-term indemnity for his business and family. Ultimately, every man behaves like the man he inherently is.

At least Seth hoped that was Deven's only reason.

Seth asked, "What about the danwei's permission?"

"I'll take care of that."

"You'll have to give us dowry."

"I'm familiar with the Chinamen's rules for Indian weddings. But let's not forget our Hindu traditions; you quietly pay for everything else."

Seth recognised a businessman better than himself, a man who didn't mix emotions with business. It wasn't comforting. But this marriage would safeguard Ida. What was left to say but yes?

Deven shook his hands and got up, "I didn't expect anything else. Now let's give people the wedding of the year. Let's show the Chinamen how it's done. Don't disappoint me."

Seth has made sure that he doesn't disappoint. He sees

the venue's glory reflected in Deven's eyes. In celebration of his daughter becoming wealthier than himself, Seth has placed statues of Ida and—after much deliberation—Harsh around the wedding tent. These statues have been carved from twenty logs of red sanders. Each log is worth rupees four lakh, and Seth plans to burn them later in celebration, to show his guests the most lavish display of his wealth.

Seth has also had cut down thirty-one sandalwood trees from the nearby New China mountains. Some trees have been used to build the mandap where Ida will sit as his daughter, others chopped down for the ceremonial fire where Ida will cease to be his daughter, one tree to make sandalwood paste to bless her in her new bridal avatar, and some trees to construct a palanquin on which she will leave her maternal home. He's had to grease palms, especially at the danwei, where Deven's contacts have come in handy. What else can a father do to show his love?

Urmila comes carrying Deven's dowry basket for Ida. The Chinese cop inspects the basket and makes Seth sign a receipt letter. As per Chinese diktat, the basket contains a gold sparrow, so Harsh can give his wife the freedom to fly; a gold horse, an animal with strong legs, so Harsh can stride his wife well; a gold deer, an animal with large eyes, so Harsh can reflect his wife's beauty back to her; and a gold dog, an animal with big ears, so Harsh always listens to his wife. The cost of this basket runs into lakhs, another move by the Chinamen to discourage Indian weddings, and subsequently, childbirth. In return, to assuage Deven and his own guilt as a bride's Indian father accepting dowry, Seth has built a Tulsi vrindavan in the lawn, inside which are three pure gold animals, each symbolic as a different blessing for the couple. There's a snake so the groom can be cold-blooded and manipulative in business. A goat so he can climb atop any failure. And a goldfish so he can swim through any tide. Each brick has been baked with an imprint of Ida's name.

"Noah's fucking ark," he hears a guest comment, as the other guests coo and caw.

But Seth is not offended. He feels this way: as if his old world is giving way to a new world, a world uncertain and unknown without Ida in it. How will he live in this house without her? What is he supposed to do for company? And love? All he has left is Kamala with her limited intellectual capacity, Vakil who stays locked in his room day and night, Urmila whom even he's scared off, Manu who's in his own world, and Ram with his simpering sweetness. How will he survive his family without Ida?

***

"Do you know why the earth revolves only around the sun? Why things grow only in sunlight? Because the sun is the first to come to the earth's life. By the time the moon is out, the earth has no more love left to give. That's why it becomes dark. That's why most rapes and murders and sins take place in the night," Manu tells no one in particular. "Why can't people show that kind of loyalty to the ones who come into their life first?"

Manu sees the plate of prasad that he was supposed to put in the mandap: sugarcane, coconut chips, cut fruit and groundnuts, and shoves a handful into his mouth. He picks out a sugarcane rind stuck between his teeth and takes another sip.

Someone shouts, "The dulha has arrived. Where's the milk?"

Manu sees the milk in a brass samovar next to his feet and spits in it. He points out the samovar to the waiters and giggles. He hears the headwaiter call two men and instruct them to "throw out that drunkard". Two men pick him up and lead him out of the cooking tent. Manu stumbles past many people and finds himself at the wedding tent. He stands alongside the swarming guests—he can't believe he's able to do this—and watches the groom's feet washed in the samovar. He snickers. Harsh looks like a beached whale finding its way into a pond.

Then Harsh stands up, in all his splendour, and walks towards Ida, goes towards God. Manu wonders: the things that Harsh has, the things that Ida's parents have given him, the heavy gold chain, the three-strand pearl necklace, the drape of jasmine threads, the heavy sherwani studded with Swarovski diamonds and rubies; where will they go when he is alone in the room with Ida? Will he place them carefully, softly, beside their bed, like a gentle lover? Or will passion take hold of him as he tears off the chain and necklace and threads? And Ida; his Ida with Harsh on top of her? Will she be weighed down with the chain and necklace and threads, or will he make her delirious with happiness?

What will Manu do with himself then? What will he do in that hour as it pours into another hour? No, he cannot bear this pain. He will kill Harsh and he will kill himself. He will burn the world. This pain, it is too much.

He starts weeping, softly.

Ida turns at that moment to look at him. Dressed in whorls of gold—her wedding trousseau stitched with thirty gold needles and spools of golden thread—she is brighter than the golden sun.

Their eyes meet, lock. Everything stops.

He cannot do anything to her: he cannot harm her, he cannot hurt her, he cannot hate her. All he can do is love her.

I'll find a way to you, he tells her without words.

Then he breaks, like lines of poetry.

***

Seth gently plants Harsh's feet into the samovar. He applies chandan paste—sandalwood and saffron grinded on a granite slab by Swamiji's own hands—and holds in his revulsion at the corns and in-grown nails on Harsh's feet.

He watches as Ida, in all her splendour, walks around the ceremonial fire with Harsh. Swamiji chants their vows in English, so the Chinese cop can understand, and leaves out any phrases that are offensive to women, especially the parts where women are referred to as cows. There will be no kanyadaan either, for it means "gifting a virgin", something the Chinamen frown upon. Seth holds back his tears. How will he now absolve himself of his sins as a parent?

Dinner is served. Seth has employed forty cooks, who've been standing over two hundred bronze pots with long-handled spoons, for the past two days. The guests are served food with one hundred silver ladles, in nine hundred silver plates, two thousand seven hundred silver bowls, and nine hundred silver spoons. For the groom and his family, the spoons have been encrusted with gold. Seth wants the wedding food to be the best that Lalbag has eaten.

It's time for Ida's bidai. Ida clutches her father and cries. Seth's heart fills up with the emptiness of her impending departure. When Seth thinks of her, his daughter, his Ida, her love seems like a net cast out for him to fall into.

All he asks her is what every father asks his daughter: Have I done right by you? She smiles at him, gently through her tears. Her fingers run through his hand, the way they used to when she was a little girl, so the father knows that he has done right by his daughter.

HARPS OF GOLD

Through a hole in Jal Nigam's water tank, Manu sees the golden moon cast a shimmer on the houses in Lalbag. He is at Lalbag's second highest point, a water tower with black reservoir tanks, which has been the bane of many an inebriated man climbing its steps and threatening suicide, in the name of love lost and *Sholay*.

Spotlights from the watchtower, tube lights from homes and starlight from the sky, fade in and out like snowflakes. There is The White Taj, looking like crystalline delight the night has bitten into. And there is Mount Akaho, smouldering with red fire like sindoor welts on the forehead of a spurned bride.

Yet, Manu's eyes keep coming back to the oversprinkle of stars that are gathered like a crown on top of Harsh's house, a mansion his father specially bought as his son's marital home. Inside it is Ida, playing wife, her feet soft and adored as they walk through her gilded cage. The house appears like a morgue to Manu, representing his love's death.

Manu takes another sip from the Chinese baijiu bottle that he's stolen from the wedding. The bitter taste of cheap firewater and paint thinner makes him gag. He takes another sip. He wants to see no one. He wants to be seen by none. So he's come here and climbed into a water tank that is filled only a few inches, enough for him to comfortably lie down in. Even the Chinamen cannot see him here.

He takes a sip, a big one. His head feels disembodied from the rest of him, as if it's floating.

Shakespeare's ghost is Hamlet's grandfather lump of love, he thinks.

What?

The water dances around him, the moon casting back its joy in gentle waves. He looks at the waves, waiting for a tune, and feels that he must oblige them. He must sing. The rust in his throat clears as his voice chants:

Gibbous this day our daily bread, and forgive us our sins.

No, no. That sounds too much like a hymn and this is not that type of moment. He recites poetry:

Like sunshine falling into water
You are the shadow behind my word
The reason for my thought
The companion to my action
You are the distance between my shadow and soul
The golden of my moon and the silver of my sun
And it is only within you that my heart sings

His voice echoes in the drum, coming back to him empty, meaningless. This is a bad poem, he thinks.

"You are mocking me," he shouts at the water gurgling gently against his cheeks.

His tears fall into the water, become one with it.

Manu takes another swig from the baijiu bottle.

... sunlight falling, bleaching your honey brain, your back a sloping hill on which my manhood bends, in the palace of my heart sits an iron throne, stone my love is my dead treasure, whorls on an emir's turban, useless lump this brogue, scallop ...

This is the tank for Ward 15 and Manu knows that its water goes to Harsh's house. He spits into the water. This pain, it is too much.

His trousers have climbed above his knees and float in front of him like a corpse. "You've taken my heart, my shadow, my soul, you fat bastard. All that's left is my life. I bet you want that too." Another swig. "You'll take it sooner or later ... so let me give it to you."

Black is everywhere and she is holding his neck. He can barely breathe. He searches the pockets and flips open a folding knife. He brings the cold steel blade to his left wrist. He closes his eyes, takes a deep breath and makes a gash. Blood, black and doughy in the murky night, oozes out.

Even this little amount of blood hurts. Like love.

He plunges his wrist into the cool of the water and enjoys its gentle licking as the tingling pain subsides. Then he crawls up and sticks his head out of the tank. Wind hits his face, hollows out his bones. His boots are wedged in the foot valve, his bottle fully drunk. The water is in the tank, holding his tears, spit and blood, sending it all to Ida's new home, perhaps to a tub in which she's splashing about with that beached whale of her husband.

"Here, take this as well," Manu says to the water. He unzips his wet pants and whips out his penis. He urinates into the tank. "I hope your cunt of a husband enjoys bathing in my piss."

There's nothing more left to lose here. It's time to go home.

Manu steps out of the tank and makes his way to the ledge. He grasps the rusted aluminum ladder of the Jal Nigam with his hands. He thinks of all the men who have jumped from here. What if he takes a step forward, into the abyss? He will fall face down into the arms of the earth. It will be over quickly. There will be no more pain, no more agony, no one to love and pine for. And Ida, she will never forgive herself for causing his death. She will live the rest of her life with the kind of pain he is feeling; his inheritance to her. But his face will get smashed and Manu knows, he is sure of this, that whenever he dies, whatever else gets decomposed or bludgeoned or ripped apart, he wants his face to remain intact. No, he cannot die this way. Not right now and not this way. He grasps the sides more firmly and begins to climb down the ladder.

One step. Two steps. Three steps. A few rungs down, his boots, wet and slippery, miss a step and he falls. He free falls to the ground, forty feet below.

You've taken away my looks, my identity, by just a glance
By making me drink the wine of love-potion
You've intoxicated me by just a glance
My fair, delicate wrists with green bangles in them
Have been held tightly by you with just a glance
I give my life to you, Oh my cloth-dyer
You've dyed me in yourself, by just a glance
I give my whole life to you Oh, Nijam

Black is everywhere and she is holding his neck. He can no longer breathe.

***

He remembers his childhood, when his mother talked to him the way mothers speak to their sons. She would bring his head to her chest, soft like brown earth. Her hands would caress his face, like the gentle sway of green grass. Her breath would cool his hair like an early morning breeze, and—no matter what he was doing—he would become quiet. After the war, her voice was gone, and only her smell of musk and smoke—like a dream that had evaporated—remained.

***

"Mother," he thinks. "Why don't you talk to me? Scold me, my dear mother. Tease me or sing to me. See my ears? Whisper anything you want into them. The world can't hear you in your son's ears. So speak mother. Show your son the way, mother. He needs you."

***

How can you be so sure of your sorrow?

***

Manu is lying face down at The Black Taj. He opens his eyes with effort, as if a tape is stuck over his eyelids. His head feels like dry pulverised powder, his wrist pulsates in dull throbbing pain, there's definitely a sprain on his right leg, and his back is cramped, as though it needs a vertebrae crutch. His clothes have dried and no longer stick to him, but they are dusty and smelly, like a corpse left out in the sun too long.

How is he here? How is he alive?

All this is too good to be true. Surely the fall must have made him a cripple? Manu tests his movements, slowly and carefully, bracing his mind for disappointments. Gingerly he opens his jaw, bends his arms, shakes his legs. He is able to sit up, slowly; he is unharmed.

How is this possible?

He looks around for answers. The red brick and mortar patchwork of The Black Taj stares back at him impassively. The earth is in sleepy carnage as the sun forces its way in, liquidating the night sky. The field is aglow in soft orange, like embers of a flame, shy in their devotion to the glory of the oncoming day. They reveal nothing.

On the floor are his red footprints, along with Ida's, but they are from their night together: what, three days ago? Usually, he sweeps away these marks of indiscretion, but this time he hasn't bothered, lacking the strength. So: here she is, part of her left behind.

There's a noise outside the wall. Someone is here. Manu thinks of running away. He's too tired. The footsteps draw closer and stop a few paces from him. He's going to be seen.

"Who's there?" asks Manu.

A Chinese cop appears in front of him. No, it cannot be! He's been marked! They've brought him here to get rid of him!

"Mai Baap, please don't kill me!" he sobs, getting on his knees. "I didn't know drinking was a crime! I will never drink again. I promise!"

She looks at him impassively. Her eyes resemble deep gashes in a wound. She's wearing an olive green uniform, a helmet, a scarlet arm insignia, and a nametag that says Mi Bingbing. Manu sees a mole on her upper lip, shaped like a cloud. It brings back a memory. She's the cop from Ida's wedding!

"You not remember anything from last night? Here—," she thrusts a thermos flask towards him. "—I get you water."

"Wha ... you're not going to kill me?" He's too frightened to be discrete.

"No," she says in a flat growling tone. "I find you nearby and remember you from wedding. You keep talking 'Ida, Ida, mother, Ida' and bring me here. I wait till you sober."

He takes the flask and obediently drinks from it. A part of his mind clears.

"You're not even going to arrest me?" he says in relief.

"No. All people—Indian or Chinese—need alcohol. It is not crime."

A thought occurs to Manu. "You carried me from the Jal to here? You stayed up with me the whole night?"

The cop gazes at him impassively.

Manu decides that he will not let the Chinamen be misunderstood and mistreated. "I can't believe it! You saved me! How do I thank you?" He rests his head against the wall, unable to hold it up straight. The cop doesn't reply.

"Xièxiè," he says.

She looks at him surprised.

"I learn Mandarin at the Olympic Chinese Classes. The one near Nandu's Tea Shop? It has a sign that says, 'Don't Be Shy, Just Try'? This way once we become a part of New China I can order a kilo of tomatoes, or ask a girl for a dance."

She smiles. It gives her face a focus, something attractive.

"I hope you enjoyed the wedding, Madam," Manu says in Mandarin. "Did you eat enough food?"

"It is nice wedding, but I not allow to enjoy or to food."

"I tell you, there's nothing better than deep-fried noodle papad with garam masala and soy sauce."

She doesn't reply.

"Did you enjoy the Chinese-Indian music we played?" he asks.

"It is okay. Chinese marriage tradition not much different from India—horoscope match, matchmaker used, gift exchange, red worn," she replies.

"You are so observant!" Manu says.

Something softens in her and she replies, "I half-Indian. I grow up China but my father be Indian. He move me to Lalbag before attack. Last few years I been here only."

"I must have seen you at Jhande Wala Park then. Every morning they blast exercise music through loudspeakers and I see a group of Chinese women from the Comi Area doing the fan dance. You ladies have so much grace."

"I not live in Comi or do fan dance," she cuts him off. Manu doesn't know how to respond till she adds, her voice suddenly warm, "You like Chinese girl? You want to go to New China and find wife?"

He laughs and then sees that she is serious. He doesn't know how to tell her that Indians don't marry the Chinese. They have a perception that they don't bathe, they don't brush their teeth, that their women are loose. Manu is at once ashamed of this subliminal racism. Because people's hearts are not ruled by people's politics. What New China is doing to India is not what the Chinamen want to do to Indians. So he says, "Of course! I'll be lucky if a Chinese girl marries me."

"Chinese girl happy to marry good man. We have few men left. Most busy with war or work or rule to marry or love." She plucks a blade of grass beneath her feet and suddenly looks sad. Her small watery eyes give her vulnerability. "But you Yindu give too much trouble in marriage. You live with parent. You want children. Divorce difficult. You make lady change last name. In China we put surname first," she says, her pupils pushing against her eyes.

He nods.

"Also, caste is problem. Indian very Yindu. Chinese women not change religion and become Yindu. Your Buddha also different."

The Indian Buddha is serene and gentle, whereas the Chinese Buddha is his chubby, jovial version. Manu takes a deep breath. He can do this. He can counter her argument, "Madam Bingbing, believe you me, he is still one Buddha. Bodhi dharma developed tea and kung-fu. It helped both nations. And caste is not a problem. Pluralism is the backbone of India. We don't force people to convert," he says proudly, to let this Chinese woman know.

She stares at him. Has he gone too far? "But yes, love is hard," he adds limply. She doesn't say anything.

Manu sees that her face is as round as the moon, and as white, as if she's used all the talcum powder in her house.

He wants her to smile again. He imagines the Chinese to be happy people, even though he's never met a happy one. He tries to lift his voice to some semblance of happiness and says, "Madam Bingbing, I read somewhere that if the Chinese hear too much bad news they get depressed. So the Communist Party is looking for morale boosters. I'm thinking of setting up a Happy TV station in New China where only happy news from around the world will be reported. Is this a good idea for your China?"

"You are funny man. Different from what I hear about Indian."

"Madam, I don't want to be an average Zhou."

"You are not—how they say in English—average Joe. In China you are not."

"I knew you people were good at heart. I knew everyone else was wrong. That's why I love China as much as I love my motherland India."

The cop snorts and moves her hand to the electric baton strapped to her uniform. "You wrong. You love China more." Manu looks up at her. Goosebumps rise at the back of his neck. Her softening was a temporary thing. "You want to live in China, correct?"

"Yes," he stammers, fumbling to collect his thoughts.

"I arrange it for you."

This can't be. Does he really want to go? He's thought about it. He's spoken about it. But ... he doesn't know. "I don't have the one million dollars required, Madam."

There, he has a way out. And, it is the truth. The one or two townspeople who moved to New China were rumoured to have paid that much to get a residence permit.

"I know," Bingbing replies. "You tell me last night your full story."

"What's that, Madam?"

"You tell me everything last night. Ida, Ida, mother, Lao Seth, Ida, blah, blah."

A tiny vial of acid spills inside his stomach and rises through his body.

He has told a Chinese cop their family secrets! What has he done?

"Please, Madam. This cannot be true. Tell me you're joking."

She gives him a stiff smile, "Seth is smart. He is rich. He no problem. You! You fool. You be poor. You have false worker permit. You and family, gone."

He falls to her feet, "No, Madam. Don't do this to us. Kill me but spare my family."

"I go. My shift over and I do overtime because of you. Chai, chai!"

The threat! She takes the flask from Manu's hand and walks away.

"Madam, spare us! Spare me! We are good people. There has to be a way!" he shouts after her.

Bingbing stops and turns around. "There is way."

Manu runs up to her. "Anything. I will do anything."

Bingbing looks up at Mount Akaho. "Get me Shiva statue."

Manu blinks at her blankly.

"You hear me?" she asks.

His mind and body are being sucked into the vortex of a nightmare.

"I don't understand."

She becomes absolutely still as she says, "Get me statue. I hand it to my boss. I get promotion. We not kill you. Understand?"

"Madam," Manu laughs in shock. It's as if his intention has taken a wrong turn and plunged into an empty ravine. "How is that possible? The statue cannot be touched. It is under lock and key. Even if someone gets to it, we don't know what will happen."

"Then get key to enclosure. You get or you die. Choice yours."

"Madam, I will get cursed!"

"I knows. We not done it yet because we not want curse. But you Indian, local, your curse not so bad." Her expression remains unchanged, like a hard straight-backed chair.

He looks at her and falls to his knees. "Madam, I beg you. Don't make me do this!"

Bingbing turns away, as if groveling is a difficult act to look at.

"I cannot betray my God, my countrymen like this!"

"No choice you have. I will call you in one week with more detail."

"How ... how do you have my number?"

"You do it or not? Yes or no?"

She leans over. Her hand is on her baton. "Yes or no? Answer me!"

When the mightiest men and the mightiest nations have fallen at the hands of the Chinamen, how will his family and he be saved? Manu thinks of their neighbour Nandini. There can be no worse fate. The words come out of him with the sharp clarity of acceptance that caged animals possess.

She leaves.

What is he going to do now?

The sun has clocked half a day of work when Manu gathers the courage to go home. He limps out of The Black Taj, his right leg trailing behind his left. How is he going to tell his parents? And Ida? Will she ever forgive him for being so foolish?

I can tell no one of what I have done, Manu decides.

He limps past the laterite ground, past the orchard and towards his house.

He enters through the back door leading into the servants' quarters, where his mother sits, slitting the stems of bright red chillies and scooping out their flesh to make pickle.

Urmila looks up from the mound of her pickling jars. She puts down the knife in her hand and stares at Manu.

"I know. I am sorry, Maa. I should've helped with the wedding. I should've come back home on time. I ..."

Urmila watches her son limp around the room. Ignoring his mother's piercing stare, those eyes, Manu walks over to their grey Changhong TV set where Humara TV is playing. It's the only channel that has not yet been banned by the Chinamen, and it's every much as ridiculous as its name. The deathly dull cooking show about Chinawallah dishes is playing with the anchor Chun-Li in her brown cheongsam. Urmila watches this only on the days that she is angry. Manu takes the remote though he knows there's no need for one. The sound has been pre-set to the same for the last four years and there is no option of switching between channels. He needs to hold something.

How could he have done this to his family? How will he save them now?

He begins to cry.

His mother, his sweet gentle mother comes to him, carrying their medicine box. She dabs her son's wrist with Dettol and wraps gauze around it. She gives it a kiss. Tears come to Manu's eyes. He holds his mother and rests his head against her chest. How do mothers find a way to love their children at their worst? Even the pain of loss and death numbs itself against a mother's love. He cannot let harm come to her.

His mind is clear, as clear the sunlight outside. He knows what he has to do.

FAST ASLEEP IN POPPYLAND

Through a lapse in God's memory, as in that of man, no one knows if the moon comes first or the sun? Does the sun set before the moon rises, or does the sun rise after the moon sets? So, in 1938, when two babies wailed to life in two neighbouring huts on the outskirts of a village near Patiala, no one could tell who came first: Seth's father, Videsh Singh, or Ram's father, Desh Sharma. To the two neighbouring families, it didn't matter. They had much to celebrate and little to celebrate with. So along they took those two little infants to be blessed by the village landlord. This landlord, with the mighty benevolence of all landlords, decreed that both the boys—to rid their families of the debt owed to him—would begin work on his farm when they had seven winters to their name.

Their destinies thus entwined, the only way in which Videsh and Desh could differentiate themselves was through their personalities. Obedient and subdued, respected in the village for never having spoken a lie, Desh was known as the moon-child. Rebellious, passionate and hot-tempered, Videsh would either cast a gentle shadow or scorch everything around him, earning him the nickname of sun-child.

Videsh also had a penchant for getting into arguments with those in authority—the landlord's servants and managers—and when they threatened to chop off his hands, like Shah Jahan had done with his labourers, Videsh would retort, "One day I will be Shah Jahan and own the Taj." Though they all laughed at Videsh he didn't lose faith in himself. He believed that after every darkness there is a light and after every night there's a morning, and so life is in a tip-in tip-out, a great balancer. Since he was born into abject poverty, life owed him levitation that would throttle him into a mid-life of riches. He already sensed life's gears shifting, as he fell in love with Rani, the landlord's daughter, who stood by her bedroom window every day between 3:01 pm and 3:59 pm, while everyone in the big house was napping, staring into his fiery eyes with her big charcoal eyes, setting them both on fire.

At sixteen, after nine years of indentured labour, Videsh decided that he'd had enough. He told Desh that he was going to the nearby town of Jullundur where money grew on men's back. "The secret is in the poppy seeds," he whispered to Desh, on the day of the moon-child's wedding. "There are fields upon fields of poppy there, waiting to be taken by men. I'll go there, buy poppy seeds, grow them, sell them for medicine, become a rich man and then—pe pe pe pe—marry my Rani."

Desh, his head filled with his to-be-wife, Jaru, and the man-that-he-would-become that night, barely heard his friend. All he asked was, "Is this not illegal, Videsh Babu?" to which Videsh chuckled and went on to reveal that his beloved Rani was going to steal from her father, thus giving him the seed capital he needed to begin his new venture.

The next day, by which time Desh had indeed become a man, he heard that the sun-child had stolen the landlord's money and run away from the village.

Videsh reached Jullundur and—with the money of the landlord filling his under-sized pockets—posed as a landlord. "I'm from the state of Mizoram," he lied. "I want to invest in a poppy farm." The Punjabi farmers didn't know what Mizoram was, and asked only whether one got booze and sex in this Mizoram place. To this Videsh said yes, having tried neither thing. They sold him an acre, then two and three, and he became a poppy farmer, learning all that there was to learn in drug medicine money.

The years passed.

Desh got busy, becoming the only sort of husband he could be, dominated, and by 1958 he had a son, Ram. Sometimes in the orange haze of a new morning, while tilling the landlord's fields, Desh would watch a beam of light crawl up the ear of a maize and think of his sun-child friend. And then, on a late evening in 1962, Videsh's father was found bludgeoned in the landlord's fields. He'd been killed, some said, not by the landlord's sons but by his own son's rebellion.

How did Videsh know? How did he find out? No one

knew. But he returned to the village on the morning of his father's funeral and stood unseen, as another son-of-a-gun lit his father's pyre. He waited till night fell, went into Rani's room and said, "It's time." They ran, away from the landlord's house, through the fields, and were spotted, of course, and chased by ten men, including Rani's four brothers. When they were close upon their heels, Videsh, without another thought, sprinted with Rani to Desh's house. Desh opened the door, heard the sun-child out, looked at the deep purple scar running down his face, and told Jaru to hide Rani and Videsh in the house without telling him where. Shortly thereafter, Rani's brothers came knocking and asked Desh if he knew where Videsh was. Desh never lied, they knew. Desh hesitated. Did he know where Videsh was *at this exact moment*? No. So he said, holding his sickle close to his heart, "I don't know where he is." The brothers went away and Videsh came out of the cowshed.

"I owe you my life, Desh Babu," said the sun-child to the moon-child, tears running down his face, past his purple scar. "And I owe you a life, something better than that of the landlord's servant. I will get you out of here. Come with me."

Desh looked keenly at his childhood friend. Wealth suited him, his belly crawled out through his kurta and his cheeks glowed. But the fire in his eyes that had once been an ember was now blazing, seemingly setting even his eyebrows aflame.

He asked cautiously, "Come where? To Jullundur?"

"Nahin," said Videsh, tracing his finger along his scar. "I can't go back there. I made too much money selling poppy seeds, more than the others. They turned against me; said I cheated them. Those stupid doped-out thurkeys attacked me, chased me out of my own land."

"Cheated them of what?" asked Desh.

Videsh looked at his simple friend and said what he knew he wanted to hear, "Nothing illegal."

Desh believed him, as he always did, and asked, "So where are you going now?"

"I am going to Lalbag, a village eight hours from here. You cannot imagine the trade in opium that goes on there. I've carried enough poppy seeds and cash to start my own poppy cultivation. Come with me. We will have a good life there."

"No, Videsh Babu. I have never left our village. How can I take my wife and son to a new place? Our life is here now."

"You want to spend the rest of your life serving the landlord and repaying his never-ending debt? Come serve me instead. I have money, more than you can imagine. I will actually pay you for your services and give you freedom from bondage."

Rani stepped in: "Think Desh Bhaiya, we'll all be together. We will have each other."

Desh flushed. He didn't dare look at Rani, the Rani of men's morning dreams, afternoon siestas and nightly brawls. The woman who brought a smile to the scowling sweating farmhands, as they took turns boasting of having seen her: one said that her limbs were longer than sugarcane stalks, the other said that her hair was shinier than a sickle, and another one claimed that her skin was whiter than cow's milk. And here she was in front of him, all long-limbed, shiny hair and white skin, as he stood unable to reply, his mouth slightly ajar.

"And Didi—" Rani turned to Jaru "—you'll live like a free woman, with a new sari for you, new shoes for your son, a kitchen piled high with makki di roti and sarson ka saag."

Rani saw that her argument was moving neither Desh nor Jaru into commitment. She looked at Videsh, the sun-child, and saw his love for her in his scarred face, in his arms that had burnt brown from hours toiling in the sun, and in the circles beneath his eyes, darker than the darkest night. With his ambitious plans forward, Videsh needed a helping hand, a loyal companion like Desh. Desh had to be convinced to come with them and she had to show Videsh how deep her love for him was, how well she understood him, what a good wife she would make.

So she lied: "I am with child. For the sake of the unborn come with us. We need you."

From her neck she removed a gold chain, on which were bunched together little gold pendants of a mango leaf, a bunch of bananas, a shunk, and an urn. She handed this to Jaru. "This is a gift from my unborn child. He too is begging you to come with us."

Jaru, whose only prized possession was a tiny gold stud she feared was smaller than her ear piercing, grabbed the chain feverishly. She glanced at her reflection in the small mirror on the wall and saw herself as a rich woman, a beautiful woman, like Rani: the Rani of women's morning brawls, afternoon envy and nightly nightmares; the woman who brought a scowl to the wives of the sweating farmhands. Could Jaru, with her coarse hands and patchy skin, ever look like her? Could she ever evoke jealousy in other women like Rani did? Would Jaru be called Badi Rani, if everyone called Rani, who was younger than her, Choti Rani? There was only one way to find out.

"How can I refuse the child of my sister?" she said and turned to Desh, "Ram's father, we cannot leave Choti Rani in this state. Ram and me want to go with her."

Late that very night Videsh, Rani, Desh, Jaru and Ram snuck out of Desh's hut. In the dark their shadows huddled together, falling on the road in which their journey together had begun, their belongings stuffed into a burlap sack, with a bulky steel cooker—which Jaru refused to leave home without—poking out like a whistle afraid of its own steam. So, on a bus boarded to Lalbag began the journey of Desh-Videsh.

By the time the sun set on their first day in this new place, Videsh bought two acres of land on which to sow his poppy seeds. While Desh and Jaru worked in the fields, lancing the poppy capsules and drying them in open wooden boxes, Videsh took the opium to a factory to be processed before selling it to a collection centre at the Western-most point of Punjab. Before winter came that year, Rani—in the zeal to prove that she wasn't lying to Desh and Jaru—gave birth to Seth on the twentieth of October, which—in the spirit of his fate that would come—was the day of the first Indo-China war, to which Lalbag—in the spirit of a fate that would never again come—was impervious. Over the years the money kept coming in and with this money Videsh bought another acre of land around his poppy field and on that he built, with his own hands, a white marble house, The White Taj. A gardener's shed at the side of the mansion was given to Desh and his family, along with a stately monthly income of rupees fifty, to which Videsh later added Ram's schooling fees. He told everyone that he sent his servant's son to the same school as his own son. That's how noble he was.

It was all going well, and like all good things it lost its shine. So Videsh, oh Videsh, he came to Desh one afternoon, sniffing a spiky, perfectly round, green globule of an opium poppy pod, and asked him, "How can I be sad even when I am happy?"

Desh, who was rolling dried opium resins into balls, looked at Videsh askance.

"All my dreams, Desh Babu, have become real and this life has become so perfect. But there is no struggle in success and my sleep is no longer delicious."

Desh looked worriedly at his sun-child friend, why was he talking like this? He saw that the scorch in his eyes had returned, like lightning that strikes after much thunder.

"Why are there are no scars to show for happiness?" Videsh added.

This could not be good.

Videsh continued, "Do you know that what we produce in these fields is even more precious than gold? If we sell the poppy for drugs instead of for medicine, like we are now, we will make hundred times more than what a Bombay gangster makes. We will be rich beyond imagination." He took another sniff of the opium pod.

Desh remembered that as children Videsh and him would often chase butterflies in the fields. It was a time of run and freedom, without the despair of money or ambition. Every once in a while Videsh would manage to catch a butterfly, and then he'd get that glint in his eyes, that glint that he was happy to the point of being delirious. It was something special, something that Desh had never had or felt, and could never imagine having or feeling. But sometimes, on days when his eyes were scorched and troubled, the sun-child would catch a butterfly, pin it to his hand and pluck its wings, let it fall to the ground. This perplexed Desh—how could someone capable of experiencing such pure happiness from something, ruin that very thing just to be cruel?

Videsh leaned over and whispered into the moon-child's ear, "Our collection centre serves as a popular drug trafficking route into Pakistan and Iran. Those men there, they are something else. What charm, what swagger! And what money they told me I can make."

"No, no, Videsh Babu," he said. "We have too much already, too much. Please listen to me. Don't get into all this."

Videsh laughed and Desh saw that his eyes were red and unfocussed. "You are worried that your workload will increase. But my brother, fear not! There is not much more that we have to do. It's easy. We take the raw opium we have, put it in a large barrel and mix into it calcium solution and hot water. That's it! See, simple no? And just for that our profitability in poppy growing will become twenty times more! How rich we'll be. How happy! Think about it."

All this time, Desh had thought that they *were* happy. How was he to know they had such problems?

"No, I tell you. This is not right. What about Choti Rani? And Jaru? And our children, Seth and Ram? What if they find out?"

Videsh looked at Desh with contempt, "This has always been your problem. This lack of courage. Thinking about other people's opinion is the surest way to do nothing with this life."

I can only satisfy your needs, not your greed, Desh thought to himself and folded his hands before Videsh. Go forth to what it is you desire.

And so the sins that Desh had no courage to commit, which Videsh had never had a problem with, started to be committed. Desh saw it when Videsh started to consume the poppy seeds he was now selling for heroin, as his land purchases grew bigger. He saw it when Videsh decided that he wanted to build a replica of The White Taj across the poppy field, but only in black marble, calling it his son's Black Taj. But five years later, before the marble inlays of The Black Taj were laid, the government clamped down on poppy production, severely crippling Videsh's business. To keep it afloat he was forced to sell his assets and the land around Lalbag, everything went bit-by-bit, and he was left with only his White Taj, the poppy field and the incomplete Black Taj. Still Videsh acted like a man of wealth: with his indulgent habits, his gifts to his wife, his son's extravagant wedding amid much fanfare. Then came the final blow: the rich industrial giant, the Pata Group, built an iron-ore factory inside Lalbag, making the air thick with black smoke. The delicate poppy buds in Videsh's field shrunk, and then died. This was the first time that Videsh realised that he may be finished; Desh could see defeat in his eyes. In anger, Videsh slashed what remained of the poppy stalks and set his field ablaze. This left a fog-like yellow haze around Lalbag for weeks after and a laterite ground as red as his eyes, as shrunken as his once-strapping body. Rani decided that despite their growing poverty she would die like a rich lady, just as she was born, and soon passed away of diabetes; the disease of the rich.

Into Videsh's eyes now poured his heart, and his eyes grew redder.

Desh had seen life born, built, wasted, rebuilt, destroyed, and he understood that happiness held no joy, sorrow no grief, and so when he took his last breath, his only thought was: what is the whole fucking point?

And soon enough the time came when Videsh was on his deathbed, stricken down by apoplexy, that people would later call a stroke. He called his son and with his upturned mouth and welded-together fingers said, "Desh and Jaru are gone now, as is your beloved mother. I too am on my way. Your only companion Ram will now be the one to serve you. Still, look after Ram and his family as you would look after your own family, for they will love you no matter where you are, but if you're alone, they will never leave you there."

Seth, by this time, was thirty, broke and a father of one. How would he look after Ram's family when he could not look after his own? Then, one day, Urmila and Ram came to his house with the gold chain bequeathed to them by Jaru Ma; the one that Rani Ma had gifted to Jaru Ma on the eve of their departure to Lalbag. "Keep it, Mai Baap. It is yours only," Ram said to Seth. Seth looked at the thick chain, struck by how Ram was smiling even though he was now poorer than he'd ever been. He looked at Urmila, her severe face still, without a smile, but not unkind, not an earring to her name, while his own wife refused to sell even a jewelry piece among her many sets. His father was right.

Seth used that money to grow cash crops in the laterite field, but nothing would sustain. He used the same land to rent for wedding functions but the guests didn't like The Black Taj lurking in the background, the ground that their heels got stuck in or the red colour that could not be easily washed off. He tried to start an export-import business in textile auxiliaries, chemicals, uncut diamonds; nothing worked and Seth continued to suffer setbacks and losses. Fortunately, his wife was new enough to be uncomplaining and his children were young enough to be undemanding of his money.

Through all this, Ram remained loyal, working diligently in the house and at all of Seth's new ventures, not asking for a salary, living happily on whatever was offered to him.

At the turn of the century the mobile industry boomed in India. Having nothing else to do, Seth began selling mobile accessories bought from a wholesaler in China, just as China was becoming known for its cheap products. It was a good business, a profitable one, and soon he was able to put an air conditioner and a flat-screen TV in every room in his house, buy his wife an expensive jewelry set every anniversary, and even feel generous enough to pay for Manu's school and college. He became a rich man.

Then in 2028, India was gripped by rumours that China was tapping the phones of its citizens, and that no one—not the common man, not even the politician—was spared. This sparked a huge outrage. Every Indian began to buy cheap phones with disposable SIM cards, changing their phone every month, some once a week, so the Chinese could not trace their activity. This was at a time when the population was expanding at an enormous rate. Cashing in on this unprecedented demand, Seth bought phones from China to sell to the Indians in order to save them from the Chinese. He expanded his mega dealership into a monopoly company called Chokia with twenty-nine stores in twenty states, including three in Lalbag. With cheap raw materials and an expanding market, it was impossible for Seth not to prosper. Money, or even the rumour of it, cast a dazzling aura around Seth and he became known in Lalbag as the man with the Midas touch. The townspeople could not afford to think otherwise, too many of their jobs and livelihood now depended on Seth. Two years later, Seth bought out the Pata Group factory, the same one that had ruined his father, and left it empty and unused, like his father. Four years later, by the time China entered India and made Lalbag a Gallic village, Seth was a millionaire.

D-RAT!

There you are, nibbling on a rotten apple, minding your own business, when suddenly you hear a swish of wings behind you. Before you have the chance to turn around—something sharp grabs you, and you are lifted off the ground. At first you struggle and you wriggle, trying to free yourself, but it is pointless. The hold on you is too strong. You climb higher and higher. The ground, where you spend the last few months of your life, becomes smaller and smaller.

Now you are scared to struggle and to wriggle. If you fall now, you will be squashed, there will be no chance of survival. If you don't fall, there is also no chance of survival, a twitch in your tiny heart tells you.

You look up and all you can see is a menacing beak, with the glint of a polished knife, and mean deep-set eyes. Your body quivers. You look down and that garbage dump that you thought was so big is now so teensy-weensy. You squeak. And go limp.

You feel the wind whistle a tune in your ears and run through your bitty fur like it's grass. Your tail swings like a pendulum keeping mad time and your whiskers are having the time of their life. That is when you realise that you're flying. You have watched the birds that come to hunt you fly, you have seen plastic bags around the garbage dump where you live prance about in the wind, you've even leapt with joy when bits of cheese and sodden apple fly out of people's window. How you've always envied things that fly! And now you, for the first time in your life, you are flying!

This is not a bad way to go.

"Did you hear me?" asks the doctor. Seth taps the heel of his foot on the leg of the straight-back wooden chair. He pats his chest. "Seth Sahib?"

"Do you know, Dr Daftari, that ever since I was a little boy, I collected coins in a glass jar?" Every time something big happened in Seth's life—the morning he lost his first tooth, the time his family moved to The White Taj, the day he started working, the day he got married—he'd put a coin into that jar. When he was little, he could afford only copper coins and then as he got richer he began to put in hundred-gram silver coins.

"Seth Sahib, we have to discuss your treatment."

The doctor is wearing a well-pressed short-sleeved brown shirt. His nails are clean and polished. The tired eyes behind his metal frames give him a studious look. Seth likes this about the doctor. Doctors should be staid, exhausted, and—therefore—respectable. But his ears have hair, sprouting like grass, and this is so surprising that it throws his entire story out of place.

"The day my Ida was born, I put a gold coin inside the jar. I tell you—" Seth chuckles "—I could barely afford it back then."

The doctor leans over his chair. "I recommend you undergo surgery to remove the rectum, which will include the tumour and adjacent lymph nodes. We have only one surgeon in town, but he can perform colostomy on your abdominal wall. Post-surgery my highly trained enterostomal therapist will take care of you."

Seth's eyes fall on the wheeled bed behind the doctor's desk. On the bed is a pristine white bed sheet fitted with a rubber sheet. The sheet is untouched. Around the bed is a movable curtain. The doctor has thought of everything.

Seth continues: "Recently I noticed that my coin jar is almost full. Only a handful of coins, perhaps three or four, will now fit into the jar. It's a sign that I am perhaps, possibly, reaching the end of my life. Only a few more moments are precious enough to put inside the jar."

"Seth Sahib, I have patients waiting outside. We need to discuss whether you'll opt for surgery."

The doctor is telling the truth; Seth has seen the line outside his cabin when he walked past the neon-lit corridor. He looks at the loan application sign-offs lying on Dr Daftari's desk. Medical treatment in Lalbag has become prohibitively expensive. The Chinamen have taken specialized doctors and nurses to New China to provide affordable healthcare for their own people. With the embargo on fuel, Lalbag's only hospital is not able to preserve blood or store oxygen. There is no access to specialized medicines. Dr Daftari is one of only two respected doctors left in the entire town. His consultations and treatments are unaffordable for anyone but the rich; exactly the way China had planned. Getting sick in Lalbag has therefore become a prelude to dying or bankruptcy or both. Still, people get sick, every day, and Dr Daftari's clinic remains a busy one.

Seth slumps back on his seat. "It's amazing to me that my life can stack up in a jar. That's all there is to my entire existence."

The doctor tugs at the hair on his ears, a nervous twitch, "Sethji, we need to focus."

Seth pins the doctor with a cheerless look; his hair tugging stops.

"Please don't be angry, Seth Sahib. I want to save you."

"I have stage four rectal cancer, doctor. What's to save? I can try surgery, radiation pre-therapy or chemotherapy, but that will give me a few months—perhaps two, perhaps nine? And if the disease doesn't kill me by then, the Chinamen will."

"Seth Sahib—" says the doctor, his voice heavy with agony.

"I'm sorry, doctor. It's not right for me to depress you like that."

"Nothing of that kind, Seth Sahib. Let's be optimistic. There are treatments."

Seth can't stand to see the look of concern on the doctor's face. He turns to the window and stares outside. While his world has shifted, Lalbag is proceeding as usual. A purple kite is flying in the sky. A hawker is peddling his wares. A lady in a pink sari is sipping on sugarcane juice. The sky is clear blue, marred only by a black mark that swishes by.

"Did you see that?" Seth asks the doctor.

"See what?" The doctor looks outside his window and turns back to Seth with alarm. "Another bomb?"

"No. A crow just flew by carrying a rat in his claws. The rat was larger than the crow."

The doctor is now looking at Seth with the full force of concern. "Seth Sahib, are you okay?"

No, he is not okay, Seth realizes. He is old. He is sick. He is about to die. But he's ready for it. He's been mentally preparing for death for four years now. With his eyes still set on the horizon he decides, "It's time for me to seal the jar, Doctor Sahib. I will not opt for surgery and hospitals and medicines. I will go in peace, the way every man deserves to go. That's the least I can do for my life."

There you are, nibbling on the carcass of a rat you've just killed, minding your own business, when suddenly you hear a squeal of tires behind you and—before you have the chance to turn around—you are squished to the ground. The tire has cut you from the middle, so your insides lie gouged out. Your wings are flattened on the hot tar and your head is at a ninety-degrees tilt that you never achieved when you were alive. Before you know it, the flock is cawing all around you—your best friend Anthony, your uncle Hari, your neighbour Biswas, even your wife-for-life Anita. Surely you were never this loud? They surround you and without further thought they start eating you. At first you are offended; they could have given you a moment to die in peace, but then you see them pecking at your dead body in ecstasy, devouring your remains so that no one else can dispose of you in any which way they please. These mobbing crows, your family, your friends, your wife-for-life, seem to be enjoying your meat, the taste of you in their mouth. You realise then that you are useful. For the first time in your life, you are bringing pleasure to someone.

This is not a bad way to go.

He walks home. Walking seems like the only thing left in the world that is not contrived. Everything else in his life seems like a pre-ordained script he's been goaded into following, the illusion of a control of his life that he does not possess, decisions made for him and his life when he wasn't looking.

Seth is not sure whether or not he's reacting correctly to dying. Is there even a way to be dignified during one's own death? He remembers the tale of Kisa Gautami, the distraught mother who went to the Buddha to bring her dead son back to life. Buddha told Gautami he'd make her son come alive if she brought a mustard seed from a family where there'd been no death. Too easy, thought Gautami, and off she went from one household to the next, searching for the one untouched by death. But every family she met had lost someone dear to them. No one had been spared the loss of their beloved. So

Gautami learnt—as we all learn—that death is the only thing we're certain to get from life.

If there's a soul in the body then, at some point, it has to be let loose from the entrapment of the body and live its own life. In that way Seth doesn't mind death, knowing that it is not the end of life, but the end of life as he knows it. He's squeezed all that he could from this lifetime, opening his mouth as wide as a child and consuming whatever the world has to offer. Isn't a full life, in its own way, a preparation for departure?

But how is he neither surprised, nor angry, nor bitter? How is he so prepared?

It's the Chinamen, Seth realises. He's lived so long in fear of death, of expecting death, that now that it's here, he can express nothing, not even surprise.

The only thing that does surprise him is his own body's betrayal. When the small red bump on his back was diagnosed four months ago, his family doctor had said that it was shingles. His brain and body had offered no evidence to the contrary. It was when he began to bleed, all through the three weeks of Ida's wedding preparations, that he finally went to Dr Daftari's clinic. A tumor was discovered in his rectum, a very large one that could, at any time, break his outer barrier. How could his body, given to him since birth, withhold all that was taking place inside him? Why did the mind reveal things that it should've kept hidden, and hide things that should be revealed?

He reaches near The White Taj. The smell of hibiscus, preserving his memories like a flower pressed within the folds of life's dog-eared book, carry him into a memory of himself: there he is, a boy in the 1960s, with a face not yet resigned to cynicism, his entity without the crisp texture of purpose, holding his mother's hand as his father carries a small bag containing all their belongings. There's his father standing atop a barren land, digging hard and long into the soil, using stones from the earth for a rubble trench, building a mansion, brick after heavy brick, breath after heavy breath, using the base as a reservoir for the water they never run out of. And then it is ready: their home, their palace, on a night when the moon seems to have sliced in half and fallen on their land like a ribbon.

The years behind him—seventy-four of them—creep up and grab him by the throat. How has an entire life passed so quickly that he can count its memories on his fingertips?

He looks at his house again. Despite the bold massing he's added to it—the colonnades on the porch, the dome where the terrace used to be, a lattice on all the windows, the bird water aviary to signify his rising wealth—at a certain angle where the porch catches the light, he can see the silhouette of his father resting on a pillar, watching him, smiling. You can take men out of houses, but you cannot take a house out of a man.

Seth remembers the way in which his father, the composite man, had fallen apart as he approached death. It was as if a bomb inside him had detonated. His purposeful life had drained out of him with no sense of purpose. The respect he had accumulated over the long years vanished in a few short months.

Men have figured out everything about life except how to die, Seth realises. We spend our entire life in fear of something or the other. Seth doesn't want that for himself. He doesn't want to die with unquiet dignity and fear. He wants to die with respect.

Ahead of him, Seth sees a murder of crows. They are circling around a dead crow, ripping apart its cadaver, devouring it, flying away with strips of raw red meat on their beaks. Crows eat each other; not sparing even their own family. This is the nature of nature. He wants to shoo the crows away, salvage the dignity of the dead crow. Then he thinks: Look at this crow. He has no more ties to this wretched earth, he owes it nothing anymore, but still he is feeding the hungry, he is able to give.

The bucolic sky with the direct heat of the sun tears up his eyes. The newness of the ancient light can no longer fool him. Seth thinks of his family. How will they survive without him? Ida, Kamala, Vakil, Ram, Urmila, Manu? Who will protect them when he is gone? That's when it strikes Seth that his death has come as a blessing. He can plan how to save his family from the Chinamen. He knows all that's left for him to do.

He goes to his study and pulls out his coin jar from the safety locker. In that, he drops a gold coin, something he's been saving for a special occasion. He seals the jar, knowing he'll never open it again. All that is momentous in his life has already become a memory, a memory that he will seal and lock away forever.

FU KONG

"It's Fu Kong," says Kulhari, the agent. His hands cup the glass of cognac, leaving masala residues from his fingertips that are dipping in and out of the peanut bowl. Seth finds this crude. He has brought this cognac to Kulhari's office as a gesture of friendship. It is his most expensive drink, a blend of half-a-century-old eaux-de-vie matured in ancient tierçons. It deserves respect. "All this war-shore, I tell you Seth Sahib, is because of that bastard."

Fu Kong is a notorious Chinese journalist who gained international fame by publishing an underground newspaper *Dírén* (The Enemy) that denounced Chinese brutality, criticised China's misdemeanors and sought to expose communist leaders, particularly those who rationalised their capitalist profits under the guise of socialist goods. His dissident voice, active for over a decade, did not agree well with the Chinese regime. In 2025, Fu Kong's house was burnt down, his tongue pulled out of his mouth, cut, and his mother raped in front of him. No one heard from him again. Most presumed him dead. No inquiry was launched. Tongues whispered that Fu Kong had walked by foot to Bangladesh and then—like any other immigrant—sneaked into India. This explained why by 2032, after The Chinawallah War, a publication by the name of *The Chinawallah Times* started showing up at people's doorstep with the same anarchist propagandist undertones of *Dírén*.

"That asshole has brought us nothing but trouble. He claims that Chinawallahs are secretly observing old rituals, our women are still fasting on Karva Chauth, our men are still cutting goats on Eid, all of them are still immersing Ganesha's statues during Chaturthi. He claims that every household has kept its temples and Gods, its mosques and churches and festivals, despite the Chinamen."

Seth nods. He's heard many times of Fu Kong's view that India's visceral religiosity is a win against New China's atheism. He's heard that by keeping God and faith alive, the Chinawallahs have not let the Chinamen entirely conquer and sever them.

"And Lalbag is the peg for Kong in this argument, the model township that has withstood the worse of the Chinese attack due to a religious miracle. He's arguing that by maintaining independence we are serving as a role model for the world. He's calling all nations to raise their arms and protest against New China. So now the Chinamen are more pissed with Lalbag. They're apparently planning a big attack on us, divinity be damned."

Seth believes Kulhari. He has a way with people, men and women who lose themselves in his affable smile and pappy eyes, find in him such comfort that they reveal themselves, reveal others. It's no wonder that he is always the first to get wind of any news. He's also a man with so many jobs that he seems to be everywhere. One of his jobs is being an importer of Indo-Chinese food. He supplies food to Chindia, Lalbag's most famous restaurant, located in the Comi Area, and one thousand loaves of bread per day for the entire army manning the border outposts. He is the only person in Lalbag who interacts daily with the Chinese patrolmen. Before The Chinawallah War, Kulhari was a small importer and now—due to embargoes and restrictions—he's become a big man. If there's war, more army men, more Chinamen, will have to be fed. He'll become a filthy rich man.

"You know the Chinamen. They do not appreciate even a little form of anarchy," Seth says. He pours himself another round from the sterling silver and crystal decanter. The decanter is adorned with a Britannia silver collar that his father had set in a half-carat diamond. Seth will miss its sparkle when he's gone.

"And what about your own business, Seth Sahib?" Kulhari asks. "How will you import and sell once Lalbag becomes New China? Your business will be completely wiped out."

"When China attacked India, I had to close down twenty-six of my stores. Still, I survived. I thrived. I'm not worried," Seth lies. "New China may have better economic opportunities but we have our civil liberties, our freedom and our choice to be happy. We are, therefore, bigger, happier and better than them. Happiness is how we will defeat the Chinamen in whatever they have planned."

Kulhari scowls. He does not like Seth's answer. It does no good for his business as an agent. The decanter, at the centre of the table, acts as a prism to colours of red, green and yellow that bounce off the man's face like convoluted feelings.

"I am closing down all my stores. I want to leave nothing to the enemy."

Kulhari almost snorts out the cognac through his nose. He leans forward, barely able to control his displeasure. "Thank God you're not my only client, Seth Sahib." He would not have had the courage to take that tone with Seth before the war. It has obviously made him a rich man. Seth is about to put him in his place, when he remembers the red-faced figure of Guan Yu, the God of War, at the patrolman's stand. It is no coincidence that Guan Yu is also the God of Commerce. After all, business is war and war is a business. He must move with the times. He lets the man continue. "I really shouldn't take names, but do you know Kabir Oberoi?" Kulhari asks. Seth remembers him. Kabir was sent to prison over an arms controversy in which he sold new-age war machines meant for India to the Chinese government. Seth himself stood as a silent witness in the case against him and was in some way responsible for sending him to jail. If he knew this, he never let on. He was a businessman first and then a person, and in business he knew that there were no permanent enemies, definitely no friends and all that mattered was permanent interest. “He has offered me double to get him out of here. Can you imagine?”

With the war Kabir will become a richer man. Why would he want to escape?

Kulhari explains, “These businessmen are facing what-what problems! Their workers think the Chinamen get better wages and better healthcare. So, half the time they go on strike! They want their children to all go to school, like those Chinese children. One of them actually had the guts to say in front of Oberoi—I really shouldn’t take names—but he said, what mistake I have made by being Indian and not Chinese? Can you imagine that fellow’s stupidity? If China overtakes Lalbag these ungrateful wretches will be happy. Then what will Oberoi—I really shouldn’t take names—but what he will do with an empty factory? He’ll be finished. Better to move now and start same business with Chinawallah workers. So he’s begging me to get him out!”

Seth looks at Kulhari’s smug face, which is happy to see another powerful man grovel in front of him. Doesn’t he know that in war and death he’ll meet the same fate as the less privileged?

Seth takes a breath and changes the subject, “So, how will this work?”

“That you leave to me. Once you give me the money, in cash, your family will be saved.”

The money, in cash, is an obscene amount. But Seth has always known that this life is a playhouse for the rich. He has seen power fail and beauty fade, but the money has stayed forever. It has bought him the centre frame of his life. He has made his bed with it. He has stuffed with it his cupboard, stocked with it his kitchen. He has used it to fill his basement when it has flooded and to fix his roof when it has burned. With the riches he's had supper with his wife, and dressed his children. Now the roof has become strong and the floor is warm, and every wall in the playhouse has a year of his life etched on it. There is nothing left for him to build with money except his family's safety.

"Where will you take them?"

Kulhari snickers. "If I reveal my secrets, then what will be left of my job?"

"Will they escape through the wall?"

"Have you not seen the bodies on the wall?"

Seth shuts his eyes. The Chinamen have hung every man who has tried, in desperation, in hope, to climb over or into the boundary wall. That's no way to escape.

"The temple?"

"Seth Sahib, you are the boss of Mount Akaho. A bird cannot fly without you knowing. You think I can sneak people out of there?"

"The bunker?"

Kulhari snickers again. "You would've found out if you'd put your name on the list."

Seth can't think of any other way that Kulhari manages to sneak people out of Lalbag and into Jerusalem.

"Let's finalise your list," Kulhari continues. He takes a long sip of the cognac and brings out a pen and paper. "You pay one million dollars, or rupees eight crores in your case, for each person. Kamala Singh. Vakil Singh. Pia Singh. Not your Ram?"

Ram.

Seth remembers the time when he was in dire need for money, and Urmila and Ram had come to his house with the thick gold chain bequeathed to them by Jaru Kaki. Seth had built his business empire with this little money as seed capital. He owes Ram everything. It was Ram who taught him that man needs not just opportunity, but also vision.

Seth then remembers a beggar in New China's marketplace, a silicosis survivor: the Chinawallah with his body like a shell, knots for fingers, caves for a stomach and cul-de-sacs for eyes. He told Seth he used to be a servant in New China. The Chinamen had crippled him because he was poor and then sent him to Lalbag as a lesson for others. How can he let Ram and his family meet the same fate? They can survive war, but they cannot survive their past, he thinks. For nothing is worse in New China than being poor. The Chinamen will come to know that they are servants, and they will inflict on them horrors worse than death. I want to spare them that. Better to have it all over in one go.

He shakes his head. Kulhari grins, like the devil. This brings Seth to his own truth: that he needs someone by his side as he dies. Ram will be the ideal companion. He can't let him go. He knows it's terrible, but he can't.

"No Urmila then, obviously?"

Urmila will not leave her Ram.

"That leaves us with one name: Manu. Will you pay a million dollars to save your servant boy?"

Seth looks at the cognac bottle. He can afford to pay for Manu. He doesn't need the money anymore. But he remembers Manu's eyes, the obvious way in which they love Ida. Does he want to send Manu to where Ida is going? Does he want them to have a chance at love? No, he knows this clearly. I will not let my Ida be ruined by a servant boy.

He shakes his head again.

Kulhari smirks, and shows Seth the final list.

"You're sure you don't want to go?"

Seth shakes his head.

"Very Mother Teresa of you," says Kulhari. "But I have found that sacrifice is man's most foolish choice."

"Then I will remain a fool," Seth replies. "But I hope that you are not making a fool of me."

Kulhari gives him a crooked smile. "Dare I?"

Seth sees restiveness in the agent's eyes. He's the kind of man who will betray someone at the time of need. But what's the alternative? So, Seth nods and hands the agent a briefcase with rupees twenty-four crores.

THE ALL MIGHTY

"Why the urgency to come to the temple?" Ram asks, his voice out of breath as they make their way up the one-hundred-and-eighty-one stone steps of Mount Akaho.

"I wanted to," Manu replies, balancing the steel tray that his mother has furnished with a brown coconut, marigold flowers, mango leaves and red sacred threads. Since his meeting with Bingbing he feels like he's walking on a flimsy film of malai. He doesn't know what he's supposed to do so he's come to the temple hoping to find an answer.

They pass one of the iconic pillars with its 10,800 bricks and its flames that leap ten feet high and refuse to die. The broken bits of stone on the pathway along which they're walking catch a ray of light and shimmer. It is like this every time he's here on Diamond Hill, Manu realises. Every part of this hill: the grass, the small trees, the rocks and the shrubs seem to glow, under the sun and under the moon. It makes him think that it is true, that the Jyotirlinga has swallowed the bomb, stored it as gems, and spread its shine like a quilt of light on the mountainside. Even nature can't resist the lure of riches.

They enter a small sanctum, which marks the end of the eighty-one stone steps and the beginning of the next one hundred steps to the temple. They take a deep bow. Each of these hundred steps is plated in gold, and above each one of them is a signboard on which is engraved a sentence from India's holiest text and the world's largest epic: The Mahabharata, in a sequential story format. It is considered one of Mahabharata's most eloquent and precise captures. Like all the other pilgrims, Manu folds his hands and during his ascent he chants each one of the signboard messages:

1. What is here is found elsewhere. But what is not here is nowhere else. So read carefully ye, for at the end, you will be someone else.
2. Thus tweet bard and minstrel, a thousand years yonder, of bygone wars, Gods and palaces of unforgotten kings. Let the mighty epic begin.
3. King Shantanu of Hastinapura to beauty Ganga is wed. Why drown our seven children, he asks. In huff, with eighth child Bhishma, she leaves.
4. Older Bhishma returns and when father loves a fisherwoman, Satyavati, he vows to life celibate, abducts three as wives for his stepbrother.
5. Amba leaves him with a curse. Ambika to blind son Dhritarashtra gives birth. Ambalika sires the sickly Pandu. Thus, Kuru gets its two kings.

6. Wife Kunti, with Gods at will, invokes three Pandu sons: Yudhisthira of Dharma's virtue, Bhima of Vayu's brawn and Arjuna of Indra's valour.
7. Hush, hush, the forgotten Karna! Son of sun. Left in basket by unwed mother, raised by chariot driver. Who knows you are first Kunti son?
8. Nakula, Sahadeva, mantras for Ashwini twins. Alas, orphans young. For Pandu, cursed by Brahmin gazelle, lusts for Madri, to death both fall.
9. Of ball and jackal cries is Duryodhana, first of hundred sons, spawn to blind king Dhritarashtra and Gandhari, his wife of willing darkness.
10. Thus in a sweeping kingdom, nestled in ancient India's breast, grow the warring cousins Kauravas and Pandavas, under sage Drona's tutelage.
11. Hastinapura rears the mighty warrior, master of arms, receiver of Brahmasira. All hail Prince Arjuna! Pride of Kuru race! The unconquerable!
12. Karna calls Arjuna to duel. Cross bows. Wronged son and the loved one mark each other as foe. Weep no more, Kunti, for your tears are dry.
13. In house of lac does Duryodhana bid to burn Pandu sons down; has tried before with poison, tongue, and his dart. For life the Pandavas flee.
14. Upon silver water and jungle wood the Pandavas hide, where wandering they chance upon Panchala, kingdom of spire and shining dome.
15. Not of bosom, nor of mother, a princess of beauty and

radiance blue, calls upon the mighty and the rich and rare. Her hand in a swayamvara.

16. Whirling discus, stubborn bow, King Drupada evokes the suitors' ire, when a gallant Brahmin steps forward and wins Panchala's princely bride.
17. It is mighty Arjuna who leads golden princess Draupadi from gem palace to potter's shed. Kunti decrees: Among all brothers Draupadi must be shared.
18. Panchali is born. Bestowed with husbands five. Pleases them all. But Arjuna in bed with another brother he spies; woe, takes another wife.
19. Pandavas and Kauravas. Tensions mount. On earth descends Krishna, the divine. Urges fair rule, peace. And into two the Kuru kingdom divides.
20. To sons of Pandu is given Indraprastha, such ruins, such their fate. But shine it to royal kingdom, they do. Proclaim Yudhisthira as King.
21. There struts Duryodhana upon their magnificent grounds, mistaking floor for pool and pool for floor. In he falls, wet. Draupadi, she laughs.
22. Deceitful Duryodhana, in revenge, invites cousin, weak, for a dice game. Yudhisthira he forfeits: kingdom, belonging, brothers, loved wife.
23. Strip her, royal courtiers shout. The Empress disrobed in council hall. Honoured elders, noble men, dear husbands, with vacant eyes, watch.
24. Krishna, the saviour, there he is! Bundle upon bundle his cloth, his blessing. Salvages honour of monarch wife, outraged body his sanctum.

25. Blazing eyes, rankled bosom, the scorch-tongue queen curses: bloody war. Her streaming tresses, she decrees, will be tied only upon justice.
26. Banished from kingdom, kinsmen, honour, Yudhisthira in pathless forest treads. Loyal wife, brothers, to thirteen years of exile, follow him.
27. Yet not suffer misfortune's icy breath. Feed brahmins. Duryodhana from Gandharvas rescue, and free Draupadi from Jayadratha. They are the Pandavas!
28. Do not doubt virtue if you do not see its results. The fruits of true virtue (and sin)—eternal, indestructible—will manifest in time.
29. Not a moment to waste, for war they prepare. Yudhisthira knowledge gains, Arjuna his celestial weapons. Twelve years, thus, draw to a close.
30. Eunuch, a cook, a counsel, stablemen, maid, these Kuru royals become. In King Virata's court pass, slowly, the final year of concealment.
31. Spots them Duryodhana in wee combat; will their victory never come? Ha, but it is after final moment that Arjuna's disguise has come undone!
32. Weary exile passed, plighted promises kept, the time has come to restore Indraprastha's jewelled throne, kingdom, to the Pandu sons again.
33. But Duryodhana, Lord of dark destruction, oh he does not yield: Surrender I will not even as much land as can be pierced by point of needle!
34. Pandavas entreat: Duryodhana, keep yours, give us only

our rightful share. No? Thence the good ones warn: Yield or perish in gory field!

35. Krishna, the emissary, counsels order, peace; begs for strife and feud to cease. To no avail, for alas, sage nor blind King no reason see.
36. Pandavas and Kauravas, never the twain shall meet!
37. War is evil, Yudhisthira thinks. To dead, victory and defeat are same. Yet, as warrior he must fight, as husband avenge shame! War it is!
38. Now prepare! To Arjuna is posed first choice: Krishna's armies or Krishna alone? Drive my chariot, says gallant Arjuna. Krishna he accepts.
39. Oh, who will Kunti choose? The abandoned aren't they easier to forgo? In first meeting with first-born Karna she beseech: My sons do spare!
40. A mother's cry who can deny? No, not even the forgotten one. He, who senses end of world, makes a promise that to Arjuna does not extend.
41. The noble grandsire, what side will he take? Duty or love, which one will it be? Ah, Bhishma, the invincible, to another Kaurava whim bows.
42. There stands blind Kuru King, on hill overlooking battlefield. Through Sanjaya's eyes and ear does he, see and hear all that's in carnage.
43. Fearsome more than tiger paws, eagle's claw, two armies form. Mighty Duryodhana with ten allied kings, ten thousand corps, Bhishma as chief.
44. Smaller the Pandava army with seven allied kings, but

no less thirsty to drink their fiery foeman's blood, tear out his heart.

45. In the sky darkness casts its eerie net, the earth folds into distant hill and dale, beasts and birds flee through echoing wood. Hark hell!
46. The Kurukshetra War, ancient India's bloodiest, eighteen days will ensue and never be forgot.
47. Blare conches, tabors, cow-horns and kettledrums, thunder more than lion roar. Tremble all. Let the fatal battle begin!
48. Brother knows not brother, father fights son. Feathered arrow pierces tongue whispering love. Elephant sears heart that sang moments ago.
49. Sword upon sword, mace upon mace, spear and axe, pike and lance. Soldiers, countless, oh so young, perish on bosom of their crimson land.
50. "You find too much beauty in the dying of men," chides Kunti Ma to Vyasa sage. "Blood decorates your epic, your music is the cry of death."
51. Arjuna to battlefield by charioteer Krishna led. Vindicate title, fight for deliverance. There beholds beloved: teachers, friends, comrades.
52. Dejected warrior prince sighs: Without kinsmen why kingdom rule? Weapons down, 'tis sin to slay. Krishna speaks. Begins: The Bhagavad Gita: Lord's Song.
53. Dwell in calm, oh struggling soul. The wise grieve neither for living nor gone. Death for the born is certain, as certain is birth for dead.

54. Body and mind, in this life, are to duty discharged. Before your end, do action to full; but pine not for result, concern it's not of yours.
55. Nowhere seek refuge, join self to self, abandon greed, without ego go to peace. Become like a sage, awake to things over which man sleeps.
56. Like smoke steals flame, desire robs sense, mind and reason. Conquer your mind for it's greater than sense, yet greater than mind is reason.
57. From anger arises bewilderment, from bewilderment loss of memory. From loss of memory comes destruction of intelligence. Thence, you perish.
58. Liberate from body, which of desire and passion is born; such a delight is womb of pain. Establish self-union or wisdom, bear fruit of both.
59. You are your own enemy, your own friend. Swing forward nor backward; succumb to pain nor pleasure, slumber nor feast, desire nor revulsion.
60. Fix gaze between eyebrows, in nostrils equal in-and-out breath. For you can overcome everything, in equilibrium, if you're balanced of mind.
61. If lump of earth and gold to you are the same, seek then only yourself. When harmony with yourself is complete, imperishable bliss you will feel.
62. As hard to curb as the wind is mind, but like lamp can flicker not without air, subdue it and find serenity. Your secret place within you is you.
63. Reborn are only the pure into blessed and wise house.

In new body you receive old body's character and must labour to make it even better.

64. Devotees in fixed resolve, come unto Me when their body is cast; they know birth no more. In doubt, oh sceptic Arjuna? Let me show you.
65. So reveals Krishna: thousand splendid suns, faces every way, beings in him contained. Deity of Deities. Arjuna joins palms: I worship Thee.
66. Harmony is wisdom bound, to sage reborn. Motion is restless, action reborn. Inertia is delusion, inane reborn. Immortal, who transcends all.
67. Demonic you are if of pride, lust, ego, power, chasing wealth. Will to three gates of darkness be led: lust, wrath and greed. Foul hell!
68. Relinquish not action for fear of pain, or delusion. Act! Do what ought to be done. Better to let go result of actions: good, evil or mixed.
69. Pure you are who worship Him, truthful in speech, divine food eat, firm of mind, give and do unconcerned of fruit. Given venom, you make nectar.
70. Passionate you are who worship gnome, self-glorification seek, bitter food eat, grudgingly give, right no wrong. Given nectar, you make venom.
71. Dark you are who worship ghosts, empty of faith, stale food eat, malicious in cause, think wrong to be right, vain of mind.
72. Your existence: tree with root in heaven and foliage on earth. Must with axe of detachment be felled, revolve like potter's wheel as per He.

73. Duty is quality born to your nature: Brahmana in wisdom, Kshatriya in prowess, Vaishya in trade and Shudra in service. Your dharma find.
74. Surrender unto Me, Arjuna, oh Vijaya, scorcher of enemies! For only to you given is this ultimate perfection of life, to settle war within.
75. Now rise disciple, Krishna says, tread the thorny path. Conquer foes, familial duty perform. Go fight, Prince Arjuna, so peace to you may come.
76. Watch tawny Bhishma slay his foes, like storm ride into enemy fray. Below wheels of chariot all felled, the chieftain is might unparalleled.
77. Tremor Pandava army as morning come: broken force, ill fare, all lost. Carnage their close for ten days. Against Bhishma what shall they do?
78. Wiping teardrop on cheek, Arjuna raises bow, to Pitamah whose shoulders he once climbed. Hail his pointed arrows, a bed for Bhishma is made.
79. Nay matter, for now commanding death's black shadow is Acharya Drona. Kaurava squad smite cowed Pandava; as fiercely does gory battle rage.
80. Amid dying and dead, Drona into lotus lair ensnares: Arjuna's young warrior son, Abhimanyu. Counts the brave heart among countless slain.
81. Deploy Pandavas an unfair mean: to Drona lie about son's demise. Destined slayer Dhrishtadyumna, in one stroke, the grieving Drona beheads.
82. He who ye all with held breath await, to conquer or die

upon battlefield comes. Karna to brother, foe proclaims: Arjuna, thy days are done!

83. Valiant and handsome, hero this is! Whence tilted chariot falls, to Parashurama's curse forfeits last hour. Gandiva, nemesis Arjuna, draws.
84. Bolt of lightning piercing heart, bathed in gore and slashed, Karna from chariot blood comes and with chariot blood he goes. Now rest.
85. Heedless yet of danger and grave, changeless in face of death, with hatred still dearer than lifeblood, Duryodhana he flees to limpid lake.
86. Found, combat with mighty Bhima wage. Hit upon thigh with mace, Duryodhana backward reels; meets his closing life and falls among the dead.
87. Before mournful shankha draws battle to end, Drona's son seeks avenge. Smothers, fair Draupadi's children, alas. Panchala Prince, all gone.
88. Mangled bodies, streams of gore, torched white tents, red fires, vultures galore. Only seven Pandavas, three Kauravas remain in name of war.
89. Sons, fathers, brothers: countless slain. Victory comes with skulls and torn limbs, tainted chieftains, wailing widows and childless dames.
90. Bhishma, Drona, Karna, Drupada, Abhimanyu, Ghatotkacha, Virata. 'Tis horror of war: win jewelled crown, sceptre with loss of saintly life.
91. Yudhisthira, void and vacant of heart: Was it all worth it, where will it end? Weary, he weeps. Know that terrible Age of Kali is at hand.

92. Where puny, fearful, hard men live tiny lives, make love with greedy mouth, fierce acts perform, their women perfect whores. That is the loss of dharma.
93. Finally, good Yudhisthira, to crown concedes. Learns society to reign, economics, politics, games. All hail King of Kurus at Hastinapur!
94. Balm nay Yudhisthira's soul: the Good Law, Horse Sacrifice, Arjuna's world conquest. For him, no more flowers, no purity. 'Tis black time.
95. Sonless Dhritarashtra, father of hundred sons, retires he to forest with queen Gandhari and Kunti Ma. Perish, forest fire, yogic calm.
96. Krishna, the cursed, on earth roams. Thence leaves human body, to Lord Vishnu dissolves. To eternal abode ascends.
97. Sit Prakshit, son of Arjuna's son, on throne, after Pandava reign. Embark then they to Himalayas. Penance. The Great Journey begins.
98. On the way their body's cast: Draupadi for prejudice, Sahadeva and Nakula for vanity, Arjuna for pride, Bhima for gluttony. Cross into heaven's gates.
99. Up Mount Meru clambers Yudhisthira, bathes in celestial Ganga, passes final dharmic test. On Indra's chariot to heaven goes.
100. Enter paradise.

The ridged steps end. Ram, Urmila and Manu put down their belongings and prostrate to the ground, bowing deeply to the Mahabharata thus told. Despite the blazing sun, the ground beneath them is cool; such is the temple design. They walk to the main temple area and get into a five-person queue standing by the registration desk. Lalbag residents have to register their names, as they are permitted entry into Mount Akaho temple only four times a year. As the registrar checks their visit history, Manu looks around.

Seth has shown his power; not only in the economy that sustains Lalbag, but also in the nifty world of religion that glues its citizens together. He's rebuilt the fallen statue of Shiva with his own money and not just any money, but eye-popping-I-am-the-second-richest-man-in-Lalbag money. The body of Shiva has been made five-feet tall and two-feet wide, almost as tall as Manu. His crescent moon, matted hair, the snake around His neck, nandi next to His feet, His damaru, His third eye, are inlaid in almost sixty per cent gold (and not just any gold, but eighteen-carat gold). Only Lord Shiva's trishul has been spared the gold extravagance, but since it's made from cinders of the fallen bomb it is highly consecrated (telling by the ash and bright orange tikkas smeared on it). Every person in Lalbag knows that the statue—more than twelve kilos in weight—is in excess of the town's entire economy. Lord Shiva's statue gleams from behind a double-level iron gate (no one is allowed near the statue), whose keys are in Seth's possession. The top level of the gate has an upside-down trishul and the bottom level has a sickle and hammer. Seth has purposely made the Hindu symbol pierce the communist symbol.

The temple is built around this statue. There is

polychromatic stain-glass and sandalwood framing, as well as a window that lights the statue from above. There are shallow-relief sculptures of Lord Shiva with his consorts: Shiva and Kali, Shiva and Durga, and Shiva and Shakti, that run-in a loop on both sides of the wall.

Unlike other temples there are no bells here and no priests singing bhajans. Walking clockwise around the statue is also strictly forbidden. The trishul, located in an enclave outside the iron gate, is the only place open to devotees and below it lay offerings of all kinds: noodles, coconuts, coins, chopsuey, roses and rice. This place of worship has the name of a temple, the quiet of a church and the faith of a mosque.

Yet, most devotees come to the temple to pay respects not to the statue, but to the Jyotirlinga, Lord Shiva's holiest shrine. As they approach the crater a silence falls over them. They peer inside the water fill to look at the three lingas: Vishnu, Brahmā and Mahesh. Most of the time they look only to confirm that the lingas are still there, so they can continue to count Lord Shiva's blessings, His continuing protection and boast stories of His legend. They come to see if the jyoti inside the Jyotirlinga, which had miraculously appeared above the water after the bombing, is still burning; it always is, though no one knows from where it gets its source.

It is here that Swamiji—guardian of the holy water—sits. He is Lalbag's oracle, Lord Shiva's conduit, his worth enhanced after the bomb that landed on Lalbag didn't kill them. His reedy body is stark naked, with his saffron robe tossed next to him. A *dhal* covers his privates. On the lower left side of the robe is the insignia of a hammer and sickle, over which someone—Swamiji most likely—has coarsely painted a red rope, as if choking the emblem of communism. Every evening Swamiji spends hours scrubbing the Jyotirlinga with white scouring powder, cleaning it of ghee and milk.

Manu hears him sing:

There will come a day,
Not too far along,
Will, blind horses with wings and
Saber-toothed bats, join in the fray
With men of clay, their eyes slit like thongs,
Marching into this land.
They will come for you, dear, your dear,
And at, long last, alas, will you know fear.

The sun's full light falls on Swamiji's face like a torched blanket. His nose and eyes, his mouth, go out of focus, as though hidden behind a cloud. In this town Swamiji reigns over the deepest fears of its people. He curses them and he cures them, blesses them if the mood so strikes him, and when he is drunk—as he often is—whatever he says comes true. It's said to be a gift that the unexploded bomb has given him.

One time, Seth had requested Swamiji to leave the Jyotirlinga, fearing that Swamiji was contaminating the holy structure and the quiet that he wanted the temple to evoke. Swamiji did not take well to this suggestion. He mumbled a curse that turned Jyotirlinga's water to blood—boiling hot blood—and made the jyoti flicker, its precious flame threatening to extinguish. The townspeople ran to Seth with fear in their eyes and it was only after Swamiji stepped back into the Jyotirlinga did the blood return to water and the flame recover its kindle. It's whispered on the streets, behind closed doors and secret alleys, that Swamiji—guardian of the water—sleeps in it, yes, inside the water where the Jyotirlinga lies, and he becomes a fish when the sun bids goodbye.

A dozen devotees are gathered near him, not too close, listening to him speak. He chants:

Yuga sahastra yojan per Bhanu
Leelyo taahi madhur phal janu

He explains: "This is a verse from the Hanuman Chalisa. It says that Hanuman used to love sweets so much that once he jumped up to the sun, orange and round and bright, mistaking it for jalebi!"

The devotees laugh.

"What this story teaches us is that sometimes even our Gods can make human mistakes."

The devotees look at each other in confusion. Surely not their Lord Shiva!

"You wonder how I say this? It is because we Indians are closest to God that we can see him better than others, in his glory and his fall, just as he can see us. Want to know why?"

The devotees nod.

"Now listen carefully, for you must not forget this. One yuga is equal to twelve-thousand years, one sahastra amounts to a unit of one thousand, one yojan equals eight miles, so *'yuga sahastra yojan'* amounts to a total of ninety-six million miles or one-hundred-and-fifty million kilometres. This, according to the NASA, is how far the earth is from the sun. Do you know why this is important? The Hanuman Chalisa was written in the sixteenth century, when China was coming out of its Primitive Age, spreading plague through its Silk Road to Europe. Even America at that time was full of Neolithic farmers and hunters. But the learned sages of India knew the exact distance of the earth from the sun. So you see why we Indians are so close to god? Because we've always been able to see his divine ways."

Everyone around Swamiji claps.

Swamiji looks around sternly, "And do you know what happens to people who question those in authority, the people who are close to god and divinity?" Everyone shakes their head. "It is said that Tulsidas was thrown into Akbar's prison after refusing to display his magical powers to the king. This is when Tulsidas wrote the Hanuman Chalisa. After forty days of imprisonment, Tulsidas began reciting the forty verses of the Hanuman Chalisa. Lo and behold! An army of monkeys invaded Akbar's town of Fatehpur Sikri. And these monkeys—as tall as me—they pulled the hair right out of the heads of Akbar's hundred wives and they threw bricks at his subjects. Such chaos reigned that Akbar himself fell at the holy saint's feet and begged for forgiveness. Therefore—" and Swamiji stands up to his full height "—always listen to the wise. For those closest to God, are closest to wisdom."

Some devotees bow down to Swamiji. Some throw silver coins into the water with a prayer on their lips. Swamiji—with no regard to their feelings—tosses out these coins onto Diamond Hill. This is an old habit of his. Strangely enough, the coins stick to the mud, despite concerted efforts of many a devotees and priests and academics to pull them out, and so they grow in number every day, reflecting the sun, reflecting the moon, adding sparkle to Diamond Hill.

Ram leads them to the trishul, on which he wraps a red cloth and smears an orange tikka, and he mumbles a silent prayer. In such hallowed surroundings, Manu cannot help but think of faith. At a time like this he needs God. He looks at the statue and feels the shock of a hard tumble, though his body is firmly in motion. How can he betray Him? How can he steal the key from Seth and give it to the Chinamen? Then he thinks of God, of Lord Ram, who doubted his devoted wife on the word of a fisherman. If God can make human mistakes, what is a human being to do?

THE GREAT ESCAPE

Seth picks up the phone and puts it down.

He wants to tell Ida that he's dying. As he first bore tidings of her birth, he wants her to be the first to bear tidings of his death, completing a circle between them. But Ida is in the throes of marriage's happiest period: the first month. The cruelty of his fate will land harshly against her. A father cannot snatch his daughter's smile, especially when it comes to her marriage; his abysmal luck.

For a moment he reels in his decision, after all he doesn't *have* to tell anyone about his illness. It can fester inside him as a secret, alongside its physical manifestation, away from public scrutiny. But plans have been made, money has exchanged hands. He will have to distance his death from sentimentality. He will have to inform Kamala and Vakil. He will have to convince them of his plan. But, if he knows them, there will be no resistance from them to be saved. This will not be difficult. Will saying goodbye be? He'll find out.

There's his wife Kamala, lounging on the chaise lounge in the living room, one hand inside a bag of Hao Pengyou kimchi chips and another hand scratching the welt of torso skin turned red against the tight band of her satin salwar. When Seth thinks of his wife he sees a showy vacuous thing, like a Lamborghini with the gas needle on empty. The kind of woman who allows her person to dissolve so completely into itself that there is nothing of her own left in her: no ambition, no capacity, no curiosity. An integument of sloth, she has packed in so many empty, layers of flesh underneath that skin, that to touch her personality, to even find evidence of its existence is highly improbable.

But when Seth's eyes had rested on her for the first time—back when her pet name was Kamar and not Kamra as Seth secretly calls her—it was this empty space—wrapped in a blue kanjeevaram sari, with a polki nose ring and a thin gold kamar-bund—that had appealed to him. He'd mistaken the cosmetic binds around her body for docility and her emptiness for mysteriousness, as all young men are foolish enough to do.

"In front of a good hunter always comes a good hunt," Videsh had whispered to Seth. Seth knew that this marriage was his father's last-ditch effort to salvage the dregs of his privately dwindling wealth by bringing home, for his only son, the daughter of Lalbag's wealthiest cotton farmer.

So, when Seth saw Kamala, he imagined her coconut-shaped head resting against his shoulders, pried open with the machete of his company and spilling its sweet juices into the crevice of his bachelor life. He saw her boil adrak chai for him in the morning, press his legs at the end of a long day, light up his dark empty room, hold his hand as they watched Sunil Dutt on screen. It was the only time in his life that he'd let logic leave that carefully guarded cage inside his heart, and for its maiden blunder Seth has a new curse everyday.

It's true that she hadn't been much to look at, with her thin long hair that coiled towards the end like a snake, and her pencil-line lips that became narrower under the onslaught of flesh. Due to her lack of beauty it was assumed that she'd possess the comeliness of a wife. These illusions were destroyed within the first few weeks of marriage, when it was discovered that she dispersed human effort only under the narrow definition of eating-sleeping-breathing-farting. Her father had claimed that Kamala was religious, but what he'd failed to reveal was that Kamala was interested in the worship of one thing: her jewelry. Every morning she would bathe, wear clean clothes, and sit in front of the temple like any other devotee. But instead of worshipping the many god statues, she would open the iron-door safety locker adjoining the shrine and pull out the handful of jewelry sets—in gold and diamond and rubies and pearls—bequeathed to her as the daughter-in-law of the house. For the next one hour, Kamala would remove each piece out of its box, gently open its swathing of soft cotton, hold it up against the flame of the diya, caress it, scrutinise it for scratches, missing prongs, fasteners and links, and then put it back in the box. Her love was so sparse that she had enough only to dispense to herself.

She knew so little of trying to please another that even with her favourite thing in the world (after jewelry, of course)—food—effort was made short: her rice clumpy, her dal watery, her vegetables singed. She suffered from sleep apnea and had to be shifted to a separate room of her own where she slept till noon everyday, unperturbed, content without her husband.

When her dowry ran short of the promised fifty gold bars, two cows and a colour television set, it was discovered that her father too was at the last leg of his wealth, as the Pata factory's iron-ore production destroyed the delicate cotton buds in his fields. Therefore, after Kamala's marriage, her parents moved up north to Kashmir and sold blankets to soldiers and, later (said the rumour mills), to militants.

"I want to send her back," Seth told his father. By selecting such a bride for him, Videsh had given Seth one more reason to quietly resent him.

Videsh looked at him, with his eyes the colour of conjunctivitis, and said, "A wife is like a child, son. You cannot send her back to where she came from. She is tied to you for eternity."

So the lies, the disappointments continued to reveal themselves, wedged between any love that Seth attempted to rouse for her. It was clear to him that Kamala was a woman in possession of such little expectation from life that she wasted absolutely no time on it. Her vocabulary mirrored a similar sentimentality, comprising a sprinkling of words, which when they came out of her mouth were ignorant and commonplace. These qualities became more abhorrent with time as Seth's wealth acquired a sheen that his wife did not.

Then Kamala produced Ida, of milk and honey. Seth saw that his mother Rani's beauty, which had skipped a generation, found itself in Ida. For producing a family member whom he could finally not just tolerate but love whole-heartedly, Seth was grateful, sometimes even at peace with Kamala. He even forgave her for her motherliness that was as vacant as her wifeliness.

That's why he's paid a million dollars to save her.

It occurs to Seth this late in his long life that marriage is like a swamp, whereas he is the river flowing past it. No matter how far the river goes, or how deep its course, it is the river that has to bend around the swamp. The swamp remains unchanged, but still manages to shape the course of the river.

Seth walks up to Kamala, with a purpose that he hasn't experienced towards her since they took their *saat pheras* around the matrimonial fire. She is watching TV with such rapture that she doesn't notice him as he sits next to her and picks up the remote from the coffee table. It is only when he turns off the afternoon show of *Chinawallah* on Humara TV—a sordid drama about the inter-racial marital woes of an Indian and Chinese couple—that she becomes aware of him.

He knows that he has her attention for a short span of time before she flakes out again, so he gets straight to the point, "I have something to tell you."

Too late. Kamala's eyes are now admiring the pink pearl bracelet on her hand, Seth's gift to her on their thirtieth wedding anniversary. It is distracting her, the gloss of these pearls. He places his hand on her wrist, to bring her back to attention, when their hands accidentally graze. It's been years, perhaps a decade or two, since this has happened, and her hands are clammy to the touch, slippery and moist. Like a corpse. He pulls away his hand.

To shake off the dread, Seth continues: "During Ida's wedding, I began to bleed profusely and went to the doctor thinking it was stress-related. It wasn't. It was worse." Now that he has to throw these words out into the open, the unknown, his loss seems elephantine. He can only manage a whisper, "I have cancer and perhaps a few weeks left to live."

He watches Kamala's face closely for a reaction. Her lips twitch ever so slightly and a look of pain passes over her face.

A tear, thank god.

"How this can happen?" she asks slowly.

"The signs were everywhere. I lost six kilos, I bled on the mattress, and I was tired all the time. The doctor confirmed it."

"That is too terrible!" She begins to sniffle. Finally, Seth thinks. Finally, there is reprieve, something to show for their years together as husband and wife. She looks at him earnestly, "You not worry much. How it matter if death come before or after? I am old Mrs. Too old, above sixty. When China come I be marked. Too many old people there, so they kill old Indians first. They take me. They take you also. We die soon anyway."

"I will not let you be killed," Seth says proudly, glad to have found the correct moment to declare his intentions. "I have arranged for you to be sent away from here."

He explains the plan to her.

"Will you go? Without me?" he asks. He's possessed with no actual desire to know her feelings towards him. He asks her this, softly, out of a morbid curiosity to extract an emotion, any emotion from her.

She doesn't say anything, her face impassive and perplexed, as though the thought has never occurred to her.

"Never mind," he says, getting up from the sofa. "You have no choice. My agent will meet you at The Black Taj at nine tomorrow morning. He will take Vakil, Pia and you. Pack only one bag, not more. Now, repeat after me."

She repeats his instructions back to him. It's an old habit from their marriage.

"Take only what you need from the house. Leave nothing important."

She touches her necklace. Seth knows what she'll be packing.

"Ida?" she asks finally.

"Her husband will take care of her. He promised."

Kamala nods but the expression on her face remains unchanged, as if not suited to emotions. Only her hands tremble, ever so slightly.

"And don't forget to pack your jewelry," he tells her with a smile. She turns to him and giggles. The husband knows that he has finally understood his wife.

In a lifetime of marriage sometimes this is goodbye.

***

Knowledge is conquest, power is conquest, and money is conquest. Everything else that lies in between these things—the unbridled and intangible—bakes the mind, produces nothing but abomination. Seth is learning that.

***

There is his son to tell.

Seth walks up to Vakil's room, taking the stairs slowly, deciding how best to break the news. Vakil is a different kind of person to deal with. And his father Seth best knows that. Growing up, he was a quiet child, unremarkable but affable, raised mostly in Urmila's presence. One dusky evening, all of eighteen, Vakil was returning home from college when he lost control and crashed his car into a banyan tree. His brains went into his nasal cavity. The hospital said he would not survive. Kamala broke her black pearl chain in agony. Seth squeezed his Chokia phone so hard that a crack appeared. Ida fainted in Manu's arms. Ram wept in a corner.

At the hospital, Urmila came up to Seth, her eyes blazing red, and asked him: what tree did Vakil's car crash into?

Banyan, Seth heard himself saying.

There. Then. Time. She said and walked away.

She was seen praying at the Mount Akaho Temple for three days after. She did not move, not for food, or water, or rest. Not even to go to the bathroom. What superpowers did she possess?

On the fourth day Vakil opened his eyes in the ICU. Within a few days his organs were functioning. After eleven days, at the exact time of the accident, Vakil was back at The White Taj.

The car, now abandoned next to the tree, was gifted to the doctor.

No one dared to ask Urmila where she had been or how she had brought Vakil back to life. When Seth finally did question her, Urmila fixed a stare on him so long, so hard, that he got up and left his own living room.

There were many inferences, many theories drawn from the three words Urmila had signaled that day, the most common being: *Then there's time*. After all, people conjectured, a banyan tree grows from host trees and, therefore, feeds off other souls. The banyan tree must have trapped Vakil's soul within its hundred aerial roots, and Urmila knew there was time to release it and put it back into his young curable body.

This excited the imagination of the townspeople. So they whispered that they'd seen Urmila and Swamiji together, walking the Mount Akaho steps, building a fire that reached the stars (in the exact location where the first flaming pillar of Mount Akaho would stand after the bomb attack) and jumping into it, only to emerge three days later with Vakil between them. Others said that they'd seen Urmila drop cobra skin into the same fire and from that had emerged a form, large, broad and slightly hunched (shaped exactly like Vakil). Swamiji had carried this form by the scruff of its neck, dipped it into a nearby pool of water (some said it was the same source of water as the Jyotirlinga) and from that Vakil had emerged, back to life. The water in the pool had turned red, they said, a deep red like blood.

After he returned from the dead, Vakil tattooed his right hand with a Shiva lingam around which was a spiral chain. A boy who had never prayed before began to recite strange hymns. He started to state that he was not a human being but a consciousness that was experiencing itself subjectively. He could not die because he was an energy force, a mere hallucination, and that he lived only in imagination, his own and that of others. Even Lord Yama in his vahana could not take that away from him.

Vakil started to lock himself in his room, hiding there for hours, emerging at specific hours and sometimes never, not even for meals or college. He came out of his room at very specific times and let it be known that he could not otherwise be disturbed. His meals were sent to his room, with breakfast at nine, after which he left for college, came back home at three for lunch, and then stayed in his room. Dinner was left outside his door at eight.

In the years after the accident, Vakil became not a son to Seth, but a big lumbering body with a silent presence and an enormous interest in only one thing: his inheritance.

Still, sons are sons and a father is a father. So Seth visited the site of Vakil's accident and built a small pond around the banyan tree, such that the water reflected the tree—with its roots in the air and its branches underground—upside down. He thought that with its seemingly unending roots the banyan tree—as reflected in the water, air and earth—would henceforth symbolise eternal life (as given, he thought privately, to his only son). But to the townspeople this was not enough; their tongues counted upon more fanciful suppositions for this tree of life. So they stood by the pond and debated: Is water symbolic of the material world being a shadow of the spiritual world? Are roots the immortal Self and branches the transitory Soul? Does the Self sit above the Soul watching it participate in the movement of evolution or does it join it in that manifestation?

To stop people's endless yammering, Seth had an epithet engraved next to the pond that said: *Of all trees I am the banyan tree.*

From this the townspeople deduced that Seth was getting into the "banyan tree business" which would be called Vakil Express, and which would plant banyan trees all around India till half the country was covered in banyan trees. Seth decided to stop caring what these men and women whispered in their own foolish corridors and live life with the simple gratitude of having a son who was alive.

When his son turned twenty, Seth tried, unsuccessfully, to place him in different divisions of the Chokia business. The vendors were uncomfortable with Vakil's heavy presence. The customers complained that he wouldn't try to sell them anything, but simply demand that they buy their products or get lost. The employees he was supposed to manage always underperformed. Seth put him in-charge of accounts and collection of payments, which Vakil undertook with startling prowess. Shortly after, he was married off to Pia Kapoor, who possessed only one virtue: she belonged to another Punjabi business family that had recently moved to Lalbag. By some twist of fate, considering that they didn't know each other before marriage, Vakil and Pia were perfectly matched. They didn't speak unless spoken to, stayed in their room, and refused even the common courtesy of producing children. Pia was rarely seen, unless she was going to some undeclared place with Vakil. On most days, no one in the family knew whether they were at home.

The townspeople whispered that Urmila had conjured Pia from the same fire where she resurrected Vakil.

***

Seth knocks on Vakil's bedroom door.

But there is no noise from within, no response, no rustling sheets or harried footsteps. Not even the sound of breathing.

"Beta, it's your father. Open the door. I have to tell you something important."

Sometimes Seth thinks about the cobra-skin theory of the townspeople regarding Vakil's rebirth. He imagines that his son is possibly a naag that transforms into a human being during certain hours of the day and spends the rest of his time curled up on the floor of his room, shedding his snakeskin with his naagin wife. Seth has watched the movie *Nagina* that stars his favourite actress, Sridevi; he understands snake life. It explains why Vakil and Pia are in their room all day, and are so quiet, detached.

Seth shuffles on his feet as he waits. His kurta is soaked in sweat, biting into his neck. He knocks again. There is no response. Again, he knocks. This could go on all day.

"I came here to tell you that I am dying," he shouts, not knowing what else to do. "Of cancer. I have a few days, perhaps weeks to live."

There is his son, towering over him. Seth startles. Vakil's eyes are misty but, for the first time in many years, they have a look of vigor in them; proof of life.

"Dying?" Vakil asks with a slight hiss, his voice thin.

Seth nods, his eyes welling under the sense of his own loss.

"I cannot believe this, Papa," Vakil says, and for a moment Seth is happy that he has a son again. "We will go to Dr Daftari and get you the best possible treatment."

"It's too late."

"Nonsense! When the Chinese couldn't defeat us what is a disease?"

Seth looks at the floor, "I have decided to accept the inevitable, beta. I am not getting any treatment."

Vakil looks at his father's face closely, seeking comprehension. Then, he understands, "Are you sure?"

Seth nods.

"Papa, this will be tough for us, but maybe this is Shiva's way of helping us prepare for something that is inevitable. We exist only in each other's imagination. We are not real. That way there will be no—"

This kind of clarity: why didn't his son utilise it in other aspects of his family life?

"Vakil," Seth stops him. "There's more. I have paid an agent to take your mother, wife and you out of Lalbag. He will take you somewhere safe where you can restart your life."

"What? But Pia and me are happy here."

"You will not be alive for long. You know we're all living on borrowed time."

"You had said that men with money and power survive everything, even war."

Seth looks his son straight in the eyes, "I was wrong. This is not a war that the rich will survive." Vakil looks at his father, blinking. It's never occurred to Seth that Vakil could simply be naïve. "The faster I get you all out of the house, the greater are your chances of survival." He adds: "Think of your mother. Think of your wife. Do you want them to be killed?"

Vakil makes no move to deny this: "You're right, Papa. We must be prepared for everything. China has taught me that we must be pragmatic." The dogmatism of the Chinese Communist Party, believing that blind obedience is to truth and facts, not to superiors or love. Where did his son learn that?

"What about you, Papa?"

Seth looks down at his feet, "I will slow you all down. If there is one thing I've learnt it's that you cannot rebuild life on death. Taking care of me will not let you seize your new life."

"But—"

"My mind is made up son. I just want you children and your mother to be safe."

Vakil hugs his father. It's the first time they have hugged since Vakil's accident.

"Thank you for saving us, Papa. Thank you for thinking of us even in this state."

In the arms of his son Seth's eyes tear up. Seth has, in his own way, loved his son as best as he could. He has fought to keep him alive. He has built a monument in celebration of his son's life. He's done all that he could for his family.

And now a father's love has found place in his son's heart. Now he can go in peace.

THE GRAPES WHO STOLE THE PLOT

His memories are a vague and foggy reflection, like condensation on his bathroom mirror. There she is, a threadbare thought, whom he remembers not as a whole but in parts, not even parts, that is wrong, but a bit here and a wobble there. The only memories that seem clear like cut glass are of the aura she evokes: cutting a lonely figure in his father's perpetual absence, her lovelorn state brimming over the empty of her expression, eyes vaguely pale, striking.

It's a cunt of a memory, Harsh knows, and it does no justice to the person who was his mother. His father, the great Deven Shah, on the other hand, is as evident to him as obviousness. His face is all pockmarks, deep gashes and scars, like a city built on skin. His body is grit, motion lines and muscular legs. In the vast net of power that he casts over many homes, many cities, many states and many hearts, a thread falls loose on his wife. She clings on to this with the resigned look of a lover hooked in love's crooked bait.

If he were a swan, he'd be gone. If he were a train, he'd be late. And if he were a good man, he'd let me be his. His mother says. Over and over again.

Whatever love her husband sidesteps, finds its way doubly over towards Harsh, feeding him as if his hunger is a personal insult to her.

A certain incident, the only one that sticks when others have taken flight, is of her standing before her vanity mirror, applying lipstick, fitting a pearl earring, singing a tune that sounds to Harsh's ears as odd, perhaps because she never sings, perhaps because he can't recall the melody or song. Is it a happy song? That too he fails to recollect, but then he soothes himself: for is singing, not by its very nature, an act of happiness? The phone rings, his father's voice blazes through the handset, telling her that he can't make it for their anniversary dinner as he is stuck at work. Or so he must have said, imagines Harsh. Because the next snapshot, perhaps later that night, perhaps a few moments after, is of her sitting on the front lawn, her lace dress sodden in the grass, holding a bottle of wine as empty as her eyes, and gazing up at the dark sky, only one pearl earring fastened to her ear, the other fallen beside her feet like a shorn slice of moon.

Glistening but alone.

"Do you see that ant over there?" she asks him. She hasn't turned around and he hasn't uttered a word, but she senses his presence. "I wonder how he became as big as me."

Harsh looks around and sees no ant, especially not an ant as big as his mother.

She has never looked as beautiful, never as fragile, but Harsh's eyes go to that patch of skin below her left eye, a grape-juice coloured birthmark that is a shade darker than the rest of her fair face. It is nothing, a quarter-size on that enormity of mother that is her, but whenever he zooms out of this strand of memory of her, the patch becomes larger and larger, consuming her face, her body, becoming all that he has left of her.

Later his psychiatrist tells him that very lonely people often envision giant ants. Ants tend to roam in groups and hence—on a metaphysical level—represent family life.

After she is gone his father says nothing, as if she is an item he's forgotten on one of his business trips. But there are new hollows on either side of his face, like something inside him has caved, folded and been permanently lost.

Harsh runs to his father. "Look what I found in the garden, Papa," he says to the great Deven Shah, holding out his hand. "A great big litchi." He expects his father to be proud of him and to tell his business associates, with their stodgy business suits, that his son has discovered something that no one has seen in their garden. But his great father, embarrassed, turns to look at the assembly of great men and says, "Son, this is not a litchi but a baby jackfruit." Laughter ripples through the men, and it does not stop, not through the long torturous years when it dawns on everyone that Harsh has none of the great Deven Shah's alacrity or business acumen. He can hear people whisper that he is only his father's shadow, while the ruthless ones whisper: he is a shadow of his father's foot.

That's when Harsh discovers how the binge of food renders his arteries insensate. So he comes to love his food. It is the first thing he thinks of when he wakes up in the morning and the last thought on his mind before he goes to bed. He grows into this tall pod of a man with fluffy arms and cornball elbows, knees that look like they are connecting some exaggerated disembowelment of lower and upper limb. Moreover, he develops man-boobs, and for that he is happy because a semblance of his mother has lived on through him. His soft, curvy body with its adequate breasts, fills that wide space left empty by his mother.

All this is told to Ida on strange honeymoon nights, where they lie in bed as they're supposed to; when Harsh's faltering, zealous lovemaking—for it's clearly his first time—is followed by no-holds barred divulgence sessions. As he talks, squirting too-fast-too-much in words as in bed, Ida turns away from his doughy body, his man-boobs. She misses Manu's taut and sinew, the way he held her. She puts a pillow between her husband and herself. He doesn't notice.

"A week after my mother died, we brought home some of her ashes in a vase for safekeeping. This guy from my school, a mean big bully who called himself Tiger, came home to offer his condolences. I was surprised to see him and even more surprised when he told me that the only way to numb my pain was to have cocaine. 'Prove to your father that you are a man", he said. He took me to the backyard, placed some powder in front of me and showed me how to snort. I did it and felt nothing but this strange itch in my nose and throat. Tiger laughed and told me that what I had was not ... not cocaine ... but ash. It was the cremated remains of my mother."

His mother's ashes have become a permanent itch on his nose. An itch that makes him sniffle, makes people think he's a cokehead. Is he?

In the first few days of their marriage, Harsh's stupidity and self-involvement affronts Ida; he speaks to her like she is a dictaphone he'll never play back. She misses Manu, more than she thinks is possible, feeling as if a part of her has ripped off and left her bleeding. What choice does she have now? Harsh knows she's married him for his money, and so he uses her for his amusement: to lay emotional traps into which she must pretend to easily fall, to get his way with everything, to win every argument, and to have her feel obligated to him for the smallest kindness he bestows upon her. She pays for every second that she spends with him.

So when that call comes, at three one morning, on that private line to which only Deven has access, and it breaks that pampered monologue of their marital suite, Ida knows a shakedown is due. Harsh turns to her, his face a half moon in the dim light of the lamp, and whimpers that a Chai sign has been found outside all of his father's factories, properties and businesses. The Chinamen are going to arrest Deven. Harsh doesn't seem surprised. Unknown to his father a union formed in his sex-toys factory, something illegal in China.

This is what Ida is told. Whether this fact actually slipped the great Deven Shah's sharp mind or it's a set-up, Ida will never know. All she thinks is: I'll be poor, and then dead. Such cruelty from a life she wanted to escape! Such misfortune! But her self-pity is allowed to go no deeper as Harsh asks her to call her father for money, to use his influence. So they've been double-crossed, her father and her. Deven has used Seth as back-up knowing things were headed south for him. No, she tells her husband. It's that or you leave, Harsh whispers harshly. His father has told him to say this and he's his father's son, a son who can finally prove his worth.

His father's imperialistic hold on Harsh vexes Ida. It occurs to her that in their few days together he's not developed for her even a small tenderness, not even the kind that people reserve for children and dogs. He can never love her. Still, Ida is not surprised.

When she was a young girl, Ida loved the neem tree in her father's garden. She loved how big it was, how wide and tall, its sheer strength. It was the only tree whose branches she couldn't touch and whose bark she couldn't climb. On the tree's highest branch her father installed a rope swing from which she used to swing every day. She would swing high, so high that Manu could no longer push her, so high that she could touch the tree's branches. And she'd shout, "I am Ida, Goddess of the Earth."

Then, during one monsoon, a tornado struck Lalbag. It carried away lampposts and cars, her school's front gate. It flooded their basement, the living room, the servants' quarters. Her family and Manu's moved up to the second floor and stayed locked there, holding each other, muttering prayers, hoping their White Taj wouldn't blow away. The wind howled with rage outside their window and door, for an entire day and the whole night, and on the second day there were horrific groans outside their window as if something—she couldn't tell what—was dying a slow death.

Two mornings later when the storm abated, she ran towards the neem tree wanting to swing again. She found out that it had fallen down, crushing their outdoor washing area. The thing that had died a slow death was her neem tree. She thought of the tree's resurrection, a miracle, for such a mighty thing could not so humbly go, but the tree did not stand back up on its roots. The neem tree lay there, like any other collapsed tree, its trunk hollow from the inside, eaten away with age, a thin black dust inside, falling apart with the slightest drop of drizzle; nothing phenomenal to show for its spectacular life. That's when Ida had learnt that most living beings do not reveal who they are from the inside.

Therefore, it doesn't surprise Ida that Deven has taught his son, as has his mother, that eventually every wife must do her husband's bidding. So, when he again demands that she ask her father, Ida looks at him, square in the face, and gives him an answer. And she knows, by the surprise on Harsh's face, that he too is learning that living beings rarely reveal who they really are.

LEASH THE DOG

Manu walks back to The White Taj, allowing his thoughts to pelt him like the wind against his face. Seth has told them to take the day off. His parents have chosen to rest. He's chosen to walk aimlessly around Lalbag, allowing his mind free rein. Will he be able to find the key and hand it to Bingbing? Will the Chinamen kill him if he doesn't give them the key? Will he be able to save his parents? Will he be able to tell Ida about Bingbing?

Manu is oblivious to the sweet smells of hibiscus that line the compound wall, lending fragrance to the dying stench of summer. He doesn't return the wave of a cheerful old man who walks past him carrying a clay pot of milky green aam panna. It's only outside the gates of The White Taj that he stops and peeks cautiously inside. Seth is standing outside the servants' quarters. What is he doing there? What's going on? Has Seth found out about Bingbing? Have the Chinamen come? Is Seth throwing them out?

Manu gulps. How is he ever going to look Seth in the eye again?

He dare not go past the gate, so he rests against the mango tree outside, from where he can see everything. He sees Seth shift on his feet. He sees Seth knock on their door. He turns towards the tree with its ancient, gnarled branches in brown knuckles. His earliest memory is of eating the mangoes that fell down from it each summer, orange orbs sealed with a patch of black nodes; little tangerine pirates. He'd climb the branches, throw down the plumpest mangoes—orange bits of sky—into Ida's arms, and watch the mango juice on her cherry-pink lips. Bud of the bud, root of the root, bark of the bark; he imagined their lives to be like two leaves falling from the tree, spiraling to the ground, printing their shadows on each other. How he misses Ida.

Seth's gaze turns to the mango tree and Manu dives behind the trunk. Has Seth seen him? He hears Seth knock again. After some time, he looks back and sees Ram come out of their carbuncle of a house; sleep stuck in white crust at the corner of his eyes. Urmila follows him. Ram walks towards Seth with a red and white cleaning cloth on his bent shoulders, hands folded in front of him as if in plea, cowering more than usual. When did his father get so old?

"Mai Baap, I would've come to you!" he says.

"Ram," Seth says dismissively. "I have to tell you all something."

He's shifting his legs. Seth wants whatever he's about to do over as quickly as possible.

Ram looks at Urmila. "Manu is not here."

Seth looks at the mango tree. Manu knows he's been seen. He comes out from his hiding place, scratching his head in apology. This is going to be unpleasant.

"Come here," Seth tells them, and they walk to the patio on the front lawn. Seth sits under the patio, hiding from the sun. Manu remembers Seth's revulsion to shade, saying that even eyes are useless under the shadow of eyelids. What's going on with him?

Sit, Seth says. Ram and Urmila squat on the ground. Manu looks uncertain. He wants to sit on the chair like Seth is. He grabs the corner of the bamboo chair but lets it go. He squats besides his parents.

"They've been sent away: Memsahib, Chota Sahib and Choti Memsahib," Seth says in a monotone. He dabs his handkerchief on the trickle down his face.

Ram speaks, his voice shrill, "Mai Baap, what are you saying?" Manu looks at his mother who gapes at Seth in surprise. He can't bring himself to react. He's so relieved that his secret is not out.

"They left today; that's why I told you all to be away from the house."

"They didn't even say goodbye?" Ram asks, his snivels starting.

Seth ignores him, "My sources have informed me that New China is preparing to attack Lalbag. They've apparently cracked some kind of code." Manu gulps. "That's why I've sent them away."

"Where?" Ram asks. He sniffles into a handkerchief.

"You know I can't tell you that," Seth replies. Beads of sweat gather on his forehead and upper lip. They look at each other. Of course he can't. The listening ears are everywhere.

"And Ida?" Manu asks.

Seth narrows his eyes.

"Ida Memsahib?" Manu adds.

"You don't have to worry about that. I took care of her when I got her married."

"There's more." Seth stares at his hand like it's a thread he wants to cut. "I have ... cancer. It's the last stage so I have maybe a month or two to live."

"Cancer? Mai Baap!" Ram shouts. "What are you saying? This cannot be true!"

His expression is that of a ruined man.

Urmila holds her husband in shock.

"That's why I didn't leave with them. There is no point."

Manu's face is torched with licks of hot emotions. Sadness, loss, pity. But strange new feelings also grip him. What are they? They're anger, disappointment, along with the heavy stink of betrayal. Here he is devising plans to escape death in the hands of the Chinamen, and there is Seth interested only in saving his own family.

He turns to Seth, his eyes wide in disbelief. "Seth Sahib, you knew the Chinamen were coming but you did not think of saving us?"

He has never spoken this way to Seth but right now he doesn't care.

"Don't talk like that to Mai Baap, beta." Ram's smile extends all the way around his face. "The Chinamen will not touch us as long as we have him."

"Baba, if they're planning an attack, they will kill us. All of us."

"As long as we have each other, we'll be fine," his father continues.

He is floating facedown inside a swimming pool where no voice can reach him.

Manu looks at Seth.

"Fine," Seth says. "If you want to escape and leave me, then tell me. I will arrange it. I am happy to die alone."

"Never, Mai Baap." Ram glares at Manu. "Don't listen to Manu. I will never let you be alone. Especially not in this condition."

"I don't want you to, Ram." Seth says, as if granting Ram a favour he's long wished for. And Ram—Ram smiles as if he's been offered the fragrance of wet grass, the shine of the moon, the caress of a breeze. How can his father be so foolish?

"This is not an opportunity we can let go, Baba," he snaps. "It's not only about you. We want to get out of here." Manu turns to his mother. "Maa, say something."

Urmila doesn't say a word, her eyes opaque, and expression sober.

"I have been with Mai Baap since we were children, beta," says Ram. "I will not leave him when he most needs me."

Manu doesn't understand his father. How can he let them die to pander to Seth?

So he rises to the full extent of his resolve, "For my sake, let's take Seth Sahib's offer. I am still young. I want to live. As a father, you have no other choice but to save your son."

But Ram's eyes are empty hollows. It's like teaching a fish to climb a tree, Manu thinks irritably.

"Mai Baap and me are like brothers," his father adds softly.

"If you are like brothers then why have we been their servants for two generations? Mother gave her only jewelry piece to Seth Sahib, though his wife has at least a hundred sets. Has he ever returned the necklace or given you anything in return?"

His father doesn't react. He looks at him as dreamily as a dandelion floating in a meadow.

"The war is happening, Baba, and it's happening to us."

"We will see then, beta. Why worry now?"

Ram is viewing New China's impending attack on Lalbag as a newsreel where everything takes place elsewhere, a way for them to continue looking into the world from behind a screen. He's refusing to let reality interrupt his happiness.

"God damn it! We're all going to die here," says Manu.

"Is that really so bad? You've had a good life," Seth says.

"Why would I want to die?" Manu asks, his eyes in genuine dread.

"What is death?"

"What is death?" Manu sputters. "Death is you, the idea that you—the body that you have, your thoughts, your achievements—will cease to exist. Who would not be scared?"

"I am not."

It's impossible to ask a dying man whether he's scared of death.

"What about the rest of us? Why do you want all of us to die as well?"

"I do not. You're my family."

"So why are you doing this to us?"

"You shouldn't worry about this so much," Seth interjects. "Death is just a figure of speech. Once we enter this world, we never leave it. We never cease to exist. Some of our ashes are strewn in the wind, so we remain part of the air. Most of our ashes are immersed in the Ganga, so we become part of the water. This river flows to the sea and the sea laps the land, so we remain part of the land. Death is not the end; it's a new beginning."

Manu gets up and turns angrily to Seth. "You're doing this on purpose. Manipulating my father's emotions so we all die! Showing us our aukaad. How can you be so cruel?"

"How can you speak this way to Mai Baap?" his father says.

"How can he let us fall into the hands of the Chinamen?"

Ram looks at his wife in exasperation, "Talking to this boy is like biting into sugarcane; you only end up losing teeth."

This line of reasoning will not work with his father. Manu tries another one.

"It doesn't matter if a cat is white or black, as long as it catches mice, right?" he asks. "We can all escape together and look after Seth Sahib in New China or Jerusalem or a new country as well, can't we Baba?"

His father looks at him quizzically and shakes his head. "We don't know how things will be in a new place, beta. And in New China the danwei may assign us some other job."

"Baba, do you know any other way to save us?"

"No," Ram mumbles slowly. "I don't."

He's won the argument. Manu smiles brightly at his father. But his father's eyes are filled with the sorrow of a man who has lost everything.

"We will not go. We will stay," Ram says, his eyes drooping further in sadness. "It is the right thing to do."

This is ridiculous.

"Seth Sahib, say something!" Manu asks his master.

"It's done, Manu," Seth replies. He gets up slowly from his chair. "There is no point in fighting your destiny."

For the first time in his life, Manu finds himself glaring at Seth. His master has emotionally played his father to lead them all into a death trap. For what? So he doesn't die alone?

"Don't do this to us!" Manu shouts after him.

Seth doesn't even notice Manu. He's lost in some other thoughts. He reaches the bungalow and shuts the door behind him.

"Baba," Manu shouts. "You cannot be fooled by this!"

Ram snivels, he is not listening to a word Manu has to say. "There is a price to pay for freedom, my son, though I hope you never experience it."

Manu turns to his mother.

"Don't let him do this."

His mother presses his hand but says nothing, her expression unreadable. Then she looks at Ram gently, for his father is someone towards whom her love finds a way even when he's at his worst. She dabs her dupatta—her fingers as pale as the moon—on her husband's sweaty face. She lifts her husband up and walks him slowly to The White Taj.

Manu's last opportunity to be saved is gone.

***

It's a time, not too long ago, or perhaps years back, when Seth and he are coming back home from somewhere. The day is so unremarkable that it has sewed shut its own memory, allowing only a thread to come unloose and flutter in the mind. Manu is carrying two baskets of cane heaped with vegetables; they must have gone to the market. A strong smell of diesel assails his memory; it must have been summer laden with the heavy heat from the goods trucks. Seth is walking along the banks of Lalbag's dried-up Yamla River, his walking stick tapping against the fire-browned stones. This used to be a river like life, full of abundance, receding and rising, twisting and turning; all that's left of it is a tiny pond. A teardrop that's survived the dessert-dry face of tragedy, Seth says. He lifts a fistful of mud from the bank and lets it fall limply to the ground. "This can be your life," he says to Manu, his baritone voice thick and husky with meaning. Scattered and forgotten. Using his stick, Seth draws Manu's name on a patch of wet mud skirting the pond. "Or it can be like this. Staying put, strong. If you let fate decide your life, it will. But it is always better to offer fate a dose of the life it has created for you."

Manu remembers.

***

Water cannot do what it feels like. It can stagnate or flow down; it cannot rise up. Water is like poverty. Air is like wealth. It does what it feels like. It rises and falls, flows and stands. Be like the air. Manu remembers.

***

Manu turns around and walks back to his quarters. He sees something standing at the front gate of The White Taj. A figure.

It cannot be.

A fist tightens around his heart.

She looks as severe as ever, as unhumorous. Her hand is resting on that electronic baton. Her mole, shaped like a cloud, is blacker than ever. What is she doing here?

Manu immediately walks to the gate.

"Madam Bingbing. What ... what brings you here?"

"You have key?"

Manu looks at the ground. His mind goes slack like boiled noodles.

"You alive because of me. They ready to kill you," she snarls. "In three days you give me key."

"Madam, that is impossible. I don't even know where the key is. It could be locked up anywhere."

"We not dumb like you Yindus. Key is in house. You have to find it."

How can Seth be so blasé as to leave the key in the house where anyone can steal it? Has he done this after his family has left? Or has the disease made him careless? More so, how do the Chinamen know where the key is? Manu shudders.

"But Madam, how will I know it is the right key? Seth Sahib has hundred of keys with him."

"It made from bomb ashes. It have trishul mark on it. You know it when you see it."

"If you know where it is, Madam, may I request you to take it yourself?"

"You stupid or dum-dum? We cannot do it ourselves or we become curse. Only Yindu and family man can bring to us key. Understand?"

Manu nods.

"You come with key to Chindia restaurant at 1 pm."

Chindia restaurant? That's in the Comi Area. He's not allowed there.

He looks at her confused.

Bingbing raises her hand in impatience, "They expect you. Come with key and you be fine. Otherwise, you die."

How can she say this with such a cavalier voice?

Manu wipes the tears he knows have spread across his eyes.

"You should not show like this sadness. It is not good for society," Bingbing adds. "You know my mother grown up during Cultural Revolution. In 1971, at seventeen age, she taken out of middle school and sent to work in collective farm at Great Northern Wilderness of China. It is place even your nightmare not go. By time revolution is over, five years later, she is labeled 'sent-down youth'—you understand? It is not good. She never recover from hardship of countryside. She then learn never to show emotion and she teach me same way. It make you weak."

Manu doesn't know what to say to this. Sorry to hear that, he adds feebly.

"I tell you so you know it is better in life to be tough person."

She is right. Where have Manu's emotions gotten him?

"Your nose bleeding," she says.

Manu looks at the clots of blood that have collected on his shirt, right above his heart, and realises that his nose is not the only part of him that's bleeding.

"Madam, please don't do this. I cannot betray my nation like this."

Bingbing leans over and whispers in his ear, "You already did. Now don't be yellow heart."

Manu looks at her with fear. This cannot be happening to him.

"Good?" Bingbing says with a finality that leaves no further room for discussion.

He doesn't reply.

"Good?" she asks again, her voice thin and menacing.

Good, Manu hears himself mumble.

It has to be done.

MADHUR PHAL

Ram looks at his wife, the woman he was never meant to marry.

His marriage was fixed to Gauri, a sweet and simple girl whose family were cleaners in the neighbour's house. Unknown to him, Urmila, the neighbourhood tailor's daughter, was in love with him. When she heard of Ram's impending marriage, she went to her parents and told them that she wanted to marry Ram. They refused, for how could a tailor's daughter marry below her rank to a mere servant. Urmila did not relent. She found the courage to go up to Videsh, who was at that time Lalbag's wealthiest and most powerful man, and say, "Please get me married to Ram."

Videsh was amused by the girl's gumption, but he refused her anyway; the decision had already been made. It was too late to change Ram's wedding plans.

Urmila didn't give up. She shared her feelings with Ram, and Ram confessed that he *had* noticed her, that he *could* love her, but he was a loyal servant's loyal son, a boy who didn't want to go against his parent's wish or those of his master.

Urmila quietly retreated, or so everyone thought.

Ram's wedding preparations proceeded as planned. Two weeks before the wedding, a strange thing happened. Gauri was sweeping her master's courtyard, as she always did, when she found clumps of dark black hair on her broomstick. She wondered where the hair had come from, but didn't give it more thought. She continued sweeping, as more hair gathered around her. It was when her mistress scolded her for leaving the courtyard dirty with hair, that it struck Gauri that something was wrong. This grew worse over the next couple of days for wherever Gauri went hair would appear. It was on the fourth day that her mother noticed a bald patch on Gauri's head and realised that it was Gauri's hair that was falling all around her, coiling like snakeskin on the mud floor of her servants' quarter. A spell had been cast! Black magic! Lock her inside the house, don't let her out, ordered her father. What will happen to our daughter's wedding if people find out, cried her mother.

When Desh and Jaru heard of this, they were flummoxed. It must be pre-wedding jitters, they declared large-heartedly, already having received the two goats promised as dowry to them. But as Gauri grew balder, whispers started. Urmila had been seen chanting at the Mount Akaho Temple for the past twenty-one days; not eating, not drinking, not talking, just chanting. Rumours flew, got confirmed: it had to be her! It had to be Urmila who had cast a spell on Gauri, cursed the poor girl to hairlessness. There was always something odd about that tailor's daughter, something mystic and unsettling, growing up around all those needles and stitches, fitting people into a mould as per her own measurement: shudder, shudder, shudder!

To confirm this theory, someone from the town took a small portion of rice, wrapped it in a cloth bag, wrote Urmila's name on it, put the bag in a nest of white ants and when the bag was eaten, said: "This proves that she is a witch." Someone else carved her name on the branch of a sal tree and when her name faded, it was taken as a sign of her culpability. The final test to confirm that she was indeed a witch was when a dog was made to drink her urine procured by a sly servant of the neighbouring villa. The dog fainted.

And so Urmila became a witch, a sorcerer, Lalbag's very own Tituba of Salem.

Have you not heard? Urmila casts her spells using the horn of a rhino, the thigh bone of a lama, a necklace made of human spine, a whip made of fox tail, an amber crystal ball and a black cloak that conceals her, lets her slip into your house unseen.

People began avoiding the tailor-master's tiny shop.

Gauri shaved herself bald and declared herself a sanyaasan.

Videsh and Desh did not know how to proceed. The wedding mandap had been paid for, as had the caterers. Only the bride was missing.

Two nights before the due wedding, Urmila came to Videsh in his dreams. She was dressed in a bride's sari. She looked at the scar on Videsh's face and said to him, "The world has scarred you and it has scarred me. We should not scar each other. Only you can stop the pain."

The deep purple scar running down Videsh's face burnt the entire night.

The next morning, his scar still stinging, Videsh said to Desh, "Our Hindu scriptures speak of the wise sage Ashtavarka. Although he was highly learned, he was hunchbacked and deformed. One day he went to the court of King Janak to impart his wisdom. The courtiers laughed at him. The sage did not get enraged for he was wise. He laughed back at the courtiers, saying that such men were incapable of wisdom since they could not see past his deformed body. Hence, they understood nothing beyond their bondage to the superficial and senseless. They were the crippled ones."

Videsh continued: "We will not be like those courtiers, Desh Babu. We will not judge Urmila for what the people of Lalbag call her, but for her love for our Ram."

Gauri's dowry goats were chopped into curry, the music band told to continue their practice and Ram was married off to Urmila.

Urmila's marriage into the dregs of a rich household, but a rich household nonetheless, gave her a reverent aura. No one in Lalbag, including Rani or Videsh, Seth or Jaru, ever spoke an unkind word to her. The people of Lalbag developed a new grudging respect for her. What a good sorcerer she was, capable of anything, protecting the townspeople from making bad personal choices like Ram was doing in marrying that bald servant girl Gauri! There was nothing left for anyone to do, other than wrap boiled rice with the ashes of a rooster in a banana leaf and keep it outside The White Taj as a peace offering to Urmila.

Urmila seemed disregardful of the hullabaloo around her. In Ram she found a devoted husband and in Manu a loving albeit impish son, and aside from performing her duties to the hilt in Seth's house, she was disinterested in the rest of the world.

Despite the stories Ram has heard about his wife in the marketplace: the mysterious circumstances under which she married him and how she brought Vakil back from the dead, he has got nothing but love from her. Like the moon watches over the earth, she watches over him. She waxes and wanes, and many times seems to be in eclipse, but she sees everything he does, in light and in darkness, and never reproaches him for it.

This love is a good thing, Ram thinks, for now she is willing to die with me when the time soon comes. She doesn't share the same wide-eyed fear of death as their son. He knows, his Urmila has told him, that when death comes, as it comes to everyone, the three of them will incarnate as rats in the sacred Karni Mata Temple in Rajasthan. In this temple, the rats are considered holy and treated as demi-gods; they ascend straight to heaven and break the cycle of life. This is an opportunity that only the world's greatest sages and philosophers, and those who fulfill their life's karma, are awarded. All they have to do in order to fulfill their karma is to stay true to their dharma of being loyal to their master.

Ram calms down as he thinks these thoughts. It soothes the bristles from arguing with his son. And so he smiles at his wife, as they strip bare Seth's room, for his master has decided to withdraw from life, and the servant, he feels, that he must follow suit.

THE AGE OF TRUTH

The time is approaching four. A large white moon hangs in the sky like a shiny tooth. It will be two hours before the sparrows begin to call. No, not the sparrows, I remind myself, for those have long fallen silent. I don't remember when exactly they stopped chirping, but I can no longer hear them herald the dawn or plop their finger-long samosa-like bodies on the ground searching for grains. They were there one day, like youth and beauty, and gone the next.

Sleep is soggy now. It flaps before me like an enemy's flag that I dare not hold.

Still, I like this darkness, for in it everything feels clean and possible. It is a place where I can be anything and imagine anything, even for my life to be different.

My stomach growls. I wish I could drink warm milk with haldi to soothe my jagged nerves, lull my body into a state of stupor. But there is no milk in Lalbag. Not since the Chinamen stopped its supply. I get up from bed, careful not to make a sound. I walk out of the front door and onto the stone path. A gentle breeze, coming in from the north, plays with my fingertips. I've been told that love comes from the north, money comes from the east, debauchery comes from the west and all that is south, is forgotten. I think of my love as I leave the path and walk back to the servants' quarters, where so much of my life and all of my happiness have been spent. I cannot let the Chinamen destroy it. They'll leave nothing of it but a pile of rubble. I bend down and rest my head against the door, as if it's my mother's caress, and—like a nightingale that beckons the dawn—I gather into me the inside of this house, all of its memory. I place it inside me like a guardian of my sanity. It is home and I cannot let it end with the finality of a full stop.

The undecided early light is nibbling into the corners of darkness with quiet dignity. It is still long before the sun will rise. The dawn air carries strains of prayers from devotees at Mount Akaho, our saviour. Dawn in Lalbag is a sight that brings solace even to my baffled eyes. But I need more than solace today. I need something familiar and reassuring. There is only one such thing.

I make my way to the mansion, past the stone path and check if the lights are off. They are. I pluck an errant leaf from the bushes. Then I walk up to the front door and open it with the house key.

My feet land on the marble floor rendered ice-cold in the air-conditioning. A chill runs through my body. I can't put on my slippers that'll slap against the marble, shake the house awake. So, led by the dim flash from the streetlight, I walk barefoot around the house. Finding balance with one hand on the wall, I wander through the study room, the dining room, the library. I open drawers and cabinets that I've never seen. But the key, it is not there. He must keep them next to him, as a man with something precious must.

I feel my way in the darkness, up the stairs.

Through the dark landscape, a slit of light appears and it grows bigger and bigger, as if a giant hand is lifting a veil off the face of this earth.

For the first time in this house, The White Taj, I feel like an intruder, as though, at any moment Seth Sahib will wake up and ask me why I'm here. What will happen if I'm caught? I've thought of no excuse. But I know that I will not be caught. Seth Sahib is alone. He is taking a medicine that lets him sleep through his own torn thoughts.

Seth Sahib is in his room, fast asleep. Looking at him makes me feel guilty, but then I think of how he has betrayed us, how he doesn't care for the people who have looked after him all his life. I force the guilt out of myself.

I scan his room that has been stripped bare after the family's departure. Where could he have kept the key? In the locker? No. The locker is lying open; empty of the money and jewels that must have been given to Kamala Memsahib.

I look at Seth Sahib's empty suitcases, which have been to better places than I have. I've never flown, of course, but I've seen the contents of a foreign land. Booze in shiny bottles, clothes with shiny labels, things I would never taste or wear, perfumes that I'd later smell on Ida. The first thing I'll do with a NIC is to go somewhere on a plane.

Maybe this is not such a bad thing after all.

The couch in his room is filled with flowers, chocolates, saris, dry fruits, a vacuum cleaner, and a crockery set. I pick up a golden box on which is imprinted: the world's finest truffle chocolates. I look at Seth. He is fast asleep, his snores—with the longevity and shock of a puppy's bark—escape his lips every minute or so. I open the box and examine the six round pieces that lay inside it like golden eggs in their nests. I've never had chocolate from a box before. The outer edges of my world expand and I want to revel in this. I unwrap one chocolate. I put the piece on my tongue and my mouth becomes liquid gold.

I look around, more determined now, and see a glass jar filled with coins. It's on Seth Sahib's bedside; as if it's the last thing he looked at before falling asleep. The coins are many—in silver, copper and gold. But my eyes spy a key. It cannot be! It is! Out there in the open! Attached to a trishul keychain, with a trishul imprinted on it. Has Seth Sahib completely lost his fear of the Chinamen?

I grab the jar and take it to the next room. I bang into a chair, then two. I stub my toe, once, then twice. I empty the jar. My hands don't stop trembling. Can I do this? Will I be cursed? Will the world stop churning? No, I can't do this. I have to. I take a deep breath and pull out the key. I tiptoe back to Seth Sahib's room and place the jar exactly from where I took it. I cannot believe it's this easy. The thing that separates war from peace is in my hands. I have the key!

Every morning, for the past four years, I have woken up feeling like I'm standing inside a lawn, or a field, where the grass towers over me like a school bully. I spend my days cutting the grass short, but when I wake up the next morning the grass is taller than me again. Day after day, every day, no matter what I do the grass overpowers me. Today is not like that. Today, for the first time in my life, the grass is trimmed and shorn down to size, swaying gently at my feet. I feel tall and powerful. With this key I can be free. My family and I can be safe! We can finally live the life we deserve.

I tuck the key into my kurta pocket and pat it for safety. I must make a quick escape. I go down, pass by the kitchen and stop at the entrance. I stare at the refrigerator, hulky like a silver beast, and hunger sweeps towards me like a wave. Damn the escape. I must first reward myself. I stick my head into the blessed brightness of the refrigerator. But there's no milk. Not even the powdered variety. Still, I'm hungry, so I scour the food items eagerly. There's cheese wrapped in translucent clothe, red like a hooker's lips, chocolate as abundant as a cancer man's tumours, green and brown and yellow pastes, thick, in tins and cans, all pouty from the outside but tasteless inside. None of these appeal to me, for these are neither my things nor my choices. I feel no sense of ownership of them. So I stand there, empty as a rootless branch. What have I done? I cannot do this to my country, my people, my family. I should return the key. I sit down on the cold marble floor and put my head in my hands.

There's a day, a day I've never forgotten, when I was

sent to escort Vakil to a newly opened video game parlour in Lalbag. How mesmerising that place was with its brightly lit interiors, enormous arcade games and the hypnotic sounds: the pings and pongs! I'd never seen anything like it. I followed Vakil around from game to game, watching as he played many games. After two hours, Vakil gave me a plastic coin: "Go play." I couldn't believe my luck. I walked carefully around the parlour, holding the coin as if it were a flying carpet that would transport me to a magical land, examining each game to see which one was worthy of my magical coin. Finally, I stopped before two pinball machines, one of which Vakil was playing on. Inside the glass-covered cabinet was a play field alive with landmarks, electric lights, an LCD as black box, a little city by itself. There were ricocheting balls of various colours, looping and spinning, whacked into the air, suspended in delicious indecision before falling or rising. I decided this was the game for me. I inserted my precious coin into the slot and the game begun. Delirious with adrenaline, ready to be king of this video game arcade, I watched as the plunger propelled the first ball upwards into the playfield. I pushed the buttons. My flippers didn't move. The ball fell through the machine, into the drain, wasted like precious time. The balls came in quick succession after that, in a deluge, as I feverishly pressed up and down, up down, up down, up down on the flippers, kicked the machine, slammed against the red, blue, green buttons, and even tilted the game in desperation. But my flippers remain locked. One by one the balls fell. They slipped past the flippers and were swallowed by the mouth of the machine. In the matter of a minute all the balls in my machine were gone.

Vakil's machine was fine, the flippers flipped with great force, buttons pressed what they were supposed to press, and the balls rose and fell, rose and fell, hitting landmarks that would light up in salute to Vakil's victory. Vakil's machine played a long jubilant song when the game ended while next to it mine ended in a whimper.

This has always been my life. Playing second fiddle to men with wealth and freedom. I am sick of it.

I run my fingers over the key. My mind becomes as clear as water, and sharp too, like sharks in the water. It is this key that will help me in my new life. I can buy a house in New China. A house with an air-conditioner where my skin can be wiped clean, stripped bare of its own stickiness, like a snake that's shed a layer. I can bathe with hot water that comes out with the mere twist of a shower handle. I can get a close shave using a fancy razor instead of that barber blade. I can drink cold water straight from the tap. Life can be better than it is now. I can become the man I'm meant to be.

Still, something inside me refuses to be still. I pick up a cotton rag and begin to clean. Gently I wipe the sofa, the chaise lounge, the coffee table, the paintings, the photos, as well as the corners that I used to skip earlier. The light from the east warms my skin. Sweat streams down my body. After an hour, my sanity is restored to me and I know that this is right. I have to save my family the way Seth Sahib has saved his. That's what men do.

My resolution stands before me in order again.

By the time I go back to bed the first light of the morning has illumined the sky. The sky is a burst of colours as if the earth has drawn a painting for my viewing pleasure. I take a deep breath in and the colours come inside me. I'm dyed with them. I feel as bright as a rainbow.

After all, freedom has all the warmth of a fireplace with none of its soot.

As the world wakes up to another day, with their exercises and children and jobs with which to fill the hours, I turn over on my stomach and shut my eyes.

CHIN CHIN CHU

They're supposed to meet at the Chindia restaurant in Comi Area, a posh sequestered part of town that Manu has never been to before. As Bingbing had said, the guards at the big gate don't stop Manu; like a mother they know when to expect him.

Bingbing is late so Manu strolls around the area and checks out the well-heeled folk. If this is what life in New China is like, he realises, it may not all be bad. He walks into the restaurant, so he can pretend that he's been here before. His mouth opens for he's never seen anything like it. It's the biggest room he's stepped into. He likes big, he realises, and he likes lamination and things that glitter: bleached wood and pendant lights and brass trimmings and mirrors shaped like portholes. Well-dressed people are on almost every table but they make no sound, as if they are mime artists mimicking the act of dining. All he can hear is the faint clanking of glasses and the slight grating of silver forks rubbing against porcelain plates. The restaurant smells of lemongrass. Where are the usual smells of thick spices and tepid fish, the noise of humanity? Manu pats the key tucked inside the safety pocket of his pants and steps out, back into the natural warmth of the sunlight, underneath which he has spent most of his life. It is soothing and he relaxes.

Bingbing is still nowhere to be seen, so he enters the adjacent naturopathy shop which has a sign claiming to treat a range of illnesses using a combination of Chinese herbs and Indian Ayurveda. The stocker, in a white coat and severe black glasses, stands next to a row of white tables. He is gluing paper signs on brown bottles: Hernia, Increase of Hips, Masturbation, Ulcer, Woman Frigidity, Tightening of Woman Part, Asthma, Painful Menstruation, Tummy Flat, Urination in Bed.

"What you want?" a Chinese pharmacist asks Manu. He looks at him as if he's a poor Indian who cannot pay for anything here. Manu randomly points to a bottle.

The pharmacist smiles. The bottle says "Enlargement of Man Power" in Mandarin. Manu smiles back at the man to show him that he can read the Chinese script.

At that moment Manu sees a woman in a low-cut red dress, her hair tied up in colourful cotton threads, the sun shining on her. She turns in his direction and he sees a mole shaped like a cloud. It is Mi Bingbing. She looks nothing like her usual self!

The pharmacist catches Manu's gaze and says, "You not needing this bottle." He replaces "Enlargement of Man Power" with "Early Ejaculation".

Manu smiles at him and steps out. He meets Bingbing.

"Ni-maste," he greets her and extends his hand. "Nice to see you, Madam Bingbing. You are looking very nice."

She bows deeply in return, folds her hands and says Ni-maste. "I be undercover so no one look." Three men turn to stare at her. Her disguise is not working. Five foot two or three inches, she is not very tall, but what she lacks in height she makes up with the rest of her perfectly proportionate body. Manu notices the cut of her sleeveless dress meant to accentuate her slender arms, it must be the body part that she is most proud of. He expected a flat chest, but her breasts push in perfect orbs against her tight dress and he imagines they'll cup neatly around his hands. He imagines her nipples to be pink and hard under that red bra whose strap he can see; he wants to place ice on them and masturbate when they tremor.

For the last two days Manu has been walking around like an axe hangs over his head, but now, standing across her he feels like his entire life is a mushy whirl of quicksand and she is the handhold who will pull him out of it. Men.

"I like your hairstyle," he says as they walk towards the restaurant.

She touches her hair in acknowledgement.

They are given a table in a well-lit corner of the restaurant, in direct path of the abrasive daylight that has found its way in shafts through the blue velvet drapes. This soothes Manu, for the rest of the restaurant seems cold and distant.

Bingbing is clearly as intimidated as him, for she

touches her head self-consciously and says softly, "It is Chinese tradition to put thread in hair and wear red for auspiciousness."

They are seated next to each other.

On the table is a thin silver vase inside which a rose has been placed. Manu doesn't know what to do with it. Should he take the rose out and give it to Bingbing? He looks around. There are roses on all the tables, still nestled inside their vase. He follows suit and leaves the rose be, for the best way to behave rich is to do exactly what other rich people do.

Bingbing grabs his right hand and says, "I have to tell you little secret before meal. My friend they all call me Xiao Zhu."

"Xiao Zhu," Manu says, allowing the words to swirl in his mouth like a spring roll.

"Yes, it mean little pig. I like to eat lot. But don't worry. Today I not eat too much." She giggles and he gives her a big smile in response. Perhaps, all along, he's liked his women feathered and twittering, as if in an aviary. "I call you Chan Chu. It suit you. You like?"

"Chan Chu," he repeats. "Yes, Chan Chu. It has a nice ring to it. I like it. And, if you permit, can I call you Chin Chin Chu? That way our names will rhyme."

Chin Chin Chu is a famous Hindi song from a 1958 movie. It was picturised at a time when India's first Prime Minister, Jawaharlal Nehru, had placed great immense in the love between India and China, making popular the phrase "Hindi-Chini bhai bhai". Four years after the song became a rage, China attacked India in their first big war.

"Chin Chin Chu? I like that!" says Bingbing.

Her eyes are full of expression today, lighting up with every smile. There's a fullness in her lips that quiver like two bows shooting arrows laced with the promise of passion. And her face is so full of smiles that it's hard to remember the semblance of her original features. This is the moment he's been waiting for, when she's soft and receptive.

"Now that we're friends, Chin Chin Chu, how about we drop this whole idea of stealing the statue, eh? We don't know what will happen. It could turn out badly for China, no?"

Bingbing's entire face transforms. "No." she says flatly. "Plan made. We go to Mount Akaho in three day. Or you die." She's back to her cop-self. Manu feels himself pulled into sinking sand that he can never get out of. There's no other option.

"Now let's go down to business," she says. She gives him a packet in which he finds a pair of scissors shaped like two butterflies, a ruler and a small glass vase. "This be Chinese custom before big job. Scissor is so our mind not separate, ruler is to show that we have land to measure, vase is for peace and wealth."

Peace, he wants to snort. But he accepts the tokens quietly.

"Thank you," he says. He never imagined selling out to the Chinamen. What can he do now?

Bingbing draws the attention of a Chinese waiter. She says something to him in Cantonese. In a minute, he is back with two porcelain cups and a pair of cherry sticks. Bingbing stirs the cups with the sticks and circles the rims with her fingertips.

"What are you doing?" Manu asks, when she offers no explanation.

She smiles and says, "This is tough time. So much to lose. I do this for good luck."

"We don't need luck. India and China have been tied together for centuries, whether it is in our fight for freedom, our common trade routes or our shared history of anti-imperialism and colonial struggles," Manu says. Better to assuage the enemy with soft facts.

"The world have changed long time since. Remember 1962 war? Our bad border? All sour thing, no?"

He tries not to react. She can't roll her r's. That's cute.

"You are looking at the glass half empty. Remember Dr Kotnis?"

"Dr Kotnis, of course! He come from India to China during war with Japan and save so many Chinese soldier life. He marry one of our woman and have with her a son. He is our hero. We have build for him statue and stamp. Chinese people, we love him."

"Well, that's the kind of Indo-China relations we should remember."

"Yes, love story of Dr Kotnis and his Chinese bride Guo Qinglan is legend."

The waiter brings them their menu and they study it in silence for two minutes. The menu has Indo-Chinese dishes, combining the best of both cuisines. Fortunately, they're written in Mandarin. Manu tries not to balk or stare too hard at the right-hand side of the menu; the appetisers here cost as much as his family's former monthly income. He can't afford it. What is he going to do?

"What would you like to eat?" she asks him.

He doesn't reply.

Bingbing takes over, "One butter chicken in soy sauce, one mutton vindaloo with pak choi, and one spicy prawn curry in oyster sauce. That I like with three spring onion naan." That's a lot of food, Manu thinks. How is he going to pay for it?

"Will you be able to eat such spicy food?" he blurts out.

On the table is a glass stuffed with red and green chilies. Bingbing takes a green chilli and puts it in her mouth. She chews it with relish. "I love spicy food."

Manu nods. "I'll have water," he tells the waiter in Mandarin.

"You Yindus don't eat anything—garlic or onion or potatoes. Che! In China the more weird food you eat, the richer you. Sea slugs, donkey hooves, dog meat, snake skin." She laughs at him.

In the naked light of day he can see the blackheads sprinkled freely around her flat nose and the fine lines around her eyes and lips. He wonders how old she is. How does one tell with the Chinamen?

"Order," she snaps. "You not pay for it. PLA pay."

In relief and without looking at the menu he blurts out, "Sushi."

He's never eaten sushi but it sounds like something exotic and sophisticated.

She sniggers. A few people turn to look at them. Manu hears a tapping sound or is it the noise of his heart thumping against the whole of his body? He wishes he hadn't spoken.

"Sushi is Japanese, Tianzhen," she sniggers. "And here chef all women. Woman blood too warm to make sushi. For that you need man hand. Men have cold blood."

Her hand runs along a bronze bullfrog statue on the table, which has red eyes, wide flared nostrils, three legs, and a coin in its mouth. Why put this hideous thing in a beautiful place?

"Chow mein and paneer manchurian," Manu says. He can't think of any other Chinese dishes.

She sniggers again, "Your Chinese food is our Indian food."

Manu can't react to what she's saying. "Xièxiè," he tells the waiter.

Bingbing looks at him and says, "I glad your classes help you. It is good thing for us. But before we talk more, let us have all ostrich logic out of way."

"Ostrich logic?"

She doesn't return his thin laugh. "Yes, a thief in state of Jin once try to steal bell and when bell ring he shut his ear thinking that no one able to hear bell ringing, if he not able to hear bell ringing. So silly, no? We think if we not listen to truth then no one else can hear it."

"Wise you are," Manu smiles uncertainly. "So you're saying that we should not be like the ostrich that sticks its head in the sand waiting for a problem to go away, but discuss any potential problems that we may have? That we must talk openly and honestly?"

"Yes," she says.

He stares at her.

"Show me key," she says.

Manu hesitates.

"Okay, tell something, Manu," Bingbing says. "What is thing which poor have, rich not have? What thing is powerful more than God and evil more than the Devil? If you eat it, you die?"

Manu's mind goes blank. He shakes his head, "I don't know."

Bingbing gives a shadow of a smile and says, "Nothing. It is nothing."

"I don't understand," he says, feeling close to tears.

"Answer to riddle is: nothing. *You* have nothing. There is nothing *I* not have. This *nothing* more powerful than God, more evil than Devil. If you not do what I say, what you will eat, what your life will be? Nothing!"

Manu gulps. He looks around. No one is looking at them. He puts his hand inside his pants. They have hidden pockets. He breaks the thread with which he has tied the key to the pocket, and brings it out. He places it on the table.

Bingbing stares at the key like it will sing to her. But she doesn't pick it up.

"Madam, it is the real thing. It has the trishul on it."

"I knows that," Bingbing snaps.

"Please take it."

He pushes the key towards her outstretched hands.

"What you are doing? I not touch this!" she says.

Manu looks at her surprised.

"We Chinese superstitious. We not touch key. Only Yindu family member can. Or we curse." A pause. "In three day you stand outside statue. At 3 a.m. sharp. You open temple gate. Then you go. We take care of rest."

"Madam, someone will see me."

"Only we see you. Do what you is told."

Bingbing stares at him unblinkingly, as though he's the bulls-eye in an archery competition.

Manu looks at the key. What choice does he have now? He nods his head.

"What will you do with me then?" he asks, his voice flat. He expects nothing from this life that he is walking into.

"You go China and teach English."

"What?" Manu asks in surprise. "My English is not the best—" Still, he silently thanks Seth for sending him to the best school in Lalbag.

"It already decided. You do job there."

Manu nods. The CPC will obviously assign a job to him. He has no choice.

"I will teach whatever I know."

"They give you house in campus. You live there with parent. They can do bathroom cleaning in university. All will be happy."

Manu nods. He hesitates but then throws it out, "Madam, I'm trying not to, but I feel terrible to have done this. Please help me! I will never live through this guilt."

She doesn't react to his emotional outburst.

"We will die without the statue," he adds.

"How it matter? You will die with statue also."

The two of them look at each other like pawns on a chessboard.

"At least with me you learn little more Mandarin. You more ready for new life."

He wants to tell her that her language has no alphabet. It is phonetically poor. The Chinamen can't even pronounce "r". He smiles and says, "You're right."

Then, she asks him, "You like dogs?"

What? He nods.

"Good. Dog meat healthy to eat. It make blood warm." Bow-wow, she adds. "Club them before they give to you rabies."

Manu tries not to let his disgust show.

"I had adopted a street dog when I was young. I don't think I can eat dog meat," he murmurs.

"I also have puppy when I was child. Small fluffy one with the soft fur. Brown soft fur. How you call them?" Her face relaxes.

"Pekingese?"

"Yes, yes. That one," she says, pointing her index finger at him in agreement. "It only dog legal in China. His right ear not there, probably someone bite it when he is baby. But to me he perfect. Above his mouth he have cute little black mark, like moustache, and on his paw is white shape like half moon. I call him Chao." Manu listens to the rest of Bingbing's story: Chao was the most loving and affectionate dog she could find and whenever she came back home from school, he would greet her at the front door, tail wagging, licking her face. She was an only child and he was her only companion. They played together and he made her laugh a lot. Then one day while her mother was napping and her father was at work, Bingbing was with Chao below the window in the living room. They were playing. Everything was going well. She went to the kitchen to get some water. When she came back she got the shock of her life! Chao was standing a few feet away from the window with his hair raised, his body stiff, growling softly at something on the windowsill. But there was nothing there! Bingbing didn't understand what he was looking at. But his eyes were fixed on that spot and whatever he saw there made his teeth snarl. She had never seen him like this. "Chao?" she said, but he didn't seem to hear her. Chao, she said again, and took a step towards him. That's when he barked and snapped his teeth, right at her. She stepped back in shock! Her Chao had never been anything but affectionate with her. What was happening?

"And then—" here she pauses and takes a moment as the scene flashes back before her eyes "—And then he, my darling Chao, my only companion, start running toward windowsill. He run so fast that I not able to stop him. And then he jump. He jump so high. Before I can grab, he jump out of window. He kill himself." There is a long silence. "Till today I not sure what happen. I don't know what he see on windowsill, what make my sweet little dog so ... so mad like that. It was like death of actor Robin Williams, he is happiest man on earth, he make us laugh, give us such joy, and he go kill himself. I cry for weeks and weeks. For days I not eat. Then I swear never to get dog again." She clasps Manu's hands, very tightly, "Still some afternoon are there when sun come through window and I see shadow of a little puppy on wall. And I promise to you that shadow have one ear missing and I feel, no I know, that my Chao have come back to me."

Manu gets goosebumps as he watches some sort of light go off in her eyes.

"Till today, Chao say to me that another dog spirit kill me. He tell me that now you kill dog for me." Her eyes become death cold. "So I kill dog. For Chao, for love, I kill."

She looks into Manu's eyes. "You do same. You kill for those you love."

What a mad evil thing to say, Manu thinks. He looks at the face of this Chinese cop and realises that there is no way he will get out of this plan alive. Manu is going to die.

MIDSUMMER DAY'S DREAMS

The day starts before sunrise and ends after sunset on the twenty-first of June when Ida wakes up to find that her room has been moved. This is not the room that she shares with her husband. Where is she? How has she moved here without waking up? Her head is the weight of an iron brick. Has she been drugged?

She gets up to open the bedroom door and finds it locked from the outside. The windows have been barred. What is happening? Have the Chinamen locked her up? Has Harsh? Why? She scrambles in search of her phone. It's not there. They've taken it.

The house is still. There's no stirring, no footsteps. Everything around her is dark.

She's alone.

She drinks water from the tap. She eats from glucose biscuit packets that have been left in the bottom drawer by whoever occupied this room before. She lays in the dark, lets it consume her, fill her emptiness. She remembers that if anyone happens to be brave or foolish enough to walk during night around The Black Taj, they comment on how dark it is. And Ida thinks: How can darkness be anything but black? In fact, this darkness is like wisdom that seeps through her eyes and into her head. It has a sharp quality and in it she can hear her every thought with clarity. She feels at one with what is inside and outside her. Memory reshapes in her head, throwing up things she had buried long ago—Manu's love for her, her father's love for her, the sense of entitlement she had towards love, carefully forgotten incidents, the things she never spoke of, didn't dare to even think about, kept off limits from the idea of the person she was, the idea of the person that her family and society wanted her to be.

On the second day of lock-up Ida is suddenly frightened by the life that she has led, the emotions that she has squandered. This marriage of convenience has been anything but convenient. Her husband's company has been prickly, his love something she tried to bring to herself only to be stabbed by the bitter taste of rejection. Why is this happening now? Now when she thought she'd negotiated safe passage, when there were meant to be no surprises? Wasn't she supposed to be on top of life's game? How does it matter, her mind tells her as the tears shed: if the Chinamen do not kill her, she'll be with love again. She'll be with her Manu. His love is like a net cast out for her to fall into, to be safe and embraced.

On the third day, Ida decides that life is a huge fire burning from afar. She cannot reach it but its smoke gets in her eyes and its ember falls on her skin, till she turns to ash and blows into nothingness.

On the fourth night she hears the sound of footsteps. She shakes under her covers. Is it the Chinamen? Have they come to take her away? The steps stop outside her bedroom door. She gets up in fear. She tries to find something to hold on to: the lamp next to her bed. The doorknob turns. She cries out. What are they going to do to her? Then silence. No one enters her room. Nothing happens. She stays awake, holding the lamp; her trembling and hungry body not letting her sleep. A few hours later, at the crisp edge of darkness, she hears someone sing, “If I were a swan, I’d be gone. If I were a train, I’d be late. And if I were a good man, I’d kill you.”

Harsh. So, it’s Harsh who has kept her locked, hoping probably to glean a favour out of Seth. What a manipulator. What a haraami. He is willing to do anything to prove he’s a man to his father. Anything but be a good husband.

And why shouldn’t she think of her husband this way? Isn’t it Harsh who said that it is ugly people who enjoy watching the sunset because they’re forced to find beauty outside of themselves? What a terrible thing to say. Ugliness should be seen for exactly what it is: for what is inside people, not outside. Her husband should be seen for exactly what he is. The offspring of his cunning father Deven. The apple doesn’t fall far from the tree.

On the fifth day Ida thinks of the Mona Lisa. What a woman! Hands folded over each other in modesty, a smile softening her face, her eyes on people but without encroachment. And then ... one day ... Ida read that the Mona Lisa was not a woman but a crocodile head with a swamp behind it. It was difficult for her to believe this. She went online for more research and what did she find? More conspiracy theories! Some claimed that Mona Lisa was the head of a lion. Or an ape. Or a buffalo. No one knew who the real Mona Lisa was.

Ida realises that things are never what they appear. When man tries to portray something, society understands it to be another thing, while it actually means something that neither man nor society can comprehend. What is the meaning behind these things that we can't see, don't anticipate, but which are lurking behind shadows to pounce upon us? Can we ever understand them? Is anything ever one thing? All day Ida thinks this.

She loses count of the days.

Then, early one day, as the sun is reigning over the shadows, she's awakened by the noise of her door opening. Ida gets up in fright, sleepy-eyed and google-faced. A hand grabs her and drags her down the stairs of the mansion. It's the male staff who welcomed her with mithai and tikka on the day she moved here. Clearly, the favour from Seth has not come through. What are they going to do to her? Are they going to kill her? Maim her? She struggles in vain but the man's hold on her is strong. She resists him. He punches her across the face. She's never been hit in her life. Her cheeks burn as if singed with acid. A tear falls from her eyes. What can she do? A woman is powerless against the physical brute of a man. She stops protesting. She is ready to be killed. They reach the door and he pushes her out of it. She hears a bang behind her. So, they're not killing her, just throwing her out. She almost laughs in relief.

Ida stands outside Harsh's house. In this bare-boned morning the mansion seems less than grand; brown water seepage clings to its walls like the claws of a hawk, tarnished like her perfect life.

"Let me back in," she tries to shout. "Let me speak to Harsh." But her jaw hurts from the punch, her throat is parched, her body weak. Does she really want to speak to Harsh? No. She has no strength for that conversation, no desire to salvage a marriage that was over before it started. Besides, this is not her home. Her husband's home is not her home.

She wants to go home. To her real home. To Manu's home. Their home. So she walks. She walks past the flower shrubs running along the mansion's gate wall: bursts of sweet-smelling poinsettias, gladioli, marigolds and arum lilies. She smells nothing. She's going home. She walks past the tall front gates and onto the main road. She keeps walking.

The sun continues its long journey from horizon to horizon, equaling in length the day and night, making this day, of all days, the longest in the year. The sun shines directly above her head. Adding to her discomfort is the smell of summer that refuses to go away, the hardened kill of heat and that stench of rot: rotting petals, rotting flesh, rotting water that assail her senses like Harsh's treachery. She is starved, parched and exhausted. Her feet are getting sores and bites. Her jaw feels stuffed with spiky cotton balls and she realises that it's swollen. The afternoon deepens. But she keeps walking. She's going home.

She sees nothing on the way, not the women who stare at her on the road, not the man who offers to help her, not the direction she's not following. Nothing. She doesn't stop until she reaches The White Taj, six hours later. Exhausted, she falls against the bark of the mango tree and gazes at her house. Home, she's home at last. She sees its Corinthian columns, its marble arch, its world full of pomp and grandeur, and thinks only of loss. Beauty and truth are all about where you set your sights upon them.

She needs to rest. She sits down below the mango tree and thinks. Once she walks into this home, her life will shift gears to a road she cannot see. Is she ready for that? Is she ready to end her marriage? Is she ready to remarry? Is she ready to fully experience Manu's love? Can she marry a man who is her servant? Can she take up with another man while she's still married? Can she live at a home that her mother and brother have left? Can she live at a house where her father is slowly dying? She doesn't know. Is what she's doing right? Does it matter? Isn't a woman's need to be loved stronger than her need to be right?

Ida gathers her remaining strength and gets up. Her jaw and feet throb with pain. She stumbles to the front door. She rings the bell. Manu opens the door and his face is in shock.

"What has he done to you? That brute. I'll kill him."

Ida falls against Manu and buries her head in his chest. This is home. She is home. "I'm sorry for everything," she says. "Let's get married. I want to marry you."

She looks up at him, but Manu startles on making eye contact with her, as if he's seen an ogre. Never mind. She hugs him tightly. And then the joy is sapped. He pushes her away.

"Listen, Ida. Things have ... changed. I ... can't explain now. But please believe me when I say I had no choice."

What, she wants to ask. Her eyes shuffle in panic as she tries to keep her smile firmly in place.

"What?" she asks.

Manu scans the room as if ears are floating around them. "Now's not the time. You look like you're going to faint. Come in."

She walks in. The house is stripped bare of almost sixty years of personal touches, de-cluttered from accumulations, left with only bare-boned furniture to keep it company. Her home is emptied of the clutter of her family, their presence. Memories, their family life, all stowed away.

Ram and Urmila stand in the living room staring at Ida in disbelief.

"Ida baby! What happened to you?" Ram says, running up to her. "Go get medicine, Urmila." He sits her down on the chaise lounge. "I'll get you nimbu paani. Some food."

"I'm so happy," Ida says quietly, when they're gone. "I love you." Manu doesn't say it back. Strange. "Come and sit next to me," she adds. He remains standing and averts his gaze. Ida notices that Manu is looking like the kind of man he's never been, the kind of man whose life is a helium balloon that has deflated and fallen to the brunt of human footsteps.

"Plato's Symposium say that God cut us in half and we spend our whole time on earth searching for this missing half," she says quietly.

Manu looks at her quizzically.

"It means that I've been searching everywhere for the one that I love, while what I seek is right beside me," Ida says softly.

Manu leans over and touches Ida's shoulder, "I made a big mistake. I am sorry."

His cavalier tone slices Ida's heart with more sharpness than the blade of a sword. He hasn't come running to her with tears, saying he loves her, vowing to bring them together, all sorrow and devotion. What has he done that can be so bad?

Ida's head drops and her voice is softer when she says, "I will save you from your mistakes. That's what people who love each other do."

Manu looks at her more fearfully. "It's too late. Nothing can save us from the Chinamen," he says.

"Anything is possible. We cannot let the enemy scare us," Ida says.

Manu looks at the floor and his shoulders shake. Whatever he's done must be shameful to him. For now, he cannot be hers.

Ida feels like she's sleepwalking from one nightmare to the next.

"I'll go meet Papa," Ida says uncertainly. She tries to get up and falls back on the chaise lounge.

"I'll take you," Manu says. No, says Ida.

We'll call him, she hears Ram say.

"How is he coping with the ...?" she asks Ram. She can't say it.

"Such a great man with such a sad end," Ram says, his voice choked with sadness. "I feel as though I'm losing my own brother. It's ... terrible." Ram snivels.

It is terrible, Ida thinks. I'm losing all the men in my life and now my father too. She feels tears roll down her face. She can't be bothered to hide her sorrow.

After a few minutes of silence, Ram says, "Don't worry, beta. Your father will make everything alright."

That's when Ida sees a tiny creature run towards her. He greets her with yelps and licks. Ida picks up her pet pug and strokes his head as he playfully nips her fingers. At least I have Lassi, she thinks.

She gets up to hold him but falls. Her right leg has cramped so badly that she can no longer move it. Lassi runs away from her. Ida puts her head on the cushion. She shuts her eyes and imagines sleep.

When she comes around she hears her father say, "I'll kill that bastard. He swore he'd take care of you. What has he done?" She says nothing. He cries softly. "But you texted me that you were okay? You should have told me and I would have picked you up from that bastard's house."

Ida can't align her face into surprise anymore.

"He took my phone. That was not me texting you," she says to her father.

"I'm sorry, my child. I didn't know he'd do this to you," Tears are rolling down his face too. He looks like half the man he used to be. "Someone give her a sip of that nimbu paani. Look how dehydrated she is."

Urmila holds a straw to Ida's lips as she sips the drink slowly.

Seth picks up his phone and dials a number. "Deven, what have you done to my daughter?"

So her father-in-law is not in prison, Ida realises. It was a lie, a setup.

She sees Seth listen to something. Fifteen seconds later he is off the phone.

"He says he sent you back because I am sick and powerless now. Because my business has gone kaput." He says this slowly, as if each word is a full stop to his understanding of life.

Ida feels as useless as a torn condom.

She hears her father chant: Hamsah shwetah, bakah shwetah, Kah bhedah hamsa bakayo? Neeraksheera vivektu, Hamsah, Hamsah, bakah bakah!

"What?" she asks.

"The swan is white and so is the crane, so how do you tell the difference?" Seth says with a smile: "When a crane and swan are both offered a mixture of milk and water, it is the swan who will drink the milk alone, because it knows the difference between good and bad, the eternal and the transient."

Ida looks sadly at her father.

"I'm sorry I couldn't tell the difference between good and bad, beta. For your sake I wish I had."

Her father, who's not been sick a single day in his life, seems afflicted with a debilitating menace of the body but also the mind, his eyes like petals drooping in the rain. Is it true that her father, her mentor and guide will die a slow painful death? Tears well up in her eyes.

Ram says, "Mai Baap ... your pants ... they are wet ... with blood!"

Seth doesn't look up from his thoughts, "Do you know that a swan's feathers do not get wet in the water? It belongs to this earth without getting too attached to it." Seth laughs, giving the two sunken boats in his eyes a lift. "There comes a point in every man's life when he must be like the paramahamsa. That is what we should become."

Ida sees a shivering anxiety pour into her father's eyes and spread, like a silent tsunami, to the faces of Manu and Ram and Urmila, to the chaise lounge on which she's seated. It swallows the walls looming above them, the exhaustion that's giving her goosebumps, the sky with its unrelenting heat. It gulps down this jittery quivering town of Lalbag.

Her father looks as if he has nothing left in him to fight. He turns to Ida, "I will find a way to save you." He turns to Urmila. "Take care of Ida."

With that he walks up to his room, leaning against a tearful Ram.

What has war done to family, to love, to marriage?

Ida feels every single day of her life come to an end with a bloody sunset.

***

He looks at Ida, concern rising in his face like a swelling tide. If you fall, you get scratched. If someone pushes you, you get hurt. His Ida is hurt, badly hurt.

Seth limps towards her and rests against the ottoman. He's exhausted, having lost seven kilos in the last three weeks. He touches his daughter gently on the elbow and she looks up at him, her eyes wide and innocent, as if she's a child. This transformation would be endearing if it weren't so shocking. It's as though Ida wants to be forgotten as an adult; as if her childhood is the only thing she can endure.

Every tree has a damaged branch that rots it from the inside. And in her tree of life that branch is love. She has to chop it off to be able to grow and move forward. So Seth says, "Forget about him. Forget that marriage. You're here now, safe with us." Seth has tears at the edge of his voice as he looks at his Ida, his daughter, made of honey and milk, for morning slipped into her mother's womb at the moment of her birth. Ida is the only person whom Seth has ever loved, who ever loved him. He feels terrible for having misjudged Deven's intentions and brought his daughter to this sadness.

Ida gives him a sad soft smile. She wipes her tears with the end of her dirty kurti and takes a deep long breath. She mumbles something as if she's not heard him. What beta, Seth asks and leans in closer. His body rips him apart but there's no alternative.

"It is but one teardrop upon the cheek of time," she whispers.

All human purpose is contained in one word: surrender. An apple surrenders to gravity and falls from the tree. The sky surrenders to darkness and becomes night. The earth surrenders to the sun and rotates around it. A mind with too much hurt surrenders to madness. For they're all mirages of this life that is always capsizing, always advancing. Nothing is what it seems. But to see this happen to his daughter, to her mind; Seth feels a sadness grip his heart so tight it can barely beat. His daughter is slipping away to a place where no one can reach her.

He's done this to her, he thinks, with the anger of tsunami waves on the shore. He's lost his daughter and he will never forgive himself for it.

He has to do something before it's too late. He has to save his Ida, of milk and honey.

There is only one thing left to do: meet Kulhari. He will go to him right away.

***

Strung high up in the sky on this midsummer's day, the sun tilts in shame to the ground and roasts the earth to cinnamon. It is a day of equality.

DOG EAT DOG WORLD

"Dig faster or I give you dog to eat," the guard barks an order. He has the face of a boy and arms the size of a man's thighs.

We are digging as fast as we can, thinks the Prisoner of War, as he loosens a rock with a shovel. But he dare not question the uniformed guard, so he avoids eye contact with him and continues digging, harder. Sweat trickles down his arms. It takes him two hours to dig a hole that's four feet across and deep enough to come up to his waist. He looks at the other PoWs, some of whom have been given rough logs to sharpen with bayonets. With the dry sound of thumps they pound them into the ground with rocks and turn them into stakes in a line around the footbridge. The PoW continues digging. His arms burn till he feels they're on fire. His uniform turns black with mud and sweat. The number 24 on it is almost invisible. Still he digs, grave after grave, with no pause, no rest. For ten hours he digs, till the last of the ancient sun's rays cast his long shadow on the earth.

Beneath the dying light the pain in his body renders his mind to daring and he asks a question, "With all due respect, Officer, may I ask for whom we're digging hundreds of graves? There's barely space for them all."

The guard snaps up his rifle and directs its nozzle to the prisoner's face. The PoW startles. He's known for a while that he's not going to make it out of here alive, but nothing prepares a man for imminent death. The guard glares at him through clenched teeth but doesn't shoot. He looks a tad bored, even though a life hangs on his fingertips, and says, "Before you embark on journey of revenge, you dig two graves. So we dig."

The PoW accepts the guard's answer with a nod. Three patrolmen on saddled horses pass them by but don't stop. The PoW turns to the guard after a moment, "I think Confucius meant that if you become revengeful you end up digging one grave for your enemy and the other grave for yourself." The guard doesn't reply, doesn't seem to have heard him. The prisoner wipes his head with a washcloth. He plunges his shovel blade hard into the fibrous topsoil and removes a large bite of soil.

Then he adds: "These graves are small, less than four feet wide. What kind of man will fit inside them?"

A foot with thick military boots kicks him hard. The prisoner falls into the grave that he's digging. His head hits a corner, as do his feet. He hears a damning crack and collapses, his five feet ten inches frame folding into itself. He lands with a dull thud. He begins to fade.

"That is how you Indian dog will fit in grave. Once you dead, how it matter whether you lie straight or curl like French fry?"

The prisoner gives a defiant spit that does not reach the guard. It dribbles pathetically down his face and that's the last thing he feels before blackness sets in.

LOVE, SCORN, EMBRACE

Manu knocks on Ida's bedroom door and stands at the doorway. She is fast asleep. Her window has been left open. Lilac petals have gathered around her bed in bunches, as if sitting atop a gravestone. Her bed is as still as a grave. She is under a blanket that covers her like a shroud, her eyes clamped shut with the finality of life's end.

Between them a patch of sunlight beams through the lace curtains in the window, the only bright patch in the otherwise dark room. Her right leg is crossed over the left, her tiny hands tucked neatly under her face, a petal crushed on her forehead, her almond-shaped eyes shut together with the kind of determination he feels in his love for her. Above her stomach, her chest falls and rises. He thinks of her nipples, pink and soft in their shell, her breasts like two large kingdoms that he would like to invade. He wants to run his hands over her body, but how can he touch her after what he's done?

Manu catches his reflection in the mirror and sees a

man different from the one he knew earlier: a traitor. But he doesn't want freedom anymore. He doesn't want the new life promised to him. All he wants is Ida, who lights up his insides like the sun. His love for her throbs inside him with a dull arthritic ache.

Everything he remembers of Ida from their childhood has this still and bright quality to it, like a spotlight. This spotlight jumps from one memory to another, unveiling his feelings to him, adding shimmer to his past snapshots of her: laughing, playing, snuggling, their first kiss. Ida is like a flame, a precious flame he's held in his hands and cherished. The flame has now brightened and he can carry it forever.

This is the girl he wants to marry. The only one. He imagines their wedding to be a grand affair, something bigger than Ida's first wedding: twenty-one logs of red sanders for statues of Lord Shiva and the couple, thirty-two sandalwood trees for the mandap, forty-one cooks sweating over two hundred and one bronze pots, thirty-one gold needles for her wedding trousseau, and in the lawn a snake, a goat, a goldfish and a deer. He imagines being carried on the shoulders of two burly bodyguards, wearing a four-strand pearl necklace, two heavy gold chains, two drapes of jasmine threads, his heavy sherwani studded with Swarovski diamonds and rubies *and* crystals! No Chinese cop to spoil the festivities. His guests gasping in surprise: You look like the richest man in Lalbag! Your bride is a lucky girl! You look like the sun prince himself!

He wants to have the biggest wedding that Lalbag has seen.

He walks up to her bed and sits besides her supine body, watching her till she stirs and opens her eyes. "You want to get up? Eat something?"

"No," she replies slowly. "Let me sleep."

She hasn't moved from the bed since coming back, not spoken to anyone. Her face is empty, a shadow of her former self, as if life has drained her, as if she's finished as a person. She's become the emotion she's feeling. She's wilting. Manu has never seen her like this. It's happened to millions, this heartbreak. But with Ida it seems more severe. It's as though she's trying to finish herself off as a memory, to never be remembered.

"You need to wake up!" he tells her. "This is not healthy!"

Her eyes widen in surprise and at once he's racked by feelings of shame. No wonder a man can never win an argument against a woman.

He sidesteps his agonising worry and asks, "Are you okay?" She doesn't reply.

"I need to talk to you," he adds. "We can take a walk? Go to The Black Taj?"

His explanation. Will that pin him to her forgiveness?

She lifts her head, says no, and drops her head back to the pillow. In a minute her entire body has vanished into the folds of the blanket.

"Ida, I know that you are angry with me. I need to explain what happened. Please come with me. It's important."

The smell of dried peonies and jasmine hangs between them like a veil.

"Fine," he hears her say finally. "I'll get ready and meet you down."

He dare not watch her change, so he goes downstairs to where his parents are. As he walks he feels like he is leaving empty silhouettes of himself behind, like one of those charts that show the evolution of man. Something has been added to him that is constantly with him and changing him.

Above the living room fireplace, his father is cleaning a photo of Seth with his family. Seth is dressed in a sherwani shaped like a fringed velvet curtain. Kamala is seated next to him, looking as soft as a cushion. Ida is in her sun-gilded bed of ornaments, giving a wistful faraway stare, and Vakil, in a suit with high collars that eat up his neck, looks like a bobbing head of smirk. They're all encased in a silver frame with convolvulus blossoms.

Manu sits down on the chaise lounge.

His father turns to Manu with the full stare of his eyes. Under his eyes are bags that carry the weight of the world. His legs shaking, Ram opens an ulcer medicine bottle and drinks straight from it. He is still upset with Manu about the way he spoke to Seth. Why does his father see only the chaff in a golden harvest?

He can't deal with him right now. He gets up as Ida comes down and ignores his father's startled expression. Ida takes one look at her family photo and shudders. It's as if someone has burnt the edges off the picture she has of her family. Quickly, Manu takes her out of the house. He walks behind her, towards The Black Taj. He watches her with as much love as a man holds when he watches his bride walk around the mandap.

They reach the mustard stalks. She swaggers like them, like drunken men coming home, tears streaming down her cheeks, covering her vision. Manu holds her. He imagines that she has never felt this beaten, this shattered. It's as if her heart has gone through a grinding machine and been spit out, pulverised, to the ground.

His guilt deepens. Still, he is trying, he tells himself. He has messaged Bingbing to take Ida instead of him. Better her than him. She hasn't replied yet. He is too scared to call her.

They approach The Black Taj. The cement floors, the brick-and-mortar ramparts, have become sticky and black, uninhabitable, the grime and dirt of many a decade behind them. In the middle of the structure, a stairway runs upward into a dark abyss, like a tornado slicing the visage of a perfectly formed landscape. An outdoor bathroom area has been built with bricks and no roof. A photo frame of Lord Shiva has been broken, but still hangs on the wall. Not even squatters will want to live here.

"You know I love you more than anything, right?" he tells her. Ida doesn't reply.

Usually the structure is silent and unmoving, like the heart of a cannibal. But on days like this, a gentle breeze thrashes against the hollows of its walls and howls, as if gripped with fear. It echoes Manu's sentiments.

"I am sorry about everything that happened, everything I'm about to tell you. You have to know that I didn't know you would be back. I would never hurt you like that on purpose." They stop walking and gaze at each other like lost lovers.

"Sometimes you live your whole wretched life in one week," Ida says, her eyes flitting past Manu and into some painful memory. Her voice is choked, as if she's swallowed the sun.

For a minute both of them are silent.

Then—he tells her everything.

Ida turns to him with the full swing of her head. Her eyes are blazing red, like they've been dyed with the colour of the mud. Manu is suddenly scared. He's never seen Ida like this. He tries to hold her. She pushes him away.

"Don't touch me," Ida replies, her soft voice harsh, pulled back from her thoughts.

There's blood around the edges of her fingernails, clotting like a quarter-moon in the sky. She's been nibbling on them, clearly unhappy.

"Let me explain," Manu says.

"Explain what?" Ida asks Manu. She raises her eyebrows till they're almost touching her hairline. Manu doesn't reply and they watch each other, paralysed. "How can you do this to my father? To your country?"

"I was going to become rich in New China, not for me but for you. I was going to find you and buy you a car, clothes, shoes, whatever your heart desired; everything that you deserve. I was going to take you to your favourite restaurants and make you the happiest woman on this planet."

"Don't talk nonsense! You're the man who lost India!" Ida shouts.

How can raindrops fall on the sun? How will she ever forgive him?

"I had no choice. She threatened to have us marked. I did it to save my family."

She lets out a sob. Manu runs his fingers from her cheeks down to her lips.

"What have we all become?" she asks.

Manu presses against her back and holds her. She's always loved this. Sure enough, she leans against him. "I love you," he whispers in her ears.

She turns around and faces Manu. She takes his face in her hands and says softly, "I know why you did it, but I wish you hadn't."

Manu's phone beeps. He looks at it and Bingbing's message stares at him with the scorch of fire. He removes his arms from Ida as if she's the one burning him.

"Bingbing is outside The White Taj. She probably wants me to go up with the key," He shakes himself, as if a heavy realization has hit him. "I will get us out of this mess. I will convince her to take you as well."

"How can you trust her?" Ida asks.

"Do I have a choice?" he asks her, eyeing her with a bovine expression. "You wait here. Don't move, okay? I will be back in a minute."

"Don't leave me alone. Not now!" she replies. Ida feels like she's been slapped across the face.

"I promise this is for the best," he says quickly and runs away.

"I'll be right back. Don't go anywhere!" She hears him shout. She's left alone.

She has never seen his face aligned into a mask of guilt that is impossible to peel, wash away or scrub. She doesn't know what to do with it. Is he really going to save her?

Ida touches her head to the outside wall. She doesn't have the strength to move.

Behind her, she can hear the sound of his footsteps. Why is he going anywhere at this black hour? In the indigo heat of the night the red dust rises like embers of a raging fire and swathes her layer after hot layer. Her mind that was as neatly divided as paper margins is now befuddled. All life goes out of her and she slumps to the ground.

This whole business of being an adult is weighing her down. She wants to put her head down on someone's lap and reach whatever destination she's supposed to without having to notice every milestone, counter every turn and feel every bump. All she wants is to hum that happy tune that delivered her from childhood to adulthood without the torridness of war and disease and lost love. Can't she just be? Is it really too much to ask?

Some lessons in life are as heavy as Mount Akaho and others as light as a feather, Ida thinks. Liquid fire fills her throat and spreads to her body, till she becomes a quivering haze. Her blood is on boil; it's so hot that she feels as though someone has thrown acid on her skin. Inside her mind Ida hears a click, like a door shutting. Darkness seeps in. She feels, and is then immediately certain, that this door will never open again.

Where is Manu? Why is he not back yet?

Corks have been pulled out of her ears and everything is the sound of brute. There is no point waiting for him, she realises. She has to save him the way he's trying to save her. Ida gets up from the ground. "I'll show these Chinamen what we Indians have. I'll teach them a lesson," she thinks.

But what can she do? God, show me some light. Her glance falls on Mount Akaho. The mountainside of Diamond Hill is glittering as if it's a lake reflecting the starry sky. Mount Akaho. The temple still belongs to her father. Shiva's golden statue, the sculptures imprinted with her face, all that is his. The trishul, the holy spear is also his. And that's all she needs. The trishul. It is good enough to kill the Chinamen when they come for the statue. But the temple is locked during nighttime. How will she get to it? Her father? No, he is too weak. The key? Manu has taken it. But there is an extra key to the gate that her father gave her for safekeeping; it's lying in the locker in her room. That's her answer!

She sprints to The White Taj. She runs to her room and opens her locker. She takes the keys to the temple. No one sees her. She runs along the dried Yamla River. I have got what I want, she thinks, smiling for the first time in months! I will take my love back from the Chinamen! I will take my life back from the Chinamen! I will take my India back from the Chinamen! I will be the woman who won India!

ALL THE GODS ARE DEAD

Sure enough, a yellow-colour Hyundai is parked near the gate. Manu cannot see inside the car, but he sees a pair of hands cupped around a match. The ends of the fingers are red in the flame of the match. They are lighting a cigarette. They look like strong hands that know what they're doing.

Manu walks up to the driver seat window and looks inside.

She rolls down the window.

"In," she says. Manu runs over to the other side and gets into the car.

He's entering a car after years. The musty smell of petrol and mildew hugs him with the embrace of a long-lost friend.

Bingbing cheers him with *Ganbei*. Bottles upon bottles of baijiu are lying on the car floor.

"Good evening, Madam," he replies. "I did not know anyone was allowed to drive a car in Lalbag."

She smiles at him like he's stupid. Obviously the Chinamen can.

"Madam, did you get my SMS? Will you add Ida's name to my list?"

Bingbing doesn't reply. She looks into the darkness.

"Do you see seven diamond point in sky?" she asks after a moment, her fingers tracing the seven stars in the sky. "The seven wise men have come. They sit on great bear and show time for wisdom."

Manu looks out at the dusky night sky and sees the Big Dipper. Science is lighting up the sky.

"It say time for wisdom, not to be foolish," she adds.

"What?"

For the first time that night Bingbing's eyes show any feeling and she says, "Moment I see her I not like her. She have too large eyes. You know what they say? Too large eyes, they see too much. Evil spirits go into big eyes. Good wife must have face flat as lake, so on that husband can rest his sorrow. Her leg must be strong to ride him well. Her eye must be small so she see thing for what it is. So nice I have small eye."

"Madam, I love her."

"I also love."

"So you understand?" he asks her.

"He here," she replies simply. "My man come at last." She looks him directly in the eye. "Xu Laong."

She unscrews the cap of a porcelain jar on her dashboard. A loud noise comes from the jar, like a drilling machine ripping apart hard earth. Inside the jar is a cricket. How can such a little creature disrupt the entire night?

She mumbles something.

"I cannot hear you," he says.

She turns around and looks at him, "We meet online few years ago, before war. He send me friend request on Renren. We message on WeChat. We fall into love slowly. He come here with army so he can take me." Her alto voice is quick and certain.

"Why did you live in Lalbag if you were in love with someone in New China?"

She puts the lid back on the jar. It's quiet again. "My mother she Chinese, my father Indian, like you. Soon after marry they not like each other and my mother she take me to live to China. I grow up Chinese. Then she become sick. I force to go to father's home. My father not bad person but he say to me that because of mother he hate Chinese. He say I hate your smelly food, your smelly mouth, your smelly language. He so 1980. He tell me I can never marry Chinese. I have to marry rich Indian. I have no home to go so I say yes. Then he become sick and tell me to marry fast so he can see me married woman type. I love Xu Xu but how to say to father? Poor Xu Xu have no money. He Chinese. If I say him then father not give me his money and property after he die. Xu Xu tell me not to worry."

Her voice becomes quieter, "Now Xu Xu in Lalbag with army. Now we marry."

Bingbing shrugs happily.

"The Chinamen ... they are here already?" Manu asks in shock.

"Of course! You will see. And hear."

Manu holds his head in dismay. This is worse than he expected.

"Look. I'm begging you. Take us with you. Save us. I'm giving you what you want!"

She snorts. "I take you. Not one more people."

"But you promised to take my parents!"

She shrugs. "Yes, your parent. If job done. No one more. Especially not her!"

"Please! It will require no work for you. All you have to do is add a name to your list. Ida's name."

"No can do," she replies firmly.

Manu feels like cottons balls dipped in kerosene are being stuffed into his mouth and ears and his stomach and groin. Everything goes soft and starts to burn.

"How can you do this to another person?" he asks.

Bingbing smiles affectionately at Manu, as if she's looking at a five-year-old child, "Do you know in China two type of people: Tianfen—the gifted one and Tianzhen—the fool. You are Tianzhen. You are nothing but bank to me, and till you do job you are—how they say in American—foreclosed, so your main customer bid you bye bye."

"This cannot be happening," Manu says. He does not feel insulted, just exhausted. He slumps down on the car seat. "You are the only person who can save us."

"Don't worry much. There was once man in North China who practice Taoism. One day his horse get lost. Man not become sad. Instead he say, 'This may be blessing.' After few month the horse return with other beautiful horse. Man not become happy but say, 'This may be misfortune.' Of course, his son fall off the beautiful horse. Man not sad, but say, 'This may be blessing.' People think he mad. One day his town become invaded. Young men fight and be killed. But his son due to injury not fight and he live. So you see my dear Tianzhen, fortune and misfortune matter of perspective."

"Please, Madam. Please help me! I am begging you!" He touches her feet. He is not proud of what he's doing but he feels like he can do nothing else.

She shakes him off, rather elegantly, and takes a puff of her cigarette. "Listen, you Yindu bastard," she says in her alto voice. "Act smart and I mark you. You go to Mongolia to shove manure."

"Go ahead! Kill me! Do it now so I don't have to watch Ida die."

"We Chinese are peace lover," she says. Manu wants to snort. "You know that we invent gunpowder? It is one of our four great invention. But we use it not for guns, no. Only for cack-boom." She joins her fingers, sends them flying into the air and then splits them while making a swooshing sound.

"Fireworks?"

"Yes, we only use gunpowder to make firework."

"Perhaps," Manu admits reluctantly. "But the saltpeter that led to the invention of gunpowder was from India. So, technically, the gunpowder was invented in India."

"Phht—you talk out of horse mouth. Don't steal invention idea, otherwise you also say that Indian make paper and printing and compass?"

"No, the Chinese invented paper, but who do you think sourced the ink with which the paper comes to life? We Indians have invented many more things than you Chinese have. We brought games like chess, ludo, kabaddi, snakes and ladder to this world. We invented the shampoo that you use so generously on your hair. We invented the button with which you fasten your low-cut blouse and the cotton cloth with which it is made. We invented the ruler that your people have used to measure every inch of our invaded land."

"If you so much love you country, then why you not go out and fight us?"

"This is not a country where the government declares war and the youth have no option but to fight it. We live in a democracy, where men can choose whether they want to give their life for their country or for their family."

"Ah! What rubbish. You are coward not to fight war."

This is not an argument he can win. Especially not now.

"Aren't you cold?" he asks her, changing the topic. The air conditioner is on at full blast.

"No," she says. "We Chinese never feel cold. They say Cheng Hanxiang, our plum blossoms, are most fragrance in harshest cold. So we never fear winter, we have noble heart. You want to see me heart?" She pulls his hand to her chest. Her nipples are pert against her uniform. She looks up at him brazenly. Her taunt is a fully ripe mango that must be squirted into someone's mouth. He pulls his hand away in shock. She laughs.

"We take this forward after job done."

"But Madam, you're not giving me what I want."

"No one care what you want. You want what we want. Get it?"

He doesn't know how to reply to this.

"You really think my people let your people live?" she adds softly.

He plunges head-down into a winter pond.

She turns to him and smiles, "I go. Do your job." She reaches over and opens the car door, "And, Tianzhen, may your Ida be killed as gently as a moth brushing past her neck."

Manu's blood freezes. Shaking, he gets out of the car. It's only when he hears the car screech out of the gate that he snaps out of his stupor and runs after it. The yellow car, with his freedom in it, is gone. What is he to do now? A broken man he comes back in and falls against the balustrade of the gate. He can't move, the world's weight on his shoulders. How can his plan to save everyone he loves have gone this way?

***

His father and mother are standing at the door, staring at him. When he walks up to them, Ram says, "Who was in the car? I have seen her somewhere. At the wedding. She's the cop! Why was she here?"

Manu looks down at the welcome mat, his brown cheeks a bright red. How can he tell his father his life's biggest shame? To cover up, he snaps, "I want you to come with me to New China. Is that too much to ask?"

"What are you going to do to get our freedom?"

"I don't want to talk about it."

Urmila and Ram look at Manu as if he's brought war to their doorstep. "Son, what have you done?" Ram asks. Manu doesn't know how to answer them.

"Manu ..." his father whimpers.

I cannot talk about it, thinks Manu. "If you're not coming then make sure you stay inside," is all he manages to tell his parents.

"What have you done?" Ram asks again. His voice is heavy, laden with grief.

King Draupad was furiously angry when his daughter Sikhandi became a man to take revenge on the great guru Bhishma. But Sikhandi did what he was destined to do. Sometimes one has to do what's in one's destiny, thinks Manu. Why can't his father see that?

Forget him, he tells himself. He has to go to his Ida. She needs him now. Manu runs out of the house. By the time he reaches The Black Taj she is gone. Where could she be? He rests his head against the gritty walls and waits for her.

He will not do it. As his eyes fall slowly to sleep he knows that he will not go to Mount Akaho. He will not betray her. He will not betray them. He will fight for his country the only way he knows how. He will die where Ida dies.

THE WOMAN WHO LOST INDIA

As she dashes up the one-hundred-and-eighty-one stone steps of Mount Akaho, past the four iconic pillars with their ten-foot-high flames, Ida remembers Coleridge's "Kubla Khan" that she'd read in school. She sings the poem to herself:

A savage place! As holy and enchanted
As e'er beneath a waning moon was haunted
By woman wailing for her demon-lover!

She reaches the gate of the temple and gently unlocks it. Then she pauses. There's a sound coming from the Jyotirlinga enclave. She ducks to the ground. Has someone seen her? She listens harder. It's a gentle rumbling sound, like that of a snore. It must be Swamiji, she realises, whom everyone says sleeps in the jyotirlinga's water itself. Him she can handle, she thinks with confidence. If he catches her, he will help her out. And perhaps later she'll gather the energy to walk to the Jyotirlinga, take a peek in and see whether he really does turn into a fish during nighttime.

In the temple area a bouquet of joss sticks send languid spirals into the air, fumigating it with the scent of lavender. Through the white threads of smoke she sees the statue of Lord Shiva, gilded and calm, ensconced in ancient starlight that seeps through the polychromatic stain-glass and ceiling window, the enclaves that house her statuettes, evoking a deep bow from her. She turns to the trishul, not glittering or shining like everything else, but still—made from the cinders of the bomb that fell on Lalbag—it is the town's most sacred entity. Ida walks up to it, her steps small and uncertain. If she is caught there will be hell to pay. Especially now that she's not the daughter of Lalbag's second richest man or the daughter-in-law of Lalbag's richest man. This warning clouds her mind like huge coils of sandalwood incense, but she blows it away. She looks around once again. The night is still. No one is about. She tiptoes to the trident and sees it covered with ash, bright orange tikkas and red cloth. She pushes aside the noodles, coconuts, chopsuey, roses, rice, the offerings lying below it, and grabs its rod, pulls on it. It doesn't budge. She sings, continuing the poem:

As if this earth in fast thick pants were breathing,
A mighty fountain momently was forced:
Amid whose swift half-intermitted burst
Huge fragments vaulted like ... vaulted like ...

She can't remember the rest of the words. These words had once been as deeply imprinted in her head as wrinkles on old hands. Still, she forgets. Logic, she must use logic to remember. She imagines the earth through the poet's eyes, this heaving beast that has in some way of this world been wronged and made vindictive, and so it spouts things: things that are huge fragments vaulting like ... vaulting like ... what do things vault like? Ah, forget it, she thinks and focuses her attention back to the task at hand.

It's surprising to her that she feels no sense of hesitancy, no sense of reproach for what she's doing. This is sacrilegious, but something in her mind has bent so much that she no longer cares about the difference between right and wrong. Digging her heels further into the ground she pulls harder. There is a small movement and a sound like a soft grunt. Encouraged, she grinds her teeth and yanks harder. A bit of the mud into which the trident is dug comes undone. There you go, she smiles to herself. She looks around and is pleased with the peace of the night, as if she is responsible for it.

With a superlative heave, in which her body surprises itself with its own strength, she wrenches and the trident comes undone in her hands. Yes, she screams, holding it up above her head, unable to believe her own triumph. Yes!

Suddenly, the night sky becomes dark, as if a veil has been pulled over it. A gush of wind swishes past her ears and lands thump against something outside. Something sinister. Ida turns around and cannot believe her eyes. The Jyotirlinga is no longer bright, for the jyoti, always burning, always protecting the town, has extinguished. What? This is not possible! This cannot be! This will be the end of Lalbag! It will be calamitous!

The trishul hits something. The statue. Behind her she hears a crash. She screams: No, no, no. The statue cannot break. But: His crescent moon, matted hair, the snake around His neck, nandi next to His feet, His damaru, all lay shattered to the ground. Five-foot tall. Two-foot wide. Shattered. How can gold break?

Says a whisper carried in from the winds: how can bomb break?

The earth trembles. The trishul in her hand turns red-hot, becomes too hot to hold. It scalds her fingers. She drops it to the ground and turns around. The hillside, it is on fire! The flames from the brick pillars are throwing flames into the sky, lighting it up, and burning it like a storm of meteors. The rest of the hill, this Diamond Hill, suddenly plunges into total blackness. Ida tries to see. She can't. And then suddenly, from Diamond Hill, comes a blinding white light. Ida covers her head and falls to the ground.

No, no, no!

When the fur of dust and ash settles, she looks up to find that the shallow relief sculptures of her father and her have disappeared. In their place are statues of fierce, thin-eyed, scowling warriors carrying swords, punch daggers and bayonets, all covered in a sparse coat of red-hot blood.

Ida screams. She remembers one of the many legends that said that at the exact moment when the bomb fell on Lalbag and the town didn't raze, one thousand Chinese farmers died in their huts in the district of Xiangchen. They paid for the saved lives of the Indians. It was said that their graves were inside Mount Akaho and that inside these graves the farmers had been training to become warriors, preparing for battle. These men were called "The Terracotta Army".

Voices gather around her, not one voice or two voices, or even human voices, but voices that seem like an army of dragonflies beating their wings together in a rhythmic chortle. But no ... no, it's a chorus, and the chorus is singing! Singing! What are they singing? She shuts her eyes to listen better:

And mid these dancing rocks at once and ever
It flung up momently the sacred river.
Five miles meandering with a mazy motion
Through wood and dale the sacred river ran,
Then reached the caverns measureless to man,
And sank in tumult to a lifeless ocean;
And 'mid this tumult Kubla heard from far
Ancestral voices prophesying war!

No, this cannot be. It cannot be. It is the rest of the poem about Kubla Khan that she had forgotten. Where are these voices coming from? She looks back at the sculptures. There is, no longer, anything there!

She falls to her knees and looks up above her to pray: save us Shiva, save our people, give us your protection one more time. The love of God is piercing her heart like a burning arrow. She hears a faint whistle from above. She looks up and sees that the ceiling has turned black, as if darkened by years of soot and incense smoke. It also seems to be quivering. What is this?

Bats. Thousands and thousands of bats. Hanging upside down they look like shreds of the torn sky. They twitch and spread their wings. Then they fly, thousands and thousands of them, above Ida's head, past her frozen body as she dares not even to blink an eye. They plunge into the hillside without thought, assured in the primal instincts that are whispered to them by this ageless land. A long deafening sound of shrill cries and batting wings fills the mountainside. Then they're gone, the bats, all disappeared, swallowed by their mother's womb.

She is nothing but a wisp of cloud burning in the earth's ancient memory.

The end is near.

19 | 47

And then the nation in half was sliced, whereupon
They came upon my mother, and her tongue slashed,
My father, they beat, hung him in guava grove,
My sister Asha, raped, and in fields choked,
My grandmother with her urine sterilised my gun wound,
For that she was burnt alive.
My pet rooster they roasted and ate its carcass as meat.
Sadly, alas, it was too late for us all.
Our bones they gathered, tied them in silk scarf,
Laid them beneath the mango tree, the mango tree,
Many decades passed and the rooster crowed,
Made a friend who its story sang.
Atop the mango tree with rooster feather in hand:
He is dead, and this forsaken country no longer mine.
For these are men without God.

LOVE

All day there's the sound of a siren screeching into his ear and streaks of smoke rising in the air. Explosions light up the sky every few minutes. The Chinamen must have found a way to Mount Akaho. He doesn't want to think about it. His Ida has been with him for too short a time to be marred by a war. He continues to wait for Ida at The Black Taj. When night comes and Ida doesn't, he goes home. The house is dark and his parents are asleep. He walks up two flights of stairs to Ida's room. The curtains are pulled back and the night sky enters her room in dark camaraderie. There is a single lamp lit in the room. Dust motes are swirling in its light like ballerinas. She is not there.

a thunderous rain cloud when armed with mail
he speaks the lap of battle
be thou victorious with unwounded body; so let
the thickness of thy mail protect thee

—Ancient Indian chant

EAT THE TIGER

"Have you changed your mind because the Chinamen are here?" Kulhari asks him.

Seth looks at the agent. The skin tags around his nose are quivering ever so slightly.

Everything on Mount Akaho has been destroyed: Lord Shiva's statue, the trishul, the flaming pillars and Diamond Hill. Gone as suddenly as they appeared. There are talks that a Chinese military radar installation has been set up on top of Mount Akaho. It's a sign, the townspeople agree, but of what? Some say that it's the end of Lord Shiva's blessings on Lalbag, a forewarning that Lalbag will soon fall in the hands of the Chinamen. Others say that the Chinamen sneaked into the mountain and destroyed everything.

Lalbag is gripped with panic. There are lines looping around the Chinese Embassy with families hoping to apply for NICs. But the Chinamen are no longer issuing them. There are rumours that the patrolmen are lopping off the fingers, ears, noses and tongues of Indians as if pruning trees. Whoever tries to escape is shot. Hundreds of bodies are hung along the border wall. The smell of dead bodies floats like a shroud over the town.

"No. I'm still staying," says Seth. "Why are you unreachable? What's going on?"

Ever since Ida's returned from her husband's home, Seth has been calling Kulhari every hour on the hour. He has come to his office a few times but it's always shut. He hasn't met his daughter in this time; Ram tells him that she's been sleeping the entire time. Seth can't face her till he has a way to save her.

"What do you think, Seth Sahib? Look around."

Kulhari's dirty little office is crammed with men, women and children; all of them desperate to escape the Chinamen. They've come with suitcases and jholas filled with cash and jewelry and TV sets; their life savings.

Seth doesn't have the strength to think about this.

"Where are Kamala and Vakil? Are they safe?"

"Everyone is fine," replies Kulhari, without meeting Seth's eyes. He gathers a sheaf of papers and hands it to his assistant.

He's hasn't answered Seth's question. Men who talk too much or too little reveal nothing. Someone pushes Seth from behind. There is no time to further discuss this.

"I have come here for my daughter Ida," Seth says. He puts a briefcase on Kulhari's desk. "Take her to her mother and brother. Do it before *they* come."

"Seth Sahib, I don't know how to tell you this ... I can't do it."

"What?" Seth asks, worry creasing his eyebrows.

"It's too late now. It's impossible to get anyone out."

He swallows from a cup, of what Seth hopes is black coffee, with a single pull.

"Think about the money," Seth whispers.

"I ... I don't want to cheat you."

"Come on. It's eight crores!"

"Our rupee is of little value. We're going to be using the Renminbi from tomorrow."

"You cannot be serious!"

"Sorry Seth Sahib!" Kulhari says. He looks exhausted.

A man pushes Seth aside and empties a pile of gold coins on Kulhari's desk. "Save us!" he shouts. "I'll give you more." Kulhari looks at the man. His assistant comes forward and pushes the man away. Another man immediately comes forward, almost toppling Seth and his walking stick. "I will pay you more than a million per family member! All in dollars! Right now!"

The assistant pulls him away as well.

Someone pushes Seth again. Seth is not used to being pushed and pulled like this. People usually step aside for him; cower and bow before him. The war has made him an equal among men. The iceberg has appeared, sinking his Titanic, threatening to drag him into the icy cold dregs where the rest of humanity lives. He feels himself toppling, losing control, engulfed.

He pushes his weight tightly against the desk so he cannot be dislodged. It takes effort, his body is weak from disease, but Seth's resolve is stronger.

"There has to be a way out! You only have to take one person," he shouts over the chaos. "I'll pay you more than all of them here."

Kulhari doesn't reply. He puts the gold coins inside a drawer and locks it.

Seth glares at him with silent menace.

"You've seen Ida as a baby. You've seen her grow up. How can you let the Chinamen do ... something ... to her?" he asks the agent.

Kulhari looks at Seth evenly. His hair is unkempt and the black unironed T-shirt he's wearing is filthy even in the dark. "The Chinamen leave our women alone. They don't rape them or throw them to the soldiers."

"Really?" Seth asks. "Why this kindness?"

"It's not kindness. They think that brown skin is dirty."

"Such vile racism!"

"On both sides."

"Tcch."

"Come on! You know war, like marriage, breaks political correctness. It lays bare the bones."

"I don't believe all this! I've been to New China," Seth rebuts. "They love our big Indian eyes. They pull them out of our women and gift them to their mistresses."

"Never! The worse thing they do is sell our women as ayahs to do jhadu-pocha."

Seth is about to argue further when someone pushes him from behind.

"Are you going to do this or not?" Seth snaps.

"See this." Kulhari lifts a piece of cloth. Below the cloth is a zip-lock bag crammed with dry ice. Seth looks more closely. Inside the bag is a dead man's hand. Seth almost barfs.

"This was delivered to me a few hours ago," Kulhari says. His expression is smeared with fear.

Seth can't look. He turns away. The pain in his body becomes stronger.

Whose hand is this, he wonders. His mind immediately goes to his—*son*. No!

"It's Fu Kong's hand, I'm sure," Kulhari says. "I've heard that the Chinamen found him and killed him. They burnt down his newspaper office while his staff was still inside. Their bodies were found at their desks." Kulhari stares at the hand as though it will leap up and choke his throat. He leans over and whispers in Seth's ear, "I tell you, it's a warning from the enemy. If I help anyone escape this is what they will do to me."

For a moment, Seth shares Kulhari's panic.

Then, he hears Kulhari shout: "Everyone, leave! I cannot help you! Get out!"

There are murmurs of protest.

"How can you do this to us?" someone behind Seth shouts.

"There is a curse in Garuda Purana for torturing the helpless," someone else shouts. "You will go to naraka where insects will crawl up your ass and bite you with venom."

"In hell you will roast in hot oil. Pigs will eat your intestines and scorpions will sting you in the eye."

"I know it is not me whom you're angry with," Kulhari

shouts. He scans the crowd around him. "Be smart. Don't fight back. Then the war will be over in a day or two, and we can go back to our lives."

It suddenly strikes Seth: could this story about the hand be of Kulhari's own device? Could he have turned into a Chinese spy to save himself?

"How do you know we will lose? We won the last time," he asks him.

"This is like that salesman who was selling his wares," the agent continues. "He said, 'My shield is so strong that nothing can pierce it.' And he said, 'My spear is so sharp that it can pierce anything.' Someone asked him, 'What will happen if your spear is used to pierce your shield?'"

Suddenly everyone in Lalbag is spouting Chinese fables, Seth thinks. Must be because *The Lalbag Times* has been publishing them on the front page every morning. The editor has clearly been following some Chinese manifesto to ensure that his newspaper is not shut down.

"What?" Seth asks.

"Lalbag is the shield and New China is the spear. They cannot coexist. Lalbag has to be destroyed for New China to exist."

Seth watches Kulhari smile at the crowd, with a flourish that is wide enough to be mistaken for amusement. The man has guts to say this out loud.

"What nonsense!" someone shouts.

Seth doesn't know how to tell them that his contact from the command post has informed him that a Chinese forward-deployed brigade, comprising three Chinese battalions with two thousand soldiers, are swiftly advancing to Lalbag. Kulhari may be right.

Everyone in the room begins to talk at the same time.

"The PLA is not even using their Air Force or Navy."

"They're only sending their Ground Force, the PLAGF, and perhaps a few Type 99 battle tanks to Lalbag."

"That's just a per cent of their total force."

"That itself runs into a few hundred thousand troops."

"Yes, they're all heavily armoured and fully mechanised."

"But in Lalbag they think they have to fight men and God. So they are carrying these surface to air missiles, in case Shiva decides to send rotating discs through the air."

Seth knows; he's heard. The Chinese command and control centres have activated troops. They've sent UAVs—Unmanned Aerial Vehicles—into Lalbag.

"Lalbag is in Code Red," Seth says simply. "Their brigade will be here soon."

"They've already put their flags on Mount Akaho, claimed it as their own."

"They're using Indian prisoners of war to dig thousands of graves around the Lalbag-China border. They're planning to kill all of us."

"No, no! They kill only when they think it's absolutely necessary. If they think someone is a counter-revolutionary they maim them, chop off their noses, arms or legs."

"Correct! The Chinamen don't want to be seen as tyrants."

"You're all fools in denial. Lalbag will not survive. We will not survive!"

"When India has fallen, then what is Lalbag? We're finished."

"It's true," Seth says. "There's a pile of forty or so dead bodies dumped near the footbridge. These men with their wives and children were trying to cross the footbridge and escape. They were killed on the spot."

"Many men were attempting to climb the wall around Lalbag. All of them were shot. The wall is lined with dead bodies," Kulhari's assistant says.

"If we try to get out of here, we will die," Kulhari says. "This war is not to be taken lightly."

"Do you even know what war is?" Seth asks Kulhari seriously. "We are not like the other sufferers of war whose lives have been ripped apart. The ones who have to survive in bunkers and ration rice and turn in neighbours, while bombs fall over their heads, ripping apart everything—legs, arms, homes, torsos, mothers, bodies—everything that was real to them a moment before. We do not have to witness tales of bestiality and terror, of able-bodied men lining up in front of a firing squad, of children's heads chopped off and thrown to the dogs, of women sliced open and thrown into ditches. We will not have to drag the dead body of your father through decimated streets. This is not war. This is just a change of office, in a slightly violent way."

"Seth Sahib, we cannot be as trusting as Chacha Nehru in the 1950s, believing that India and China were best friends, placing faith in Chou En-Lai, even as the Chinamen came pouring over our mountains and showed the world what wimps we were. This is war. Not 'Hindi-Chini bhai bhai'."

Kulhari is like a wounded bull with its horns aimed perpetually at the matador.

"It was a different time, son. People showed solidarity during the first war with China. Most of them were cornered into patriotism. Men would line-up to enlist in the army and serve the nation. Women would throw gold chains and bangles from their windows to raise funds for soldiers. Have any of you done that?"

"Wars are not carbon copies of each other, Seth Sahib. They are not consistent from one to the other."

"You are right only about one thing, Kulhari," Seth admits. "This is not a war we can win." He's heard that Lalbag will be nothing but a heap of stones. The stones will be hewn into blocks and carried off by the enemy to build a statue of Chairman Mao on top of Mount Akaho.

"Of course we are finished!" Kulhari says, breaking into the noise. "And who is left to save us? My sources have told me, and I have sources at the highest level, that the EU, US, UK and Russia—" he counts each of them off with each diamond-ring-studded finger "—will stay out of this conflict. Their economies need Chinese goods."

The room falls silent. It's as if they can only be silent spectators to their own abuse.

Kulhari continues: "Why would anyone mess with the Chinese? Lalbag is not even a dot on the world map. *The Times* is reporting that a fight has broken out between laughing Buddha and tranquil Buddha. Without our Lord Shiva the world thinks we are a joke."

"What about the UN?" Seth asks.

"China is a permanent member of the Security Council, so the UN will do nothing," someone quips. "They will publicly condemn these attacks, only if there are human rights violations."

"But there *are* human rights violations. The Chinese *should* face public outlash."

"They might. But it will not involve the US. It's the Bay of Pigs situation all over again with the goddamn US. Always too busy fighting their own battles to care about a war whose blood doesn't spill on their soil."

"*Chalo*, war or no war, it's the end of time. Kali Yuga is coming to an end. Vishnu will now show his last avatar as *Kalki*, the destroyer of darkness, and Satya Yuga will begin."

"Lord Kalki will be glorious, like a lion coming down from heaven."

"Stop talking nonsense," someone snaps. "Do you know what they will do to us, if we survive?"

Everyone in the office shakes their heads: are there no Indian survivors or does no one know what's become of them?

"I've heard that they're doing to us what they did to Tibet."

"That's impossible. They've practically wiped out Tibet from the world map, made Tibetans a minority in their own country, destroyed all their monasteries and killed more than one million Tibetans since invading them in the 1950s," Seth says.

"And they repress them. Tibetans are imprisoned for

sending an email outside the country, for flying the national flag or for using the two words: human rights."

"I think India is a different conquest for China, a different nation, attacked due to a different agenda. We will probably not go the Tibetan way."

"We will not. Their conquest strategy has changed and it's brilliant! For each country they unify with New China, they pick men and women advocating unification and give them key posts in the Chinese government, keeping the countries appeased and in check," Kulhari says. So that's his game, Seth realises, pretend to be a China sympathiser so he can work for the CPC.

"And they will not stop with us. Now that they've got India, they've won the psychological war. The Chinamen want to claim back territorial lands that they believe belonged to them from the time of the Qing Dynasty. Their next stop will be the mighty nation of Russia."

"Of course," Seth scoffs. "After their takeover of India, they'll have the political, military and diplomatic power to intimidate Russia that has become very unpopular with its many enemies."

"A reliable source, one who can be of a stature only slightly below The Chinese Premier himself," Kulhari says, "has informed me that the PLA has offered the richest men of Lalbag quarantine status. China wants to rebuild captured states using the smartest and richest Indians. Those with NICs—only them mind you—no children or parents or spouses or brothers or sisters, no servants, no uncles or aunts—will be picked up tonight from the bunker and taken in an army truck to a secret location outside Lalbag. When the town has been conquered, they will be brought back here to continue with their businesses."

There are murmurs around the room. Someone shouts, "I have the NIC."

It's Amar Sandhu, a businessman who owns a steel factory. Till recently he counted himself among the wealthiest and most powerful in Lalbag.

"It will not be easy, Sandhu," Kulhari warns. "To keep your business you will have to appoint Chinese management and operational heads. Half the company profit will be given to the government—"

"Fucking socialists!" someone shouts.

"—thirty per cent will be pumped back into the business, ten per cent will be for the local government, and ten per cent will go to the owner."

"Ten per cent? Ten? That is nothing. How will I feed my family?" Sandhu asks.

"Your family will not be with you, remember?" Kulhari says.

Sandhu's face crumbles, along with his knees. His two teenage daughters hold him up.

"And I hope the survivors are ready to eat tiger penis," Kulhari says.

He looks around the room as though he's walking among daffodils.

"Tiger p-penis?" someone asks.

"Yes. Tigers are a symbol of courage, bravery and strength in China. The wealthy even hold 'tiger feasts' where they eat tiger bones, tiger eyeballs and, of course, tiger penis, while drinking tiger blood. They believe this enhances their performance in the boardroom and bedroom, that it cures everything from weak eyesight to impotency. It is a status symbol for the elite. Rich Chinawallahs will be expected to serve this at business dinners. So say the rumours."

A woman from the back of the room shouts, "There is also a rumour that if you paint your house red, the colour of communism, they will not kill you."

"*Lal*bag will turn red," someone shouts. "Ironically enough."

Someone laughs.

Seth turns to Kulhari, "They'll turn our democracy into a capitalist caste system?"

"Of course they will! When the Chinamen have nothing left to eat, they eat the rich."

"War is not a dinner party, you know," someone says.

"The phrase is: Revolution is not a dinner party. Mao said it," Seth says.

"Seth Sahib, do remember your old friends if we need your help in New China," says Kulhari.

Seth turns his head slowly to the agent; "I have no intention of going to the bunker or painting my house red, my *dear* friend. I was born on the day that China and India first went to war, and if I have to die on the day they go to war again, I will die happy. But I will not leave Lalbag."

The truth is sometimes more important than fear.

Kulhari looks at Seth in disbelief.

"I came here for my daughter," Seth continues. "Now if you can't take her away, can I take her to the bunker instead of taking myself?"

"No, this option is only for businessmen. Nobody's family will be allowed in."

"With this kind of attitude how will we survive the war?" Seth says.

"Only snakes survive war," Kulhari tells him.

"What does that mean? What about all the people you've been saving?" Seth asks him.

Kulhari looks up at Seth with the expression of a politician on a lie-detecting machine. What inappropriate act is he hiding?

That's when it strikes Seth! He grabs Kulhari's T-shirt with the full force of anger. "Where is my family? What have you done to my wife and son?"

Kulhari's assistant grabs Seth from behind. Everyone watches in silence.

Kulhari raises his hand. His assistant lets go off Seth.

Kulhari wipes his sweaty forehead with his T-shirt. "Seth Sahib ... the truth is ... I don't know, okay?"

Seth feels his eyes sizzle with the anger of coal. "What the hell does that mean?"

"It means that ever since the statue has fallen my sub-agent is not reachable. I don't know where any of my clients are."

How can this be? Seth imagines his son as a rotting mutilated corpse that flashes on people's TV screen, with its bludgeoned face and wide-eyed surprise. How can his safe passage for his family go awry? He grabs Kulhari's T-shirt again and whacks his face.

"I'll kill you, you bastard!" Seth shouts.

"How is this my fault?" Kulhari asks. "You were guarding the temple! You were supposed to protect the statue. You failed! Now you're blaming us?"

Seth feels the force of life come out of him. He has sent his family into the jaws of death. He lets go of Kulhari and steps back, into the crowd. He has sent his family into the jaws of death. Kulhari is right. He was supposed to protect his people. Now that he thinks of it, he doesn't remember when he last saw the temple gate key. After Kamala and Vakil and Ida left, he emptied out his belongings and left them lying around, without a thought, without a care. He put the keys in his coin jar, as a sign of its momentousness in his life, and has not seen it since. He cannot even remember if it's still there. Could someone have stolen it from his room?

He can't be here. Seth lets the pull and push of the crowd lead him to the door.

"Everyone, everyone! Get out! We cannot help you," he hears Kulhari say.

"What will we do?" someone asks.

"Do nothing. Keep your head down! Tell no one of your plans. Pray!"

"Whom do we pray to?" someone asks.

"Pray to the Chinamen that they don't kill us all. Be prepared that those of you who live will be on the streets in a few days shouting slogans in their praise and glory."

"How dare you, you traitor!" a man shouts.

Seth wonders what else can be expected from a man who siphoned money from a Children of Fallen Soldier's Relief Fund during the *2016 Poonch Skirmish* of Pakistan with India.

"Enough! Get Out! Out!" Kulhari's assistant shouts. He begins to push the men and women and children out. As they scramble out of Kulhari's office, a man asks: "Where is God when you need him?"

"Haven't you heard? All the Gods are dead," Seth says. "We are now men without God."

Some bullets are shot before the battle begins.

THE BIG DRUM OF LIFE

Manu pauses. His entire life has been spent standing outside this door in reverence and service to his master's. Muscle memory forces him to knock, wait and then enter. Ram is facing the window looking out at Mount Akaho. In the low mist over the hill, an orange glow broods, as if the shrubs and grass are on fire. No one knows what exactly is happening on the hill. No one dares go there. Only the birds fly in and out of the mist, trusting that in the hill they will meet no harm.

"Baba, have you seen Ida?" he asks his father.

But his father hasn't heard him. The expression on his face is odd, uncertain, as if the big drum of his life has toppled and he can no longer strike it in the right position. His shoulders are slumped and his gaze forlorn; as if he's viewing a painting drawn by someone else. He looks like the saddest man on earth.

Manu has a sudden urge to reach over and touch the thin wisp of hair stuck to his father's wrinkled forehead.

"Baba, are you okay?" he asks gently, afraid that his father will desiccate under his touch, scorch with the slightest edge in his voice.

His father turns to Manu with a faraway look, as if he's been brought back from a nightmare. He's wearing one of Seth's old tweed jacket from which emanates a singed odour like that of tobacco and rock salt.

"Is everything okay? Why are you in Vakil's room?"

Ram blinks and Manu sees that his father has only now seen his son's face float in front of him and registered him in his mind.

He brings his face next to his son, and pulls down the lower lid of his right eye. It reveals veins like pink thunder on the white valley of his eyes. "Look how pale I've become. Before the statue fell the skin under my eyes was red, redder than a cherry, and now ..." He turns back to the window.

Manu doesn't know what to say.

"Do you know what's happening in Lalbag?" Ram asks him. Manu shakes his head. "I went to the market today, and all shops are being looted. Fridges, tires, washing machines are lying on the road. Cars have been abandoned. The roads are almost empty, people don't want to be seen or heard. Black paper has sealed the windows and doors of many homes, in fear of a bomb attack. A curfew has been declared. Everyone is saying that the Chinamen are here."

His sentences flow one into another, as if he's taken a deep-rooted sorrow, chopped off its end from both sides and hurled its murky anguish onto Manu.

"There is a reason God did not create doors or maps, life is better without man-made boundaries," his father says. His voice is a whistle that's been caught by the wind. Manu feels there is a chasm wider than the sky between them.

Ram's eyes fill up with tears. He leans over and motions for Manu to do the same.

"Last night, Gauri, you know, the woman I almost married, came in my dreams. I dreamt that her hair was falling again and she went bald. No one would marry her. She became a beggar. Even her family had abandoned her. All these years, she's been alone in this world. I felt terrible. She looked up at me and cursed me! She said the Chinamen will kill me first to avenge her."

Manu touches his father's shoulders, his concern for his father bordering on panic for his Ida, "Baba, I have to go and find Ida. Why don't you rest?"

"Rest?" his father says and looks around. He pushes Manu's hands away from his shoulders and walks furiously across the room. "I'm so scared that the Chinamen are here, that I jump every time I see someone. They could be hiding anywhere."

"Stay indoors. You will be safe at home."

"The greatest war that a man fights is in his own home," Ram replies.

"Don't you trust in God, Baba?"

"Not anymore," his father says sadly. "In war it is the devil who knows everything and God who is in the shadows."

He walks to the doorway. He puts an ear against the door

as if to detect someone else's presence. "Do you think they're here already?"

Manu looks around. He sees nothing. Hears nothing.

"Baba, no one is here."

"Hush son, when a knife appears in a Chinaman's hand, eventually it slashes something."

"Baba?"

"You don't worry, beta. I finally understand what you have been saying. I will save us," Ram leans over and whispers, as though the enemy is listening.

"What can we do?"

His father's eyes trust his mind, for they've taken on an intensity Manu has never seen. "A lion should not concern himself with the voice of a sheep. We will fight!"

"Fight? With what? Kitchen knives?"

"We will see. You don't worry. I will protect you."

The nation is on fire and his father wants to burn down his own house.

"Baba, we cannot fight. They are ten times our population! They are armed. We can do nothing but surrender or run!"

"I will protect you," Ram adds. He turns back to the window, absorbed by his own thoughts. His father says nothing more, as if he's capped a bottle pickled with a motley collection of strange ideas.

Can one man save another from his ravaged mind? No.

Manu has to find Ida.

He walks around the house. Ida's room is still empty. He can't see Seth anywhere. He finds his mother in the kitchen.

She is cooking peshawari chicken in the pot, his father's favourite.

He walks up to her.

Urmila looks up at him and her normally assembled face is in disarray.

"Don't worry," Manu says. "We are safe inside the house."

He smiles and feels a thin line stretch across his face.

She wipes a tear from the corner of her eye.

Manu walks over to her body that is as stiff and straight as a rod and puts his arms around her.

For the first time in his life Manu's life rubs away at him. He feels as wrung out as a piece of cloth rammed against a washing stone. The house, despite its size, bears down on him like a prison cell with barred windows. Manu walks out of the kitchen in a daze.

***

Better to have three winters than a summer like this.

***

Later that afternoon, when the sun is swallowing the earth, Manu decides that he needs to find Ida, curfew be damned. He opens the front door of his house, steps out to the porch and walks past the front lawn. Behind the curve of the bushes lining the driveway, right next to the gate, he sees Kamala staring straight at him.

What is she doing here, he wonders. How has she returned from New China? Has she come to meet Ida?

Manu places his hands in his pocket and walks up to her, "Ni-maste, Memsahib! Back so soon?"

She doesn't reply.

"You shouldn't be here. The Chinamen are here. Do you know that a curfew has been declared? The police are shooting people on sight. There are riots in the town, people's charred bodies are thrown about, looting and rampage, vehicles set aflame."

There is no sound from Kamala. She keeps staring at him without blinking.

"Memsahib, do you know where Ida is? I've looked everywhere for her," he adds, suddenly nervous. Why is she not talking back to him? He walks to the lawn and behind the bush to speak to Kamala properly. "I'm going—"

But there is no body to talk to.

Kamala has been killed. Her head is chopped off.

The War Mantra

Here I am staring at a blank sheet. I alone can cause peace. All I have to do is type two words: Truce Declared. The war will end. There will be no bloodshed. No rapes, no orphans, no widows, no arms raised. The world will be in quiet churn again.

But I cannot do that. Not to you. I'm sure you know why.

The Life Mantra

I'm clean. Very clean. I like to put things back where they belong. If I pick up a bottle it is returned to the exact spot from where it came. In this way I leave nothing unwanted in the world, I leave no trace of things that don't belong. I start from zero and return to zero. As carefully as I keep the bottles back in their place, I also watch their contents decline. And in that drop I see my life passing by. It's the same thing with time. It's present but not palpable. A circle without a drop. Let's end this time; so it begins.

PARIPLAVA

THE STORY THAT BEGINS AGAIN

When I come to my senses, a day or three later, the mountain is a mound of charred rubble. The water from the Jyotirlinga has encased my body in the cool protect of the mother I never had. I get up slowly from the ground where I've been hurled with the explosion and shake off the scales that envelop my body when I sleep here. No wonder the townspeople think I turn to fish at night. Correcting them is like separating yolk from the egg: it leaves you with less than what you had. It's not worth my effort.

It's difficult for me to walk. I turn my feet over. Second-degree burns have blackened the soles of my feet. My ankles and calves, hands and arms, my ears have not been spared either. Soon gangrene will set in and bring me to my knees. Still, I am alive.

I bow to the Jyotirlinga, "Thank you for saving me, again."

You're welcome. Now go.

"Go where?" I ask and pick up my robe, wrap it like bandage around my burns.

There is no answer. I turn around and see, to my horror, that the ground is moving. Before I can blink it quickly swallows the Jyotirlinga. No! I lurch forward.

Let it go. In the age of truth it will appear again.

Where the Jyotirlinga now rests, only a patch of mud remains with grass sprouting from it. I bend forward, lean to the ground, and clasp my hands in prayer for the dearly departed, our dark age of Kali Yuga.

Now go forth.

I get up and turn. The wind guides me to the statue area. I turn to it ... but ...

Lord Shiva has fallen. Gold has turned to ash. The brick pillars have been flattened, spewing ash like molten lava down Diamond Hill.

"The statue is dead," I say. "This is impossible! It is dead."

Hush!

"Why has our Shiva been taken down?" I ask in fear. For I can feel fear too.

Hush, they will hear. Be careful of what you speak.

I look around to see if there are ears floating around us, listening in for a whisper of sedition. Is it too late? Have I inadvertently informed the Chinamen of India's greatest fall? Oh well, all the king's horses and all the king's men couldn't put Humpty together again. Soon enough they would have come, fallen God or not, those four-score men and the four-score more.

Something is moving, very slightly, a few feet away from me. It's her: the daughter of The Lord of Lalbag. Made of milk and honey. She is sitting, actually not sitting but trembling, amid the rubble and stones. The sounds that come from her are more like deep sobs than screams. The mountain has blown away the clothes from her body and the soot has turned her body as black as the night, as naked as the day she was born. Next to her is a pile of red shiny sari. I have seen her wear this at her wedding to which I was not invited. The trident is in front of her, shining red. With its light falling on her black body, she looks like a lighthouse in the middle of a giant tsunami. I see that she is responsible for all this.

Go to her.

Really? I have stared at her through the shallow relief sculptures that line the wall of the temple, but never before have we spoken, not exchanged a glance. It's not meant to be, I think, not in this life.

Go.

Clearly, I am wrong. I walk up to her, my feet like they're striding on a bed of coals.

She looks up at me as if I'm a clap of lightning emerging from dark clouds. Nightmares have pooled around her eyes, rings like the bark on the aged tree of her face. Her body is a maze of dark blood. Next to her is a stone on which is drawn The Dark Mother, Goddess Kali. Her entire right hand is tattooed with a Shiva lingam around which is a spiral chain.

She is The Chosen One!

What do I say to her? I look at Diamond Hill. *The Earth will guide us to wise words.*

I start: *You destroyed the trident and broke the statue.*

A gust of wind blows past her hair. She blinks in confusion. The voices have whispered to her. It's the first time because her eyes widen in dismay.

You have awakened The Giant, I continue.

—I know.

For this you must pay.

—I understand.

The moon is full. Many men die when the moon is full.

—I can see.

You are partly lucid. Good. It means they have not completely taken over your mind. The Broken Lord must protect you.

—Praise Lord Shiva!

The corpses have clawed their way out of the mud with their swords, punch daggers and bayonets. They've turned into warriors of The Terracotta Army.

—I saw.

The warriors must be stopped or this war will get bloodier. We must give them blood before they come to life and suck out all of the town's blood.

—My blood?

Yes

—Praise the Mother!

Are you ready?

She nods, yes.

"It's time for samhara." Destruction, I tell her.

She gets up, stark naked.

I wrap my robe around her body.

—And you?

I look at her sari on the charred ground. Red. So fitting. We smile at each other.

Slowly we walk, gently, soft is the ground beneath our feet. There I am dressed in her red wedding sari, there she is covered in my robe with the hammer and sickle.

With the creatures around her, inside her body, gripping her mind, she has acquired an ethereal quality. With her cheeks flush with tears and her eyes luminous, she has never looked as exquisite. If *they* hadn't taken her, the enemy would have. Violation would surely have come to a creature as magnificent as her, no matter how loathed the local women were by the Chinamen.

We walk down the gilded steps where the Mahabharata has been singed away and replaced by the Cantonese battle cry: Hi-yo! Hi-yo! Go all out! No one told you to be poor!

The day is just beginning to show, like a pregnant woman filled with the abundance of life. The sky is like melted butter with an orange yolk smeared across it. There is complete silence. The birds are all gone. Yesterday they were here—cawing and chirping and tweeting—and today they've upped and left.

Birds feel death as we feel life, I tell The Chosen One.

—Or, the Chinese have eaten them. It's not just cats and dogs that they like, but also parrots and crows and pigeons.

You've only seen that the sky is empty, but look closer. Our walls and grounds are empty too. For they've taken the lizards, cockroaches and spider eggs. It *is* an army of the thousands.

The Chosen One knows all. She is wise.

—What about my family?

They will not survive the war. You know this.

Tears form around her eyes.

—Without them I will not go.

Now is the time of God, I tell her. Then silently I add: God justifies everything. Let them go.

—Of what use is such wisdom to me now, Swamiji?

Wisdom has never been of use to anyone. The finest trick of the wise is that they let no one know that they exist.

She still looks unsure. I sing—

Only gold and silver, Men of clay seek,
Not knowing how soon they will break.
Not knowing that to the final destination,
They walk hand in hand, the weak and the strong.

Comprehension rises in her eyes like a high tide and she bows her head like the moon, nods her assent.

We go.

I will pray for you when you go your way.
May the sword not fall upon your head.
May it not tear the arms of your beloved, nor
Mutilate the legs that carry you to the pyre.
May it fall silent in that time before your last breath.
I will pray for you to go softly, tread gently, oh,
Man without God, When you walk the last mile.

TRIUMPH OF CADAVERS

The killer has carved out the inside of her head, emptied it except for the eyes. Her ear lobes have been chopped off, probably for their solitaire diamonds. Manu takes the grief of losing a person he's known all his life and uses it to weep.

He looks back at The White Taj. What he needs to do now is to save Ida. What will they do to her if they find her? He needs to save Ida.

He runs to The Black Taj, where he had last seen her. There's no one there except Seth, fast asleep on the floor. His father has told him, in a voice like thunder on a clear summer day, that Seth has self-banished himself from The White Taj, as punishment for not saving his family, and moved here to die. He has bid Ram and Urmila farewell, and forbidden them from coming here. Manu has never seen his father so fraught with anxiety.

In defiance of the Chinamen's ban on hanging clothes in open spaces, Seth has hung his pajamas outside the window, where they flutter in the wind. It's his last act of rebellion. The pajama is his David in the army of Goliaths. Manu gives a sad soft smile. He looks at Seth. His skin is pallid, his face sunken and his bones eating into themselves; his is a body in mutiny. Manu resents Seth for not even trying to save Manu's family, but for too long Seth has been *Manu's* family. He walks up to him slowly and touches his feet. It's his final goodbye to Seth and he hopes he can see him again in the other world. Then, Manu is off. He has to find Ida.

Ida might be in the marketplace. It's the only place he hasn't looked. He will go there.

His area, The Royal Mason, seems untouched. The Chinese have not yet been here. Still, the streets are deserted. The houses in Royal Mason seem empty too as if their residents have all left. Where could they have gone? A lot of the houses have been painted red. Most houses have a chai sign. Why are the outer walls of all houses painted? Manu walks past these. Despite the stillness around him, he has a distinct feeling that he's being watched. Somewhere behind the stain-glass windows and deserted streets, someone has their eyes on him. It's then that he notices that most houses have blackout paper on the glass panes of their windows and doors. He doesn't understand this. Do the owners think that the enemy cannot see their houses because paper has been put on them? Because even in this early evening light the houses shine bright like beacons. He almost laughs.

Manu wonders why he hears no bombs, like the last time, and remembers that the Chinamen want to show the world how easy it is to conquer this little town since its men are now without their God. He's heard that this is a town they want to preserve, like a well-pickled memory, and turn into a museum that will showcase to visitors the might of the Chinese soldiers. Therefore, the People's Liberation Army of China has done away with sophisticated militarisation, and decided to use foot soldiers, rifles, swords, hand-to-hand combat and—if it comes down to it—grenades.

In the distance, the clusters of small buildings in the residential area are still and eerie, erect like tombstones. Have the residents been forced out of their homes in the middle of the night and taken some place to be killed?

The second he steps outside The Royal Mason, Manu hears explosions and the crackle of small arms. He hears shouts and screams, the sound of shelling. He turns to the faraway west side of Lalbag, with all the factories, and sees flashes of light appear and disappear like a Morse code. The Chinese soldiers must be in that part of town. He sees white fires coming out of some factories, orange at the base, ending in long whirls of black smoke. Even from such a distance he can smell things burning: tires and cars and human flesh. He imagines a worker trapped inside the factory, his body on fire. To go directly from life to the cremation ground, no respite for the body to lay on cold stone awash with tears from loved ones; is there a fate worse than that for a man?

He hears sharp whistles and crackles. It's not safe for him to be walking in the middle of the road. The flying embers or shrapnel could easily maim him. He ducks behind cars that have been abandoned. The smell of gunpowder and burning flesh stings his nose. Smoke reaches him. For a moment he can't see anything. But he hears the sound of men running past him. Are they Chinamen? The smoke clears and Manu sees that they are ordinary civilians, weeping, hands and legs bleeding, searching for each other, crazy with confusion. Manu sees a man with his daughter and son. They're hiding their faces. They cannot stop crying. A yellowish secretion is pouring down the father's shirt.

What terrible tragedy have they just witnessed?

The sound of gunfire and artillery shells comes from deeper south. Manu doesn't stop to listen. He's accustomed to this sound, having often heard it from near the border wall. He falls on a pair of slippers. He gets up and continues walking. He will not stop till he finds Ida.

He passes streets filled with families who have loaded their possessions on bicycles and carts, ready to flee. But flee to where? They're trapped. They shuffle instead of walking, shoulders drooped, crying softly.

Manu reaches the town square. Evidently, the Chinamen have been here. Everywhere there are signs of war. There are bullets and slippers lying all over the streets. Billboards have been pulled down. Bright red Chinese flags hang from electric poles and lampposts. Dust has accumulated on abandoned cars like cremation ash. Many car tires are missing, their windows and windshields broken. An ambulance is partially on fire, a fire too wasted to allow its full rage. Manu sees a school bus with bullet marks on it. There are a few knapsacks thrown outside it. He cringes. From a tannoy he hears the Chinese national anthem blaring on loop: *Arise! All those who refuse to be slaves! Brave the enemy's fire! March on! March on! On!* The streets are streaked with a bloody sludge.

Manu stops. It's too much. These are the streets he grew up playing on. Where has his childhood gone? Where is home?

He hadn't expected it: this war. Not in this way. He's heard it from within his house where it's easy to think that the violence is less brutal than its noise. He's seen his streets empty but never imagined that the people who walked it this morning now lay with their throats slit in its gutters.

He sees a man lying stiff on the ground. His leg is on fire but the man is still; he makes no noise. Manu wonders whether he can gather wet sand and throw it over his burning limb. But the man is dead. Clearly, there is no respect being given to the dead in this war. Manu will not let it be this way. He removes the man's dust-caked body from the middle of the road so that no one runs him over.

He walks on ahead. A tear falls from his eyes. Where is Ida? He needs her now more than he ever has. He wants to say "I love you" and hold her, at least one last time.

It's the time of day when the earth is nearly done swallowing the sun and in the growing darkness, Manu sees a mountain where Jhande Wala Park used to be. He walks closer to it and balks. The smell emanating from the mountain is repulsive, the stench so unbearable he can barely breathe. But something draws him to it, the power of the flame to a moth. He sees a hand, then a leg, hair, blood. This is not a mountain but a mound of dead people, their bodies thrown on top of each other in a pile!

Manu falls down in shock. He grabs his stomach by its sides, leans forward and retches onto the ground. Dead people, his friends and neighbours, familiar faces, now lay splattered in blood, their eyes wide open in surprise as if Manu has played another trick on them, their hands—which he's held—open as if begging for God, skin waxy like that of the apple they've shared together. A body—Nandu's body—stands out. A knife is lodged into his stomach and his skin has closed in around it, as if trying to swallow the knife.

Manu looks around. Surely there must be someone to help them. The Indian Army? Police? But Lalbag is in a state of lawlessness. There are no local cops; he's heard that the police station has been burnt to the ground, though he doesn't have the strength to walk to the South to confirm this. And their nation's army belongs to New China. There's no one to save them.

The town where he's grown up has been turned upside down and all its contents spilled out into an abyss. Lalbag has become a skeleton of itself.

Suddenly Manu sees an army jeep with loudspeakers. He ducks behind a car and holds his breath till they pass.

All along, everyone had said, even the most cynical, that the Chinamen would not kill, they would not destroy, they would only intimidate. So why has it come to this? How has it come to this? What lie has been told, what secrets made, what ego offended? Who has become rich, who poor, who turned poet and who soldier for it to come to this?

With his mind heavy with questions, heart heavy with sadness and his body in a state of faint, he walks on to the marketplace. He walks, no longer searching for Ida—what are the chances of finding her?—he walks because he doesn't know what else to do with himself. Everything is a blur of fire, smoke, bullets and dead people.

The ditches are filled with carcasses: men, women, children, babies, dogs, birds, no one spared. Chokia and most of the other stores have been looted. The shutters of every shop have been pulled down, and their banners have broken or fallen. Their glass display windows are shattered, emptied of their content, whether by the owners, looters or the Chinamen, he doesn't know. Outside most of the stores he sees broken plywood cupboards, single-door refrigerators, stoves and gas burners. Standing in place of Nandu's tiny tea stall is the drum in which Nandu used to boil tea. The tealeaves are still inside it, coagulated like a wound. The board with the mural of a Chinaman and Chinawallah shaking hands is still up, along with the inscription, "War no more, cooperation will build a new nation". Fucking lies! Manu goes to kick it and sees next to it a gutter from which a hand is coming out. Harsh. Oh God!

Still. It's Harsh. "You deserve it," he shouts to the corpse before a howl escapes his lips and he stumbles to the ground. At least it's not his Ida. He wants to retch once more, throw out that feeling of disgust, but nothing comes out.

He can't go any further. He's seen too much. He sits down on the ground. Sadness seizes his body with the full extent of its despair. Tears fill his face with such abandon that he can't bring himself to open his eyes. He lies down weeping and shouts, "Take me also! Take me also!" He hopes the Chinamen hear him and shoot him. Death has to be better than this grief. He hates the Chinamen: "You fascist bastards!" And Bingbing? She must have reported him to the authorities by now. They must be on their way to The White Taj. That means his parents are in danger. The thought of this wills him back home. Manu gets up, with an effort, and runs.

Running among the dead makes Manu think of his own mortality. He imagines himself walking along, ticking items off his grocery list, and the next moment his limbs flying through the air, his eyes gouged out, his insides disemboweled like Kamala. Is this how it ends for everyone?

Manu passes the small pond around the banyan tree, the site of Vakil's accident. The red sandstone slabs around it are lying shattered to the ground. The water in the pool has turned red and viscous. It has corpses floating on it. There is blood on the epithet engraved next to the pond, leaving only these words visible: *Of all I am.*

An emaciated goat is scarfing a laddoo amid the ruins.

His stomach catches. He can't run any further. He needs a minute's break. He sits down next to the pond. Watching the gentle laps of the small waves, Manu feels that he, the Immortal Self, is watching the transitory Soul of the dead bodies, for are they not from the same tree of life? He sees the water reflect the tree, the world upside down, the water symbolic of the fact that the material world is a shadow of the spiritual world, a cycle of—ironically—eternal life.

Suddenly, behind him, Manu hears something cute, like a Korean rap song. His ears perk and sharpen. No, he is mistaken. These are the voices of the PLA soldiers, singing. They are marching straight towards him. At any moment they will see him and snuff him out. Manu looks around. There is nowhere to run, nowhere to hide. The voices are getting closer. There is no way to escape this. What should he do?

In panic, Manu dives into the pond. He hides in the red water. But they are coming nearer and it is still not pitch dark. They will see him. What should he do? He ducks below a corpse—he cannot believe he's doing this. The belly of the corpse is empty and whatever nerves and blood vessels are left are surprisingly soft and malleable, gooey though everything around Manu is equally so. He can barely breathe but it's better than losing his breath altogether.

And there he stays long after the voices are gone and the road becomes silent once again.

Shadows all over the world are hacked with one deft sweep of the sun and it becomes night. Stars tuck into blankets of clouds and sleep in the sky. When the clouds pull away, the stars wake up and twinkle again.

The soldiers are somewhere near the town square which means they can reach The Royal Mason in twenty minutes and his house in half-an-hour. His family. Manu needs to inform them immediately. He cannot let them meet the fate of the townspeople. He lets go of the corpse, gives it one long sad look, and jumps out of the water. His clothes are wet, his sodden shoes heavy on his feet, but he manages to sprint home. Here and there he falls, not knowing if it's a hand he's tripping over, a leg or a tree branch. At one point he thinks he sees Vakil's hunched body in a drain, but even for that he doesn't stop. He keeps running.

Manu reaches The White Taj, covered in the blood and insides of a corpse. Outside the house he sees the sign of chai. Where did this come from? That horrible Bingbing. He shuts the gate behind him and runs to the lawn, where he hoses himself down. It's dark. The Chinamen may not immediately see The White Taj with all the trees that line it. They may not see them if they are in total darkness. He runs into the servants' quarters, shouting out to his parents, "Switch off the main electricity switch. Put blackout paper on the windows. Quick! Hurry!" Does this make sense? It doesn't matter.

There is no answer. Where are his parents? He panics. He runs into the mansion, from the living room to the kitchen. A disturbing thought strikes him: there is no hiding in this house. He runs up to the first floor, shouting, "Baba, Maa! Come out! The Chinamen are attacking Lalbag. They've reached the town square. They'll be here in a few minutes. Come out! We need to go."

He knocks on the doors of all the rooms and enters, but all the rooms are empty. Have the Chinamen taken them?

Manu continues shouting: "They're killing whomever they find on the road ... burning all the shops ... dragging people out of their homes. It's a massacre. There is looting. People's throats are slit. No one can escape alive."

There is still no response from his parents. He bangs the walls of the house furiously.

A shout. It comes from the bottom of the stairs. Manu looks down to see his father running down the steps. He is carrying a sword. Behind him is Urmila. Her long dark hair is open till her waist, red streaks of powder are running down her forehead like a fountain, and black kajal is smeared down till her nose.

His mother looks at his father askance. Tears stream down her face. Manu's mother turns to Manu for help.

Manu feels as though he's switched one horror movie for another. But he has to pull out of his situation and into his parents' before it is too late. With great effort he runs to where his father is and holds his arm.

Ram turns to him, "This is the only way for us to win this war, get back our family. I thought you would understand that beta." He has the face of someone who has never touched alcohol and the expression of a raging drunk.

Manu looks at him with a stupefied expression as if, all along, he thought of him as a dewdrop in the first flush of morning and instead he's turned out to be thunderous rain. How did his dreamy father finally wake up to the reality of war and death?

Ram holds out a ceremonial sword. "Remember this? It's from the eighteenth century. Aurangzeb used this sword when he was facing the mad elephant Sudhakar. This will protect us."

The sword has a metal hilt decorated with gold inlay and a knuckle guard with overlay work. The blade is curved, set in steel with a watered effect. On its pommel is engraved the incarnation of Shiva in his fiercest form, Bhairav. Seth was gifted this by one of his associates back when its only use was decorative. The sword is exquisite.

"Baba, why would India's most bigoted Muslim ruler use a sword with a Hindu God on it? This is not Aurangzeb's sword, it is a cheap rip-off from chor bazaar in old Bombay."

Ram startles and scowls at his son. "Does it really matter where the sword came from? It's a good sword that will hack off the head of anyone who tries to come near us."

He takes out a forward curved sword from his kurta. "You can have this sosan patta so we can fight together."

Manu doesn't take the sword. Ram glares at him.

"This is not the time to be lazy," he says. "Men from all over Lalbag have armed themselves with whatever they can find to defend themselves and their family. We must too."

Manu doesn't move. Ram puts the sword back in his kurta. Suddenly he perks his ears, sniffles his nose and turns to Manu, "Can you hear the wind?"

"The wind? I don't hear any wind," Manu says and then listens more carefully. He hears the sound of many feet marching on the ground at the same time. "They're here," he shouts in disbelief and horror. "The Chinamen are here! We're going to die!"

"Don't be scared! I will stop them."

The reality of what his father is going to do dawns on him.

"Baba, you have to stop! The Chinese are ruthless. They will ... kill you."

"No one can stop me now," Ram says, a smile spread across his face.

Manu feels like he is talking to an abecedarian who is learning the letters of the alphabet for the first time. Where has he got this great and misdirected sense of courage? He leads his father to the couch and forces him to sit down. He can feel his father's bones beneath his fingers. When did he become so thin? He pleads: "Please don't go outside. You will get killed. Let's stay here till it's all over."

"No," Ram says and gets up.

Manu catches his father by the arm. "I will not let you go!"

Ram bites his son's hand. As Manu yells in pain, Ram sprints towards the front door.

"Stop," screams Manu. Why is his father going deeper into tragedy?

But Ram, gentle peace-loving Ram, beloved husband, beloved father, beloved servant, runs past the porch and past the driveway, not sparing a glance for his old home, the servants' quarters. He steps out of the front gate and runs onto the street. Manu and Urmila chase after him. They cross the front gate and stop in shock. Ahead of them, to the left, a platoon of thirty soldiers is advancing down the street in a ragged line. They look like a peasant army, armed with clubs, swords and rifles. All of them are carrying knapsacks on their back. Many are quite young. Some are wearing platinum facemasks.

There is nothing to do now but watch silently, in horror, as Ram runs towards them, holding the sword up in his hands. The men do not seem to notice him, as if he's a housefly.

Then Ram shouts, "Don't move another step or I will kill you."

The soldiers don't stop. They keep moving as though they haven't heard Ram.

Maybe they can't see him in the dim light, thinks Manu. After all, most of the streetlights have been broken—Manu had seen glass lying scattered below most of them on his way home—making the street dark. The other houses in Royal Mason are also in complete darkness.

Will Ram be saved? Urmila and Manu look at each other, their jaws soften: maybe the Chinese are kind and not killing everyone as rumoured. Maybe they will spare Ram.

By the time they turn back a soldier has taken out his Browning, removed the clip, and deftly loaded it. His gun is raised to Ram's head. There is not a moment's hesitation when he fires. In the blink of a second, time rises into a lifetime and snuffs out a living breathing shouting thing.

"No!" screams Urmila.

The soldiers turn and see Urmila and Manu. Manu turns too, not sure if the shock of seeing his father killed is greater than the shock of hearing his mother's voice.

Still, Manu puts his hand over his mother's mouth, drags her flaccid body inside the house, locks the front door, and switches off all the lights on the way. He walks up the stairs to the second floor and into Vakil's bedroom. He locks its door and runs around locking the windows, praying, foolishly he knows, that the soldiers don't follow them.

The march of footsteps comes closer and closer to The White Taj.

He pushes his mother, still flaccid, under the bed and ducks in beside her.

The night is silent as if all living things have ceased to exist. Manu can only hear the breath on his mother and him. Even her sobs have been struck dead in the quiet.

The front gate creaks open as strong sturdy footsteps click on the cobblestone driveway. The soldiers laugh and exchange jokes that Manu cannot grasp; they must be speaking in Cantonese. Perhaps the sign outside the gatepost: Accident Porn Area has amused them. That's good. An enemy who can laugh, cannot kill. He hears a crash; the soldiers must be breaking the statues of The Ecstasy of St Teresa. And soon thereafter, splashing. The soldiers must be at the lily pond in the gazebo. What are they doing inside the pond? What are they doing to the goldfish? Manu remembers rumours of how the Chinese swallow live insects and reptiles and fish. He shudders. There is more laughter. The soldiers are enjoying themselves and in no hurry to reach their intended victims. Do they know that there is nowhere that Urmila and Manu can run to?

Manu pulls his mother closer to him.

Someone breaks open the front door. "What a fancy house," he hears a soldier growl in Mandarin. There's a crashing of glass on the ground floor. Manu hears some footsteps on the back porch and some more instructions in Mandarin that he cannot understand. They are taking over all sides of the house. A few shots ring from the orchard and the laterite ground. A few of them must have seen The Black Taj and are crossing over to it.

Ida, my poor Ida, Manu thinks. The love of my life. So close and yet so far. He's left her once again in her hour of need. This fills him with regret. He's a coward for not finding her and saving her.

His mother's nails dig into his skin, breaking him out of his reverie.

There is some laughter from the ground floor, this time with a slightly sinister tint. The Chinamen will not climb up so many floors, he thinks. After all they have the town to capture. Surely their time is better spent than killing a servant boy and his mother?

He hears some angry shouts, a few instructions. The smell of gasoline hits his nostril.

The footsteps recede. And then Manu smells smoke.

Their house is on fire!

"Let's go, Maa! We can jump out of the balcony and into the orchard. I know they're out there but maybe they will not see us. It's dark. We can run. We can run up to Mount Akaho." Urmila says nothing. "Maa, let's go! We don't have time!"

Though her eyes are brimming with tears, Urmila meets her son's eyes. She presses down on his hands.

"We'll be killed! We will burn to death!" he tells her.

Urmila doesn't respond. Manu looks into her eyes and sees that they are twinkling like a clear night sky. There is no fear. Manu can see things that his terror is not allowing him to.

She is right. There is no point. There is no escape.

There is smoke outside the door now. Manu looks at his mother. The serenity in her face communicates what her words don't.

"I'm not ready for this," he tells his mother.

She brings his head to her chest, soft like brown earth. Her hands caress his face, like the gentle sway of green grass. Her breath cools his hair like an early morning breeze, and he becomes quiet.

"Your clothes smell of sunlight and musk," he says to his mother.

She smiles at him.

"Is the end near, Maa?"

Urmila turns towards the sky outside the window. She brings her son closer to her. The end is near, she says. But it is always the beginning for someone else.

***

Seth is on the mattress, writhing in pain. He knows death is near. He is prepared. He doesn't want to die hiding like a coward in The White Taj, with its walls and doors and concrete and bricks. He wants to die in the open, where his father's dreams had once been, a place where he can be easily found and finished.

He hears the sound of footsteps outside the black walls. The footsteps are curiously synchronised, marching to the strains of their own beat. They are here!

"Ida," he says, "My child. Come to me. I don't want to die alone."

No one comes forth. He remembers: Ida is gone. His family is gone. He is alone in The Black Taj.

Or is he?

Inky Pinky Ponky. Father had a donkey. Donkey died, father cried. Inky Pinky Ponky.

His father's love, it's hovering above him.

Videsh says: *Good to see you, son.*

Seth replies: You too, Baba.

Is this the best way for you to go?

Seth laughs, "Every way is a good way to go, for its the only way to go."

Whether you come to a place to live or die, says Seth, the things you do are the same.

Something outside explodes in loud devastation. It sounds like the eruption of a volcano or the awakening of a giant slumbering beast. Has Mount Akaho been destroyed?

Still the voice does not quiver, it does not stall; it asks:

This war, couldn't you have done something about it?

Men die every day in sport, on the road, from the top of buildings, inside their homes, but the world calls it war only when men die on the border.

Still, old men must stop dreaming up wars for young men to die in.

No, men need martyrs.

Now it's his turn to ask: Will I get jalebis in your heaven?

His father laughs, his laugh throaty and full, as if still stuffed with poppy seeds.

Then there is silence. His father, the sun-child, is gone.

Seth looks up from the mattress and sees a man in saffron robes sitting atop a white horse. The man has a sword in his hand. The sword is red-hot. The white horse has wings. The man's face is blurred so Seth cannot see it. But he knows it is Lord Kalki, the destroyer of darkness, on his swift horse Devadatta, Lord Vishnu's final avatar, descended on earth to end the demon age of Kali Yuga and usher the era of truth, the Satya Yuga.

There will be no more darkness.

Seth sees his pajamas fluttering uselessly in the wind.

"In the end it's all for nothing, isn't it?" Seth asks.

The man's sword glints as if the light of a soul has fallen on it and then he is gone.

SAMHARA

Mount Akaho explodes.

And from out of the mountain's mouth come thousands and thousands of snakes. His snakes.

From the mirror in Vakil's bedroom, that faces Mount Akaho, Urmila sees Swamiji and Ida walking together amid the rubble and stones. He's in her red sari. She's in a robe. The trident she's holding is shining red. The spiral chain on her right hand is whirling fast. The stone in his hand, on which is drawn Goddess Kali, is smouldering with an orange glow.

Urmila blinks in astonishment: The Giant has awakened!

Behind them she sees an army of His snakes gather. They slither under the full light of the moon, following Ida.

As the ash settles, Urmila stands up in disbelief.

Ida's long dark hair is open till her waist, red streaks of powder are running down her forehead like a fountain, black kajal is smeared across her eyes, and three horizontal lines of ash are on her forehead—the tripundra tilak.

"She is glorious," Urmila whispers, "like a lioness coming down from heaven."

And then, suddenly, Ida turns blue, like the Lord!

Urmila gasps. And then bows down towards Ida.

"What are you doing, mother?" Manu asks from under the bed, coughing as the fire reaches their bedroom door. "Our end is near."

"The end is near for them, *beta*. Which means it's a new beginning for us. Rise."

"*What?*"

"Lord Kalki is here, the destroyer of darkness. Now we will win India back."

"*How?*"

"Look."

Urmila points to the tripundra tilak that has emerged on his forehead, and turns to the mirror to see her own. She smiles.

Urmila begins to chant. Manu comes out slowly from under the bed.

The fire outside their room stops. There are no more flames. No more smoke. There are no more soldiers. The White Taj is saved! They are saved!

How?

As Ida walks through the streets of Lalbag, the snakes slithering behind her, the corpses rise. Dead bodies rise from the footbridge, the border wall, the graves, the gutters, the Jhande Wala Park, the pond around the banyan tree, the drum of Nandu's tea stall. They rise and they follow her, her army getting larger and larger, stronger and stronger.

Of all I am.

Seth rises from the mattress.

Ram rises from the street.

Vakil rises from a drain.

Pia rises from under a tree.

Kamala rises from the bush.

They all have the tripundra tilak on their forehead.

Ida stops. She turns to her army. They all stop. In a voice that echoes around Lalbag, she says: *The streets of Lalbag will not be streaked with the bloody sludge of its own people, but of those who dare attack us! Let Lalbag turn red with the blood of our enemy! Jai Hind!*

Jai Hind, her army shouts back. And off to fight they go.

The snakes bite the foot soldiers of the People's Liberation Army of China, and down fall the astonished soldiers to their death, their platinum facemasks, knapsacks, grenades and rifles turned to dust. How do you fight an enemy that can't be defeated?

The bodies of humans turn to the warriors of The Terracotta Army, with their swords, punch daggers and bayonets, and destroy them with a punch or a kick or a slap, turning them back to mud. Down they fall to nothingness.

Not one Chinaman is spared.

There. It's over. The guns are silent. The enemy has fallen. There are no more Chinamen in Lalbag. There never will be. Just as there never will be another attack on the great nation of India. No one would dare now!

It is the unknown that defeats our enemies. And keeps them defeated. The Indian flag turns on a flag post, flying high again, a sign to the Chinese of India's victory.

They gather at the gate of their home, at The White Taj, cheering for Ida, cheering for Lalbag, cheering for India, cheering for their beloved Lord Shiva!

"Ida, you are our India—without the N and I in China. You saved us!" shouts Manu victoriously, as Ida's colour changes back to normal. The snakes are also gone though no one asks where.

They cheer again.

"But we are all dead," whimpers Ram. "We all died."

"We are not dead. We are our Immortal Self, the ones who will live an eternal life," says Vakil. "The cycle is complete."

"But ..." says Seth.

"I'm so glad this secret is out finally, Papa! It's such a relief."

"What you mean?" asks Kamala.

"I have been a zombie since my accident. A zombie human-snake actually," says Vakil. "Urmila saved me from death by turning my human form into a zombie form. And she did the same for us now—only this time we are immortal thanks to Ida."

They all turn to Urmila who looks away.

"How can zombies live? Love? Be happy?" asks Manu.

"Pia has been one too, since our marriage. Urmila turned her into one so we'd be happy," continues Vakil. "Didn't we live? Happier than humans? Trust me, this is good for all of us."

"I can't believe it," says Manu, as realisation dawns on him. "We are zombies, all of us. Zombies living in a zombie town."

"It's better than being dead, no?" Pia hisses.

"We can be together now, forever," Ida tells Manu. Manu smiles.

"But who will protect us now?" asks Seth, changing the subject. "Mount Akaho has been destroyed! Lalbag is nothing but a heap of stones. Even The White Taj has turned black in the fire!"

Ida turns to her father and says gently: "The stones of our ruins will be hewn into blocks and carried off to build a statue of Lord Shiva. A statue as large as Mount Akaho, in His honour."

Seth bows and smiles in relief.

"And, you ... you have finally got your Black Taj, Papa."

They turn to The White Taj that has indeed turned black in the fire.

"But there is no time to rest," says Vakil. "For we must now free the rest of India and bring it back to us from the clutches of the enemy."

They all hail and cheer: *Jai Hind*! India will be free again and no nation shall ever dare to attack the mighty nation whose God protects it with the ferocity of a mother with her child.

And so, Kali Yuga comes to an end and Satya Yuga begins.

In a few hours dawn will penetrate the sky, recreating what dusk dissolves.

For that is the way with war and peace.

—THE END—

ACKNOWLEDGEMENTS

As I pen down these words of gratitude, I stand in awe of the monumental 10-year journey in bringing this novel to life. *The Man Who Lost India* has been my most demanding book to write, but I am grateful for the challenges that sculpted my resilience, the triumphs that crowned my perseverance, and the unwavering support that sustained me.

First and foremost, I extend my heartfelt thanks to my parents, Sujata and DC Pant, for being my anchors through the highs and lows of this creative odyssey, and for travelling with me across China while I was researching the book. Your boundless belief in my dreams and constant encouragement fuel my perseverance.

To my husband Sahil Kanuga, who always stands proudly by me with enduring conviction and unmasked elation. Thank you for saying this novel is what brought us together, lending a sweetness as you do with everything in my life.

My baby girls, Amara and Aria, my little inspirations—you count reading your mother's book titles among your first words, and I hope my words always make you proud. Your laughter and innocence brought joy into the writing process and served as a constant reminder of the importance of storytelling in connecting generations.

I am also filled with profound appreciation to have the incredible team of Simon & Schuster championing my labour of love. My heartfelt thank you to my prodigious editor Sayantan Ghosh for immediately and wholeheartedly falling in love with the book. Your acumen and dedication transformed the novel into something truly special, and I truly couldn't have asked for a better advocate of this book. A special nod to the brilliant Rahul Srivastava and Abhay Singh for your vision, passion and insights. And for crafting a visual masterpiece that captures the essence of my story with unparalleled creativity and brilliance, a big thank you to the extraordinary book cover designer Pinaki De.

To my fellow writer Anuja Chandramouli, whose resolute encouragement during breakfast at a literature festival, spurred me to bring this book to life. You were my right thing at the right time.

To my readers, who grow in size and pride, thank you for being there through all my genres and all my years. Your connection to the characters and the story is the ultimate reward for the countless hours poured into crafting each sentence. If I have made any mistakes or gaffes in the book, I humbly ask for your forgiveness. Know that I tried my absolute best keeping you in mind. I hope I make you proud.

To Lord Shiva, the divine presence who has quietly guided and blessed me throughout my life, I offer my sincerest thanks. I hope I have done you justice. The sanctuary of your blessings has been my source of strength during moments of doubt and the beacon of inspiration when hope seemed to elude me.

I am profoundly grateful for the collective effort that brought these pages to life, and I hope you enjoy reading and sharing this labour of immense love, resilience and hard work.

Om Namah Shivay and Jai Hind!